Syssi

Ever since Syssi had heard Jacki recount the vision that revealed the atrocities the cartel monsters had committed, she couldn't shake off the rage and frustration that clung to her like radioactive sludge.

The monsters had slaughtered those poor villagers just because they could. There had been no one to defend the defenseless. The atrocious act was probably perpetrated to serve as a warning to others to keep their heads down and comply with every demand the cartel thugs made, even if they asked that virgins and babies be delivered to them to be violated or sacrificed to whatever demon they served.

If the Eternal King learned what level of evil the gods' creations were still capable of despite all the progress that had been made, he would order that the entire planet be destroyed. It wouldn't be because he cared about the pain of innocents, but because he would be disgusted and ashamed of what his people had created. Humans had been enhanced with the help of the gods' superior genetic material, and the king wouldn't want creations like these to exist and mar the gods' reputation.

Syssi reached for her daughter. "Ready to see Nana, sweetie?"

As she lifted Allegra, her daughter's soft breaths whispered against her neck, easing some of the tension, and the baby's sweet scent soothed the turmoil in her head. Slowly, the tight coil of anger and frustration unraveled, and the warmth from her daughter's little body seeped into her own, relaxing Syssi's stiff shoulders and releasing some of the vise-like discomfort that had settled over her heart.

Glancing up at her with eyes that appeared to know more than they should, Allegra grabbed her favorite rag doll, hugged it to her chest with one hand, and waved with the other at Kian. "Go, bye-bye."

It seemed like her vocabulary was growing by the day, but it wasn't surprising that she was learning to speak earlier than other babies her age. Allegra had started communicating clearly with only minor changes in pitch and sound almost from day one.

"Daddy is coming too." Syssi smiled, hoping that Allegra's excitement over seeing her grandmother would distract her from sensing the turmoil raging inside her mother.

"Are you okay?" Kian's forehead furrowed with concern.

Damn, Syssi had been doing her best to hide the storm raging inside her from him, and so far, it had worked. Her mate wasn't the most empathetic fellow, but he knew her well, and the only reason he hadn't seen past her composed façade before was that he had too much on his plate. The last thing he needed was to deal with her emotional meltdown on top of everything else.

Her only option was to fake it and deflect his attention to another subject.

Syssi plastered a bright smile on her face. "I'm excited about tonight's wedding. I have no doubt that Anandur is planning some goofing around. I just can't imagine what he will come up with."

Kian grimaced. "Neither can I, which worries me. Hopefully, he will think of his bride and not embarrass Wonder in front of the entire clan with something too outlandish."

"Maybe you should have a word with him when you guys meet for whiskey and cigars later?"

Kian chuckled. "I'm afraid of bringing it up in case he hasn't thought of it, and he gets the idea from me."

"Good point." Syssi kissed their daughter's cheek.

"Na-ni," Allegra said with a commanding tone and pointed toward the door.

"Are you excited about having breakfast with Nana, sweetie?" Syssi asked.

"Na-na." Allegra nodded.

Syssi was excited, too, but for reasons of her own. Finally, she was going to see the amulet that had enhanced Jacki's prophetic ability and enabled the rescue of the surviving victims.

It scared the hell out of her, but she was going to touch that thing anyway.

Hiding her anxiety and fear from Kian hadn't been easy. If she were still human, he would have smelled her emotions and realized what her calm façade was hiding and what she was planning, but she was immortal now, and the emotional scents she emitted were not as strong as they were when she was a human.

Kian didn't want her to touch the amulet, and she wasn't too eager to do so either. She wasn't sure she could stomach what Jacki had seen, but if there was a chance that she could discover the identities of the masterminds behind the atrocities, she was willing to suffer through the horror so she could provide the information to Kian, and then he could mobilize the clan to wipe them off the face of the Earth.

Kian made it to the door first and held it open for her. "I wonder if my mother has told Allegra to call her Annani or if she picked it up from others."

"She repeats what she hears." Syssi managed to keep her tone casual as she entered the wide hallway. "That's why I call your mother Nana or Grandma when Allegra is around."

"Yeah, I do too. But she still says Na-ni more than Na-na."

"It's confusing." Syssi stroked Allegra's soft hair. "The two sound so similar."

The small talk was helping, but her heart was still racing as fear mixed with excitement.

"Mama?" Allegra put her tiny hand on Syssi's chest, her big eyes scanning her face with worry.

It was much more difficult to fool Allegra than to fool her father.

"Yes, sweetie." Syssi kissed the top of her head. "Mama, Dada, and Allegra are going to Nana's cabin, and your aunts and uncles will be there too."

She knew that hadn't been what her daughter had tried to convey in her one-word question, but she had to keep Kian in the dark about it for a little longer. If he guessed her plan, he would give her another lecture about why she shouldn't touch the amulet, saying all the things she knew to be true and couldn't dispute. The visions would upset her, she wouldn't be able to sleep for weeks or even months, and it would affect Allegra.

It already had.

There was very little that escaped their daughter's notice. She might not understand much of it, but she sensed and internalized her mother's emotions.

"Nana." Allegra pointed at the door on the other side of the corridor.

The Clan Mother's cabin was the most luxurious on the ship, but Syssi couldn't tell the difference between theirs and the goddess's, and it didn't really matter to her. What mattered was that she had her family with her, the one by birth and the one by marriage, and she felt incredibly blessed and guilty.

She was experiencing many of the classic symptoms of survivor's guilt even though she hadn't lived through what had happened to those villagers.

The poor women on the lower deck had lost everyone they loved in terrible and gruesome ways, and then they had been violated by the monsters who had done it.

Thinking of them and their immeasurable suffering made Syssi's skin prickle with heat, and the tips of her fingers tingle. It was an odd and disturbing reaction, given that she was immortal now, and her blood pressure wasn't supposed to spike when she was upset or angry.

Perhaps it was the rage she was trying to stifle for the sake of her husband and daughter.

The monsters were dead, torn to pieces by the Guardians, and that gave her a small measure of satisfaction, but vengeance wasn't enough. It couldn't bring back all the innocent people they had barbarically and sadistically slaughtered, the children, the mothers and fathers, grand-mothers and grandfathers that they had maimed and violated before killing.

There was no erasing the images Jacki's words had etched on her psyche, and they were going to haunt her for the rest of her immortal life.

That was why touching the amulet and taking the risk of summoning a terrible vision no longer terrified her as much as it should.

Syssi was already traumatized just by what her mind was reconstructing on repeat from Jacki's account, and her sleep was disturbed because the images haunted her in her dreams, so if she could gain more information by exposing herself to the amulet's power, things shouldn't get markedly worse.

As Kian rang the doorbell, Syssi hugged Allegra tighter, plastered a bright smile on her face, and summoned courage she didn't feel.

All the females in the cabin she was about to enter were so much more resilient than she was. Annani and her daughters were strong and brave, Jacki had nerves of steel and seemed almost unaffected by what she'd seen in the vision, and Syssi refused to be the only weakling who couldn't face suffering and horror without falling apart.

The door opened, and Oridu bowed deeply. "Good morning, Mistress Syssi, Mistress Allegra, and Master Kian. The Clan Mother awaits you at the breakfast table."

Frankie

〜

F
rankie opened the balcony doors, stepped outside, and inhaled the fresh ocean air. "It's such a beautiful day." She leaned her hands on the railing, lifted her face to the warm sunlight, and closed her eyes to shield them from the glare.

Dagor's footsteps sounded behind her, and a moment later he leaned over her back, placed his hands on the railing next to hers, and enveloped her body with his.

"You are beautiful." He nuzzled her neck.

She laughed. "You're such a flatterer."

"It's true." He peppered her neck with tiny kisses that were tickling and sweet at the same time.

"I love your lips on me." She giggled when he touched a ticklish spot under her ear. "I love your hands on me, too."

"Oh, yeah?" He moved his hands from the railing to her waist and started a slow trek over her ribcage. "Like this?"

The effect was instantaneous, and she considered getting back in bed and continuing what they had been doing through most of the night.

They had hardly slept, in part because Amanda and Dalhu's wedding had ended so late and in part because of the strenuous activities they had engaged in after returning to her cabin, but thanks to the effect of Dagor's venom, she'd woken up quite early and was feeling great.

She pushed her bottom against his groin and gave it a little wiggle. "Do you think I can get away with not using the wheelchair today?"

Groaning, he pressed against her from behind. "I don't know. If you were healing on your own, would you be ready to walk around less than twenty-four hours after getting shot?"

"Maybe." She leaned her head against his chest. "But since everyone knows that we are together and that you are pumping me full of your venom, they will attribute my rapid recovery to its healing properties."

"Good point." He scraped his fangs over her neck, eliciting a shiver of delight. "Just remember to say nothing about the thing that Kian insists on being kept a secret," he whispered.

"I don't blame him."

The tiny quantity of Dagor's godly blood had been a miracle cure, healing her gunshot wound in hours instead of weeks, but it was also a big secret for a very good reason. If people discovered what Dagor's blood could do, even his godly powers wouldn't keep him safe. He would be hunted down, and his pursuers wouldn't quit the chase until he was caught, no matter how many casualties they sustained in the process.

He was a god with mind control powers and superior physiology, but he was not invincible. Even a god had limits, although she didn't know what those limits were.

Not yet, anyway.

They still had so much to talk about, so much she needed to find out about her alien lover, and there were only seven days left on the cruise.

After it was done, they were supposed to go their separate ways, but she was working on a plan that would allow them to be together without either of them having to sacrifice their objectives.

Well, saying that she had a plan was a little presumptuous. She was still trying to come up with ideas on how she could be a Perfect Match beta tester remotely, but that qualified as working on it, right?

Turning in Dagor's arms, Frankie leaned against the railing and looked into his mesmerizing blue eyes. "Why don't you just thrall me to forget that you gave me your blood?"

He winced. "I don't want to thrall you. I love that you know who and what I am and that I don't need to pretend to be someone I'm not."

That was so sweet it deserved a kiss.

Lifting on her toes, she wound her arms around his neck and planted a soft kiss on his lips. "I love it that you can be yourself with me, but erasing the knowledge about the blood transfusion from my mind is not going to change that. I will still know that you are a god, and that you love me and that I love you back."

He smiled, but it looked a little forced. "I don't want to keep secrets from you that I don't have to. Fates know I have enough of those."

She frowned. "What do you mean? What secrets?"

Also, why had his smile looked forced when she'd said he loved her? Had he had a change of heart?

No, that wasn't likely. Dagor wasn't the kind of man who said things he didn't mean.

Not a man, she corrected herself. A god.

Well, a more accurate term was an immortal alien with super-mind powers, but saying that she had a god for a boyfriend was cool, even if she could tell practically no one, so god it was.

If only she could tell Margo about him.

Perhaps she could call him a god jokingly?

Toven had compelled her to refrain from saying anything about gods or immortals to anyone outside the ship, but she might say that Dagor was a god in bed or that he was as gorgeous as a god and get away with it.

Dagor shrugged. "I'm a trooper. A lot of what I know is classified information that I'm not allowed to share with you or anyone else."

He'd told her about his mission to find some missing pods that were supposed to have some Kra-ell settlers in them, whatever that meant. Was the identity of those people the big secret, or did he have more clandestine missions that he couldn't talk about?

Tilting her head, she looked into his eyes. "Who would I tell? Even if I could talk about you and the immortals, people would think that I was tripping on drugs. Your secrets are safe with me."

Dagor

"I know." Dagor dipped his head and kissed the top of Frankie's nose. "But that doesn't change the fact that I was sworn to secrecy about the things I've learned, and I can't break my vow just because the woman I love is curious. I trust my parents implicitly, but I won't reveal any of that to them either."

Smiling, Frankie lifted her hand and cupped his cheek. "That's okay. There are plenty of things I don't know about you that you are allowed to tell me. Once we exhaust those, I'll start nagging you about the other stuff, but it will probably take years for us to get to that point."

Dagor's mouth suddenly went dry.

They didn't have years, not unless Frankie transitioned, and even if she did, the only way they could be together was if she gave up her dream of working for Perfect Match

Virtual Studios and joined him on his pod recovery mission.

It wasn't fair of him to ask her to give up everything that was important to her to be with him, especially since it was not going to be fun for her. Frankie wasn't the outdoorsy type, and she would quickly grow tired of sleeping in a tent on frozen ground.

On second thought, though, it could be fun keeping her warm.

She tapped a finger on his temple. "What's going on in that head of yours?"

"Breakfast," he lied.

"I don't want to go to the dining hall." She made a pouty face that was so cute he wanted to kiss her again. "I want to be in the sun and breathe fresh air. Can we go to the Lido deck instead?"

"Sure. We can have Bloody Marys and pretzels for breakfast."

She narrowed her eyes at him. "Are you being sarcastic, or do you really mean that? It's hard to tell with you."

"I mean it, even though I should probably insist that you eat something nutritious. Do you remember what happened the last time you had drinks and snacks on an empty stomach?"

"I fainted." She smiled sweetly. "But that's not going to happen now that I have your blood and your venom in me." She pulled on his neck to bring his lips to hers. "You are injecting me with vitality." She chuckled. "In more ways than one."

His semi-hard erection swelled in an instant. "Perhaps we can skip breakfast, and I will inject you with some more of my vitality. I have plenty to give."

"Oh, I know." She kissed him on the lips. "But now that you've planted the idea of a Bloody Mary in my head, I crave it something fierce. Besides, I need to call Margo. If I don't, she's going to interrupt us in the middle of your vitality transfusion."

Reluctantly, he let go of her and took her hand. "What are you going to tell her?"

"A highly modified version of the story." She followed him back inside the cabin. "I can tell her about the treasure hunt for the amulet, but I can't tell her what it did because then I will have to explain Mey and her echoes and Jacki and her visions. Instead, I'll tell her that it was just a trinket Kalugal had planted ahead of time for us to find. The cartel thugs will be a group of robbers, and I won't tell her anything about the rescued women or about the monsters' well-deserved fate." Frankie frowned. "Although once we collect Margo in Cabo and she comes on board, she will learn the truth, so I need to be careful and not lie too much. I'll have to come up with a creative way of omitting the incriminating details while still staying close to the truth."

He nodded. "Good plan. What are you going to tell Margo about your injury? There is no trace of it left, so you can just skip it."

Frankie laughed. "The more important question is what we are going to tell Dr. Bridget. Can you claim that your godly venom is much stronger than that of the immortals and that it healed me?" She stopped walking and turned to him. "What if we tell her that you bit me over the wound? That would have delivered the venom's healing properties right where I needed them and sped up my recovery, right?"

Frankie hadn't even lowered her voice, so it was good that most of the ship's occupants were still asleep, and the corridor was deserted.

"That's not a bad idea. The only problem I can see is when someone else tries it, and it doesn't work. Bridget is a smart lady, and she will figure out that we lied."

Frankie shook her head. "She won't. Bridget knows only five gods, and that's not a big enough sample on which to base a scientific claim. Each Dormant is different, and each god has different powers, and that could include the potency of their venom. She will have to take our word for it."

"You are one smart lady, Frankie. It scares me a little that you know how to manipulate truth and lies so well."

"I will never lie or manipulate you." She gave his hand a squeeze. "If I do, you will know because you can peek into my mind."

"But I won't do that because it's an invasion of privacy. I will just have to trust you."

"That's the spirit." She smiled brightly. "Trust is the foundation upon which a good relationship is built."

Kian

K ian was surprised to see Lokan and Carol at the large dining table his mother's Odus had set up.

It was supposed to be a family breakfast, and although Lokan was his cousin, he wasn't part of the inner circle like his brother was.

While Kalugal wasn't a member of the immediate family either, somehow, he had managed to insert himself into the family and clan leadership without putting much effort into it. He had done it with his intellect, charm, and natural leadership skills.

Kalugal's men worshiped him and liked him as a person, so perhaps it made him an even better leader than Kian.

Kian didn't doubt that he had the respect and loyalty of his clan, but he wasn't as well liked as his cousin, which was fine with him. Managing the clan affairs and keeping his people safe was much more difficult than what

Kalugal had to deal with, and being liked was not a priority.

Besides, charm wasn't one of Kian's attributes, and neither was faking it.

Toven and Mia were also seated at the breakfast table even though they weren't part of the inner family circle. Annani had probably invited Toven because of his familiarity with the ancient Mesoamerican cultures. He might offer some insight into the amulet and its origins.

Syssi's parents were there as well, and as Syssi handed Allegra to Annani, Anita shook her head.

"You have her all of the time." She reached for her granddaughter. "I hardly get to see her."

Smiling, his mother kissed Allegra's cheek and then transferred her to Anita. "If you retired and moved into the village, you could see her whenever you pleased."

Syssi's mother chuckled. "Adam says that the day I quit, I'll die, and he's probably right. Knowing that I'm needed, that what I do improves and often saves people's lives, motivates me to keep going."

Annani nodded sagely. "I cannot argue with that. Having a purpose is essential to one's mental health, especially for immortals and gods."

"My grandparents keep busy while being retired," Mia said. "They have their hobbies and their friends, and they enjoy taking it easy."

"Nothing wrong with that." Anita stroked Allegra's hair, curling the soft strands around her finger. "Why didn't they come on the cruise?"

Mia shrugged. "My grandmother can't tolerate being on a ship. On top of being seasick, she gets terrible migraines. They decided to spend the ten days in their Pasadena home and enjoy time with old friends that they haven't seen in a while."

As the chitchat continued about things that Kian had no interest in, he scanned the faces of his family members, noting the changes in their expressions following yesterday's events.

With the wedding behind him, Dalhu looked like a new man. The stress he'd been under for the past several weeks was finally gone, and his marriage vows to Amanda had gained him approval from many who had been still suspicious of the former Doomer.

Lokan always looked stressed, which was understandable given the danger he was in due to his association with the clan and the undercover work he was doing for them.

Thankfully, his father had shipped him off to China, so he wasn't under constant scrutiny as he would have been if he'd remained on the island. Still, it had to be nerve-wracking to straddle the fence like that, and Kian wished he could just tell his cousin to cross over permanently, but he was the only spy they had in the Brotherhood, and they couldn't afford to lose that connection.

Kian doubted that Areana knew as much as she thought she did about Navuh's dealings, but even if she did, he didn't think she would have told Annani anything about them unless they included a direct threat to her sister's life. Regrettably, his aunt loved her psychotic mate and would never betray him.

"I still can't get over how gorgeous your dress was," Carol said to Amanda. "When Lokan and I finally get married, I want your designer to make my dress."

Amanda pulled out her phone. "I'll get you her contact information right now."

"By the time we get married, the designer will probably be dead," Lokan grumbled under his breath. "Humans don't live that long."

Carol cast him an amused look. "Don't be such a pessimist. The Fates might resolve things for us sooner than we expect."

"What things need to be resolved?" Syssi asked.

"The island, our post in China, and the designer label that started as a cover for Lokan's work with the Chinese authorities but has become my life's passion."

Annani listened to the exchange with a small smile lifting her lips. "I do not see why any of these things should have an impact on your wedding ceremony. You can tie the knot right here on the cruise. We can squeeze you in for a lunchtime wedding."

Carol shook her head, causing her golden curls to flutter around her face. "I told Lokan that we can't get married as long as we are in danger. I want to feel safe when I pledge my life to this rascal." She nudged his arm playfully.

Annani's smile slid off her face. "The only place I feel safe in is my Alaskan home, but to be frank, I do not feel completely safe even there because safety is an illusion. The trick is to be vigilant and not to let fear paralyze you and prevent you from living your life."

Annani

B oth of Kian's brows hiked up nearly to his hairline. "You don't feel safe in the village? That's news to me. Besides, since when have you been concerned about safety? Given your track record of shenanigans that have kept me awake at night, I assumed that you were fearless."

Annani smiled. "I am a goddess, so there is not much that can harm me, and the odds are in my favor, but since nearly my entire family got wiped out in a single act of terror, I know never to let down my guard. If I had not been vigilant back then, if I had underestimated Mortdh's irrational disdain for me and, by extension, for all females, I would not have fled in the nick of time, and I would have died along with everyone I knew and loved."

As Toven's sigh from across the table drew her attention, Annani turned to him. "I am sorry for bringing up a painful subject. Even five thousand years are not enough to blunt the pain of our loss."

He nodded. "It comes and goes. Sometimes, I manage to forget and enjoy the life I have with Mia, my children and grandchildren, and your entire lovely clan. But sometimes I'm crushed under the painful memories." He inhaled deeply. "I also carry the pain of entire civilizations wiped out of existence despite my best efforts to save them. I can't grasp the savagery, not in humans and even less so in Mortdh. As a god, he should have been above the ape-like savage impulses, but I guess that in his case, it wasn't innate but a form of insanity."

Kian chuckled. "No one thinks otherwise. Mortdh's insanity is a well-established fact."

Syssi put a hand on his arm. "We should change the subject. This is not good for the children."

She was right. Allegra and Evie were too young to understand what was being said, but Phoenix was older, and she was smart for her age. Listening intently to the conversation, the girl had worry in her eyes.

Annani waved a hand over the spread on the table. "We can continue talking after breakfast. When we are done, Okidu and Onidu can take the girls to the other room and watch them while Jacki shows us her amulet."

"Good idea," Jacki said. "I left Darius with Shamash in our cabin because I don't want my son to be anywhere near that thing when I take it out of the box." She turned to Amanda. "The same goes for your children."

Alena rubbed a hand over her rapidly growing stomach. "Perhaps I shouldn't be here when you bring it over. It might affect my baby, and I don't want to take the risk."

"I agree," Orion said. "We will either leave or join the girls in the other room."

"I'd rather leave." Alena turned to Syssi. "We can take the children with us."

Syssi hesitated for a moment before nodding. "Will you be okay watching over the three of them?"

Alena grinned. "Of course. It will be my pleasure."

"I'm very curious to see the amulet," Syssi's father said. "Would it be okay if I take pictures?"

Jacki scrunched her nose. "I'd rather you didn't. Some nutcase somewhere might see the photograph in one of your photography books, recognize the amulet for what it is and come looking for it. The thing has the ability to absorb the life force from the slain, and there are plenty of monsters out there that would slaughter thousands to imbue it with power."

"Uhm," Syssi cleared her throat. "We agreed to save the talking for later, remember?"

"Oops." Jacki covered her mouth with her hand. "I forgot. Let's change the subject to something happy and upbeat so I don't slip again."

When a long moment of silence stretched across the table, Annani's heart contracted. They were all searching their minds for happy topics to talk about and could not come up with a single thing. It was not because nothing good was happening in the world but because it was difficult to think positively after what had happened the day before. Annani had not heard all the details yet, and she had a feeling that things were even worse than what she was imagining.

Given how stricken Syssi looked under the fake smiles she was trying to cover her distress with, she might have talked with Jacki and gotten more information. Another possibility was that Syssi's empathic nature made her more sensitive to the suffering of others than anyone sharing the breakfast table with her.

"I have just the subject," Amanda said. "Wonder and Anandur's wedding tonight. Who wants to bet on Anandur wearing a garter under his tux pants and tossing it at the bachelors after the ceremony?"

Kian chuckled. "I'm not betting against it, and before you ask, he hasn't told me anything."

"You know what would be great?" Mia said. "If Wonder came dressed as Wonder Woman. After all, that was the inspiration for her name. It would be so cool."

As all eyes turned to Amanda, she lifted her hands. "Don't look at me. I'm sworn to secrecy. Besides, I want it to be a surprise. Wonder hasn't given me any instructions or asked for anything specific. She said that she trusted me to come up with stuff she would never even think of. She's very easy to please."

"She is," Annani agreed. "Back in Sumer, when she was still Gulan, she was a very gentle and amiable girl." She smiled. "I was the wild one, and my parents hoped that her easy-going nature would rub off on me."

"Did it work?" Jacki asked.

Annani laughed. "Not at all. I continued to come up with wild schemes, and poor Gulan was in a constant state of panic. I mean Wonder. She does not like to be reminded of her former life. For some reason, she is ashamed of having been my servant even though I never thought of or treated her as such. She was my best friend."

Gulan had been Annani's only friend. The palace guards she had played games with had included her in their play-time because she was the princess, and they had to do what she asked, not because they sought her company.

"There is no shame in being a servant," Syssi's father said. "And being the handmaiden of a princess is a very honor-able position."

"Indeed." Annani sighed. "Perhaps it is more about her waking up from stasis as a different person than her years in my service."

"Tula is very different from her older sister," Carol said. "There is nothing timid about her, and she thinks very highly of her position as Areana's companion and confidant, and rightfully so."

Leaning back in her chair, Annani sighed. "I envy you for having seen my sister and Tula, but I do not envy you for what you had to go through to do so. I am not as brave."

Carol's eyes widened. "I don't believe that even for one moment. If you could have, you would have jumped at the opportunity to have a fabulous adventure."

"I am not sure," Annani admitted. "Your so-called adventure almost got you killed."

Syssi cleared her throat. "It seems like we can't have a conversation for longer than five minutes before it touches on a subject that shouldn't be discussed in front of the children."

Annani cast her a fond smile. "You are right that we should let the girls enjoy their innocence for as long as we can. At some point, though, we should stop shielding them from the ugliness of this world. They need to start building up their resilience or they will be paralyzed by the first crisis they face."

Syssi blushed, probably thinking that Annani was criticizing her for being soft, but that had not been her intention. Anita and Adam had not coddled Syssi when she was growing up. She was just a sensitive, soft-hearted soul.

Jacki

Once breakfast was over, Alena and Orion took the children to their cabin, and as the door closed behind them, Jacki leaned back in her chair with her coffee cup in hand and turned to Lokan. "Now, you can ask me whatever you want."

He arched a brow. "How did you know?"

She shrugged. "I don't need a paranormal talent to figure out what's on people's minds, and that includes immortals. You kept glancing my way, opening your mouth, and then closing it. Obviously, you wanted to ask me something."

"Yeah, I did, but Syssi kept reminding us that we shouldn't talk about upsetting things in front of the kids. Carol and I heard the main points of what you saw in your vision, but how did you know that it happened recently or that it happened at all? You could have seen the future."

"I just knew." Jacki leveled her gaze at her brother-in-law. "But that's not the real question, is it? You want to know how I convinced everyone of the veracity of my horrific vision, and then had them chase after the kidnapped women and tear the monsters who committed the atrocities to pieces with their fangs just based on what I told them, which could have been untrue."

Next to her, Kalugal shifted in his chair and squared his shoulders, ready to defend her, but Jacki didn't need his intervention.

"Yes," Lokan admitted. "I don't doubt what you saw or that those monsters were guilty of everything you said they were. The women you rescued are proof of that. My concern is that it was done based on a vision, and we all know that foretelling should be taken with a grain of salt."

"I'm not a compeller, and I didn't force anyone to accept my vision as truth. I'm not a convincing orator, either. I just say things as I see them without embellishing or diminishing anything. That's why I was believable when I described those horrific acts of cruelty. Still, Kalugal would not have ordered the attack without first peeking into the minds of several of the women and seeing exactly what I saw in my vision."

Annani lifted her hand to get everyone's attention. "If you are up to it, I want to hear it from you, Jacki. I heard a highly censored version from Kian, but I do not need to be coddled, and I want to know if there was anything in your vision about who ordered the massacre and the sexual assaults."

As horrible as that was, it hadn't been the worst of it, but evidently Kian had chosen not to tell his mother in order to spare her tender feelings.

Jacki wasn't as worried about the goddess's ability to handle the information as she was about Carol's.

Across the table, Carol was chewing on her lower lip and winding a curl around her finger, releasing it, and then winding it up again.

Jacki hesitated.

Carol was a survivor of torture and repeated sexual violation by a sadistic Doomer. She'd not only survived but had also become an undercover agent and gone on a highly dangerous mission. Still, Jacki had no doubt that she carried deep emotional scars.

"Carol, sweetheart. Perhaps it's better if you wait out on the balcony while I tell the Clan Mother what I saw."

The tiny blond shook her head. "Don't worry about me. After what I've been through, I'm no longer naïve or soft-hearted. I know the depths of depravity monsters can sink to."

As tears prickled the back of Jacki's eyes, she shook her head. "No, you don't. What I'm about to say is worse than anything you can imagine." Bile rose in her throat as the images played before her eyes, and she knew that verbalizing everything again would feel like acid was eating her from the inside, but hiding evil deeds to spare people's feelings was wrong.

The good people of the world needed to know because evil needed to be stopped and wiped off the face of the earth.

"I want to hear it," Carol said. "I'm a survivor, I'm brave, and I don't cower under the blanket, hiding from monsters. I kill them before they can get me."

"As you wish." Jacki sighed. "But don't say I didn't warn you."

When Jacki was done talking, all the males had their fangs fully extended, Syssi, Nathalie, and Mia were sobbing, Amanda was crying quietly, with rivulets of mascara running down her cheeks, Sari's eyes blazed daggers, and the Clan Mother looked infinitely sad.

But Carol looked catatonic.

Jacki took in a deep breath and turned to Lokan. "I think Carol needs some fresh air."

"We all do." He helped his mate up and walked her out the open balcony doors.

"How do you do that?" Syssi blew her nose into a napkin. "How are you so strong? After what you told me yesterday, I couldn't sleep all night, and you didn't even tell me the worst parts. You didn't tell me about what they did to the children, the babies." As her sobbing intensified, Kian pulled her onto his lap and wrapped his arms around her.

Jacki closed her eyes and then immediately opened them as the horrific images flooded the space behind her closed lids. "I'm only as strong as I need to be to do the right thing."

"And what's that?" Amanda lifted a cloth napkin and wiped her mascara-stained cheeks.

"Rally the troops, rescue the survivors, and go to war. I did all three."

Frankie

"Good morning, Mistress Frankie and Master Dagor." Bob grinned, flashing his metallic teeth. They were just two convex strips of metal with grooves etched into them to mimic the look of the real thing. "What can I serve you today?"

"Two Bloody Marys and two bags of pretzels, please." Frankie leaned over the counter and scanned the various snacks. "Unless you have something more nutritious to offer."

"Peanuts are a good source of protein." Bob reached with one of his long arms to snatch them off the overhead conveyor. "I also have roasted edamame beans, another good source of protein."

"We will take both," Dagor said. "Two of each."

"Of course, master." Bob put four bags on the counter and then reached for two glasses to mix the Bloody Marys.

Frankie tore into the roasted edamame bag and shook some into the palm of her hand. "That should do it, right? Since it's nutritious and all that."

Dagor chuckled. "I'm not an expert on human dietary needs, but I doubt Bridget would approve."

Frankie shrugged and shoved another palmful into her mouth.

"Your drinks are ready." Bob pushed the two tall Bloody Mary glasses toward them. "Enjoy."

"Thank you." Dagor took the drinks and turned around to scan for a good place to sit. "Shade or no shade?" he asked.

He was wearing his sunglasses, so the bright sunlight wasn't a problem, and he wasn't concerned about skin cancer either. That wasn't the case for her, though.

Frankie had forgotten to put on sunscreen before leaving the cabin, and she needed to stay out of direct sunlight to protect her skin. Once she turned immortal, if she ever turned, she could do whatever she wanted and not worry about the consequences.

"Shade," she said.

"Thank you." Dagor rewarded her with a smile. "I prefer shade, too."

"So why didn't you say anything? It's not all about me, you know."

"I'm trying to be a gentleman." He walked over to a table with an umbrella opened and put the drinks down. "It's my job to take care of your needs to the best of my ability."

Huffing out a breath, Frankie sat down on the chair he'd pulled out for her. "It's my job to do the same for you. Next time you have a preference, please let me know. It might work for me or not, but at least I won't choose arbitrarily without taking your needs into consideration."

Dagor smiled. "Is that part of the list of things you wanted to talk to me about?"

She had forgotten all about it.

On the way to the ruins, she'd promised to give him a list of acceptable and unacceptable behaviors, but with all that had happened since, it was no wonder that it had escaped her mind.

"I don't really have a list," she admitted. "But if I had one, this would be on it. We need to learn as much as we can about each other, and the only way to do so is to be open about our likes and dislikes. We will have to figure out things as we go, and if you want, you can take notes."

Dagor was the type of guy who would actually do that. He liked everything neatly organized in the appropriate boxes, and anything that was out of place bothered him. She was willing to bet that he was a neat freak and added that to her own mental list of things she needed to learn about him.

"I keep it all up here." He tapped a finger over his temple. "So far, I have two items. One is to never leave you sleeping without letting you know in some form where I went and when I will be back. The other one is to express my preferences if I have them. Anything else that you can think of?"

"Many things, but since I can't think of them off the top of my head, we will have to address them as we go." Her gut clenched with what she was about to say next, but her expression was firm. "Hopefully, we will have plenty of time to do that on our trek through Tibet."

His eyes widened. "You want to come with me?"

She shrugged as if it wasn't a big deal. "You can't abandon your mission, but I can postpone my beta testing internship or perhaps assist in some way remotely." She grimaced. "Regrettably, I'm not a girl of independent means, and I need a way to earn a living while we are searching for the missing pods."

For a long moment, he stared at her as if she had grown a pair of horns. "You don't need to worry about money while you are with me, but finances are not the main problem with your very generous offer."

Frankie hadn't planned on blurting out her idea to Dagor before she had a concrete plan, and she blamed her impulsivity for that. "Finances are important to me because I don't want to be completely dependent on you for every purchase I make. That will just not do. But other than that,

I see no problem with me joining you on the mission. Gabi is going, so it's not like you can't take civilians with you."

"You are still human, Frankie. And even if you start transitioning soon, it will be weeks before you are ready for a grueling trek."

So that was his problem. She was a weak human, and she would hold them back.

"I get it. You don't want me to slow you down. But maybe I can join you after my transition is complete and I'm back on my feet? I could fly out and meet you somewhere. I'm sure there are airports in Tibet."

"Not where we are going."

Dagor

Dagor hated the uncertainty of their situation, and he hated putting Frankie in a position where she was planning to give up her dreams to be with him.

"Let's not talk about it now, okay? It can wait until your transition starts."

Her brow furrowed, and she assumed the stubborn expression he dreaded and loved at the same time.

On the one hand, it meant that Frankie was going to argue until she won, and he would have to accept things he didn't want to, but on the other hand, he loved her confidence and her ability to stick to her guns.

"We don't have the luxury of time." She huffed out a breath. "Besides, you are the one who needs everything planned out."

She'd got him there, but how could he make plans when it wasn't clear whether or not she could turn immortal?

What if she couldn't, though?

What if she remained human?

He was in love with Frankie. He couldn't just forget her because her lifespan was so short. It was better not to think about it just yet. Why worry about something that might not happen?

"I wish I could make a plan, but everything depends on you turning immortal."

Frankie narrowed her eyes at him. "So, what are you saying, that you will just leave me if I don't transition?"

"That's not what I'm saying at all. What I meant was that we can't plan for the future without knowing the outcome of your induction. Plans that will fit Frankie the immortal will not fit Frankie the human."

Deflating, she sank into the chair. "Yeah. The same things are going round on a loop in my head. Perhaps we can make two plans, one for each outcome."

That was actually not a bad idea.

"What happens with your job offer if you don't transition?"

"They erase my memories of gods and immortals, which will probably include this cruise and you." She winced. "Toven says that he's very good at that, and he can leave some of the memories and just change a few details. Maybe

I would remember meeting you and falling in love, but not the fact that you are a god."

He nodded. "I get that part, but what about the job? Will they find you something else to do that is not in their village, or will they just leave you to find something else on your own?"

"I guess Toven can get me a job in one of the Perfect Match studios. Why?"

He smiled and reached for her hand. "If I know where you will be working, I can find you there, and even if they erase me from your memories, I can make you fall in love with me all over again."

Her eyes softened. "And then what? You will pretend to be human?"

"Yes. Hopefully, we will find the missing pods, so I will be free to spend time with you."

"For how long?" she whispered. "You're not going to age, and you can't keep thralling me every day to not notice that you look exactly the same years later."

"Thralling is not my only option. I can also shroud, but you are right. If I don't tell you the truth about me, I will have to thrall you every time we are intimate, and that means daily. I can't do that. You'll need to know who and what I am and accept me all over again."

"I'm sure I will, but I don't want you to suffer, and you will suffer if you have to watch me get old and die."

Dagor lifted his glass and emptied what was left down his throat. "It's my choice to make. The only choice you have is to either love me back or not. And don't think for even a moment about pretending to not want me just to save me heartache in the future."

She chuckled. "Am I that transparent?"

"To me, you are. You have a noble heart beating in your chest, and you think of the well-being of others before you think of your own."

"You think too highly of me." Frankie took another sip of her Bloody Mary. "I'm not that selfless. What about our children, though? Will they be born Dormant or immortal?"

Dagor swallowed. "If we are blessed with children, they will be born immortal."

The thought of fathering hybrid children had been foreign to him only days earlier, but witnessing the wedding ceremonies and observing the two little baby girls at the family table had changed things for him, and what once had felt like 'hell no' had turned into 'hell yes' or at least 'hell maybe.'

"Oh, boy." She took another sip from her drink and then licked her lips. "Then you will need to hang around long enough for them to become adults so you can guide them on how to remain undetected."

"I plan on doing that regardless of whether we have children. I don't think I can live without you."

"Oh, Dagor." She leaned over and kissed him on the lips. "I love you too much to let you suffer when I die. I'll have to make you fall out of love with me."

"Not possible." He cupped her cheek. "You don't have it in you to be mean to me."

She arched a brow. "You wanna bet?"

"Sure." He clasped her hand. "What are you going to give me when I win?"

"What do you want?"

He leaned over and whispered the prize in her ear.

She laughed. "You are so naughty."

"Is it a 'yes'?"

"You got yourself a deal." She shook his hand. "What do I get if I win?"

"You won't win. Not this time."

Syssi

S yssi sincerely considered asking one of the gods to remove the memory of what Jacki had told them, and if that made her a coward and a weakling, so be it.

She doubted she could continue functioning with that horror movie playing on repeat inside her head. She did not want to raise her daughter in a world where things like that could happen. But what were her options?

Move to a colony on Mars?

Suddenly, the gods' planet didn't seem that bad. Peace and security were worth sacrificing some freedoms for, right?

Not that it was an option. The gods thought of immortals and all other hybrids as abominations, and they were not welcomed on Anumati.

"Can I get you a glass of wine?" Kian asked quietly.

"I need something stronger than that, but I doubt it will help. What I need is a brain scrub to erase what I just heard."

"I can help with that," Annani offered.

Syssi shook her head. "I can't. I have to be strong."

Maybe she would take Annani up on her offer after touching the damn amulet and getting a dose of visuals to supplement what her mind had already supplied.

"I can be strong for the both of us," Kian murmured. "You don't need this crap to keep you awake at night."

"Yes, I do. I owe it to the victims."

"Dammit, Syssi. I need you to listen to reason. Please let my mother erase this ugliness from your mind and ease your burden."

She shook her head. "If all of you can handle this, I can as well. I have to."

Mia let out a long, shaky breath. "I can't handle this, and I will gladly accept Toven's help to erase the past twenty minutes from my mind. I know it's wrong, but I can't let this poison me from the inside. I want the bliss of ignorance."

But that was the problem. So many people were ignorant, most willfully so, because it was easier to believe the lies than acknowledge the ugly truth.

Syssi refused to be part of the uninformed masses, even if it meant sacrificing her peace of mind. "I'll take that drink." She lifted her head and scanned the room for the Odus. "Okidu, can you get me a giant margarita, please?"

"Of course, mistress." He bowed and rushed to the bar.

Amanda lifted her hand. "Make me one too."

"I'll get the whiskey." Dalhu pushed to his feet.

He had responded to Jacki's retelling the same way all the other males had, with glowing eyes and elongated fangs, but while Kian, Andrew, and David wrestled theirs under control, and Kalugal's, Toven's, and Lokan's had retracted halfway, Dalhu's were still fully elongated.

It was ironic that Syssi found Dalhu's rage reassuring.

The answer to violence shouldn't be more violence, but sometimes nothing else worked to eradicate evil and protect the innocent and the defenseless, and Syssi was glad to have the powerful warrior on her side.

Her father eyed the gods and immortals with fascination rather than trepidation, which was good, and her mother looked like she was on the verge of tears, but she did not allow them to fall.

Anita had always been an iron lady, the cornerstone of their family, and Syssi wished she had half of her mother's resilience and strength. She was also glad that her mother hadn't commented about her being overly sensitive like she used to when Syssi was a teenager.

They were nothing alike, and it had always been difficult to reconcile their different personalities.

Perhaps being a doctor had hardened Anita, or maybe she had chosen to become a physician because she had that hard core inside of her that Syssi lacked. It was no coincidence that Syssi hadn't followed in her mother's footsteps and had chosen to major in architecture with a minor in business. Neither field involved any human drama.

When Dalhu was done pouring whiskey for the guys and Sari, Okidu handed out margaritas to the rest of them, save for Mia. Even the Clan Mother accepted a glass with a salty rim and slowly sipped on it.

Taking the large glass with her, Annani leaned back in her chair and looked at Jacki. "You did not say anything about who was behind the attack other than the cartel thugs. They are known to be vicious, but usually not to such an extent. Did you notice anything that would indicate they were being directed by an outside force?"

Yeah, they were probably possessed by demons.

Syssi couldn't imagine a society that produced such monsters. It was beyond gang wars and drugs and even trafficking. Who were their mothers? Their fathers? Who had raised such twisted creatures?

"I didn't," Jacki said. "All I got were visuals of the attack. There might have been some clues, but I was too overwhelmed and shocked to notice anything else."

Annani nodded. "That is perfectly understandable, dear."

Syssi felt in her gut that touching the amulet would make her see more, but maybe it wasn't a good idea to do it with Carol in the room.

She and Lokan were still out on the balcony, but they would no doubt come back inside when Jacki brought the amulet to show them.

"Let's see that amulet," her father said. "I'm curious to see the thing that has caused so much trouble."

"The thing didn't do it." Jacki rose to her feet. "It was only a tool, and it helped us rescue the victims. Still, remember not to touch it with your bare hand. Use a cloth napkin."

"I don't have any psychic ability," her father said when Jacki ducked into the bedroom. "I can touch it as much as I want and not get any visions."

Her mother patted his arm. "It's better to be careful, Adam. You never know. Perhaps Syssi got her paranormal ability from you. She surely hasn't gotten it from me."

"I wish that was true." Her father cast her a reassuring smile. "But I'm not a Dormant."

What if he was, though?

They had never considered the possibility that her father could be a carrier of the immortal genes as well. Perhaps Dormants weren't as rare as they had initially believed, and the affinity Dormants and immortals felt for each other increased the chances of Dormant pairings.

Not that it mattered. Both her parents were way over the age of attempting to transition safely.

Kian

"Ready for the big reveal?" Jacki opened the box and pulled out a cloth bundle.

"Very much so." Syssi's father pushed to his feet and walked over to look at it over Jacki's shoulder.

She put it on the dining table and carefully peeled off the layers of fabric without touching the object itself.

It was a big piece, definitely not something that would be comfortable to wear around the neck, but it was impressive, and Kian could imagine a male priest wearing it over his bare chest.

The opal in the center was the size of a large potato, and it most likely weighed two pounds or more. The color was magnificent even as it lay dormant on top of the fabric wrapping, and Kian was sure that if he dangled it from its chain, he would see even more colors as the light hit its polished surface. Most of it was orange, making it appear as if it contained fire, but there was also red, green, and yellow.

Holding a napkin, Adam reached for the amulet and lifted it by its chain. "It's heavy."

Jacki nodded. "It is."

As the amulet swung from Adam's fingers, the opal reflected the light as Kian had expected, and the colors seemed to swirl like there was something alive in it. A pulsating heart or a vein.

"Creepy," Andrew murmured, echoing Kian's thoughts.

"What's written on the edges?" Amanda turned to Toven. "Can you read that?"

The disgusted expression on his face indicated that he wanted nothing to do with the artifact, but he leaned a little closer, squinted, and then pulled out his phone and snapped a picture. "It's been a while, and I'm rusty. I'll try to decipher the writing from the photo, but I can guess what it says. It's something along the lines of beseeching the gods to accept the sacrifice, and in exchange, grant the wearer either prophetic powers or victory against their enemies. It's always the same. Blood and more blood." He leaned away.

"I don't sense anything nefarious from it," Syssi said. "Maybe it was drained after the vision?"

"That's possible." Jacki sat down, leaving the amulet in Adam's hands. "When I touched it, I felt as if I was being zapped by a bolt of lightning, and I let go of it immediately. I held it for no longer than a split second. The vision appeared right away, and in my head, it lasted a long time, but I was unconscious only for a few moments. Then, when I wanted to find the victims, I put it around my neck, and it was more of a hum than a zap, a steady flow of something that communicated in sensations of hot and cold. If I was on the right path, it felt warm, and when we veered off, it cooled down." She chuckled. "An ancient GPS."

"Then it's probably safe to touch." Leaning over, Syssi started to reach for it, but Kian grabbed her shirt from behind and tugged her back down. "Don't touch it without protecting your skin." He took his folded napkin and handed it to her. "Use this."

"Fine." She cast him a glare.

"In fact, there is no reason for you to touch it at all." He was still holding on to the back of her shirt. "You can see it perfectly well from where you are right now."

"Here." Adam walked around the table and laid the amulet in front of Syssi. "Now you can examine it to your heart's content without touching it."

"Thanks, Dad." She peered over the thing as if she was trying to decipher all of its secrets. "It's gaudy, but I don't sense evil. Not that I know what evil feels like."

"It gives off a sense of foreboding," Nathalie said. "When you feel anxious for no reason and think that you are going crazy, there is evil nearby."

As everyone turned to look at her, Kian wondered if there was anything to that. Nathalie had described how he felt on most days, so did it mean that evil was lurking nearby all of the time?

Yeah, it kind of did.

He had Doomers to worry about, missing Kra-ell twins that were so powerful they could enslave the entire planet, Kra-ell assassins that were after his mother and the twins, and the Eternal King and whatever he would do to Earth once he discovered that the human population had grown to eight billion people and that their technological advancement posed a threat.

"Is this something you learned from the ghosts?" Amanda asked Nathalie.

Nathalie nodded. "The first one, Tut. He said that evil was everywhere, hiding in plain sight and pretending to be something else. Evil is a great liar because it has no scruples, so it can be very convincing." She sighed. "As a kid, I thought that he was mean, and that he wanted to scare me so I would be dependent on him, but he was right."

"What kind of a name is Tut?" Sari asked.

Nathalie chuckled. "Tutankhamun, but I think he lied about it. There is no way Tut was an ancient pharaoh."

"Who knows?" Annani said. "He might be. Tutankhamun was an interesting fellow. Very smart and pragmatic even though he was just a kid at the time."

"You knew him?" Sari asked.

"Of course. I knew most of the world's great leaders."

Syssi

As everyone's focus shifted to Annani, Syssi's remained on the amulet.

While the goddess regaled them with tales of ancient Egypt's religiopolitical climate at the time of the young pharaoh Tutankhamun and his predecessor Akhenaten, no one was paying attention to what Syssi was doing, and she might be able to touch it without anyone trying to stop her.

"The shift to a monotheistic religion nearly drove Egypt to economic ruin because its economy was based around the many temples of the different gods they worshipped." Annani sighed. "Akhenaten was too progressive for the times. The world was not ready for his lofty, elitist ideas. While he had gathered around him in his new beautiful capital city all the intellectuals of the time, which included all the priests from temples across Egypt, the common people of Egypt were left with no guidance, and things started falling apart. After Akhenaten's death, Tutankhamun reversed the move and restored Egypt to its former glory."

It was all fascinating, but Syssi was listening to it with half an ear while trying to control the trembling of her hand as she reached for the amulet.

Perhaps instead of taking it in her hand, she should only touch it with her finger? But which part should she touch, the opal or the casing?

Maybe she should stop being a chicken and just take it in her hand?

"Tutankhamun died at nineteen," Annani said. "But he managed to accomplish a lot in the ten years he ruled over Egypt."

Kian released an indignant huff. "A nine-year-old saved the country from economic ruin?"

"He was aided by his great-uncle, Ay, the real mastermind behind the restoration."

It was now or never. Kian was busy with his mother, and no one was looking at her. There would be hell to pay later, but she had to do it.

Closing her eyes, Syssi extended her hand and smacked her palm down on the amulet.

The vision was so instantaneous that it knocked her off her feet, and she felt herself falling backward, but she didn't hit the floor. Instead, she was floating over a scene and watching events unfold from above like she had done countless times before.

The main difference was the speed with which it had happened, and her full awareness of what was going on.

Syssi was both in the scene she was witnessing and in Annani's cabin on the ship.

Six males were gathered around a map in a dimly lit room, all armed to the teeth and looking dangerous. They were speaking Spanish, of which she understood only every fifth word, and then two of them switched to another language she didn't understand but recognized as the bastardized version of Sumerian that the Doomers spoke.

One of them approached the map and drew a red circle around one of the villages, and as he spoke, she suddenly understood what he was saying as if he was speaking in plain English.

"Make an example out of them so all the others tremble in fear and give us what we demand without a fight. We don't tolerate disobedience."

As the other four exchanged glances, Syssi hoped they would argue against the command or at least look uneasy, but when they turned to their co-conspirators, the four grinned with so much malice in their eyes that they looked more demonic than their masters.

"Sí, señor."

The Doomer clapped the thug on the back. "Kill everyone, except for the pretty girls they refused to hand over. They are worth a lot of money to us. You can have your fun with them, but don't damage the merchandise too much. Just break it in." He laughed. "Surprisingly, virgins are not in high demand these days."

The vision winked out, and Syssi gasped, "Doomers."

"What about them?" Kian barked.

She was in his arms, and he was looking at her with fury in his eyes.

Oh, yeah, there would be hell to pay, but that was okay. Once he heard what she had to say, he would forget about being mad at her and get busy correcting the grave mistake they had made.

"Doomers were behind the attack. They control the cartel. If they come to investigate what happened to their monsters and find the remains, they will figure out immediately who disposed of them, and they'll come after us."

Only a bunch of hungry jaguars, lions, or immortals with fangs could have torn those monsters apart like that, but the big cats wouldn't have buried them.

It wouldn't take a genius to connect the dots and follow them to the only tourist group who had visited the ruins that day and then to the ship they had come from.

"Crap." Kian let out a breath. "What do we do now?"

"We turn around," Kalugal said. "We need to burn the bodies, or rather the body parts, before they find them."

Pushing out of Kian's arms, Syssi moved back to her chair and emptied the last of her margarita.

"Was it bad?" Jacki asked. "What did you see?"

"I saw six monsters planning a horrific attack and smiling about it."

"There were six of them?" Kian filled a glass with water and handed it to her.

"Two Doomers and four cartel thugs."

"How do you know they were Doomers?" Kian motioned for her to drink up.

She took a couple of sips and put the glass down. "Visions are strange. They spoke in Spanish to the thugs, and I understood a little of it but not enough to make sense of what they were saying. Then, the two Doomers switched to their own language, which I don't understand at all, but I know how it sounds. Then they spoke to the thugs again, and although it was back to Spanish, I heard it as if it was plain English. They ordered the thugs to make an example out of that village so no one would ever oppose them again, and they told them to take the pretty girls because they're worth a lot of money."

Kian

Kian was doing his best to contain his anger, and yet he was doing a piss-poor job of it. Syssi was casting him fearful looks that cut him worse than anything she had revealed, but he couldn't bring himself under control.

It was her right to do whatever she deemed necessary to enhance her visions, and he could hate it as much as he wanted, but he couldn't stop her from doing that or be angry at her for using her Fate-given talent to help the clan.

Her latest revelation might save them a lot of trouble, provided that they made it to the burial site before the Doomers discovered what had happened to their henchmen.

"I need to tell the captain to turn around." He raked his fingers through his hair.

"Tell him we forgot someone," Jacki said. "He doesn't need to know why we are turning back, right? The less he knows, the better."

"I don't need to tell him anything. He will do as I ask." He pushed to his feet and offered Syssi a hand up. "Do you want to come with me?"

She hesitated for a split second. "Sure."

"I'm not mad," he said when they were outside the cabin.

"You could have fooled me. You still look mad."

"I'm angry because I hate when you put yourself in danger, but I also hate that I make it more difficult for you. You have every right to use your talent as you see fit as long as you don't hurt anyone else in the process. I just wish you didn't hurt yourself."

"I don't." She smiled and stretched on her toes to kiss his cheek. "Not really. I might seem fragile, and maybe I am, but I'm not a coward. What was the worst that could have happened? I would have seen something even more disturbing than what Jacki recounted? So what? If I couldn't live with it, your mother or Toven could have erased it from my brain."

He shook his head. "You know that it doesn't work like that. Remember the women we freed from the Doomers and took to Hawaii?"

"Of course. What about them?"

"Vanessa said that erasing their memories wasn't enough. They still remembered their trauma subconsciously despite the thrall, and the dissonance between what they felt but couldn't remember was detrimental to their mental health. They needed to work through it the conventional way."

Syssi let out a breath. "I didn't really plan on getting a memory wipe, but it was comforting to think that I had the option. Jacki must be made from solid titanium to handle what she saw so well. I'm grateful to the merciful Fates for sparing me the gruesome images and only showing me the demons at the planning stage. Perhaps the Fates, or whoever else is responsible for visions, know what each seer can tolerate and grant them glimpses of the past or future accordingly."

"That's possible." Kian stopped at the door to the bridge. "I might need you to court another vision."

Syssi looked at Kian, barely able to contain her astonishment.

Who was this man, and what had he done with her overprotective husband?

"Of course," she said quickly before he could change his mind. "What do you need me to find out?"

"We need to find where the Doomers are based and how many of them are involved with the cartels."

"I'll try, but you know how visions are. I might not get the answers to my questions."

"I know, but so far the Fates have shown you what you needed to see, so I trust that they will do the same now."

"I love you." She lifted on her toes and kissed him on his lips. "You're incredible."

A grin spread over his face, and he wrapped his arms around her, cupping her bottom. "I know, but it's always nice to hear. Tell me why I'm incredible."

"Well, there are the regular reasons, like the breadth of your shoulders, the shape of your lips, those tight glutes." She rubbed herself on him like a cat on a scratching post. "But what I admire most is your steadfast commitment to go against your instincts and not try to stifle me. I know how difficult that is for a caveman like you."

"You have no idea what a herculean effort that is." He reached for the door handle. "Let's take care of informing the captain of the change of plans, and then we'll go back to the cabin and try again."

Syssi nodded, but her stomach churned with unease at the thought of touching the amulet once more.

What if this time it showed her things she could never unsee?

Annani

⟨◦∽◦⟩

After Kian and Syssi had left to talk to the captain, the conversation continued in hushed voices, but Annani didn't take part in it.

She was still trying to compose herself, and it was proving difficult.

Living through most of human so-called civilized history, she'd witnessed atrocities such as Jacki had described before, but that did not make it any easier to process. Especially since she had truly believed that humanity had been going in the right direction and that kind of evil was never to return.

She had been wrong.

Humans were still savages, too easy to incite into committing terrible crimes against others either by ideology, religion, greed, or rather all three woven into one hateful motivational force to destroy.

The Doomers were not responsible for all of it, but enough.

The thing was, she had a feeling that the ultimate responsibility was with the gods. They had engineered humans to be easily influenced so they could control them effortlessly, and that back door into human minds was what made it possible for evildoers to turn otherwise ordinary people into monsters.

Were the Eternal King and the Anumati establishment aware of that? Was that the reason they viewed hybrid children born of unions between gods and lesser species as abominations?

As half-human, immortals suffered from the same vulnerability to virulent ideology, and that was made clearly evident by the disciples of Mortdh.

She used to believe that there was hope for the Doomers and that there was a way to undo the brainwashing and turn them into decent people, and that was why she forbade her people to execute the captured ones and put them into stasis instead.

Once Navuh was taken down and replaced by a progressive leader, she hoped those Doomers could be rehabilitated. Without the constant brainwashing and indoctrination, there might be a chance for them.

But perhaps she had been wrong.

Maybe there was no salvation for their souls. Perhaps Navuh's propaganda created fertile ground, but the poisoning was done by their own evil deeds.

Not even Navuh would have ordered the gruesome murder of children. His goal was global domination, and he was ruthless in attaining that goal, but he wouldn't have bothered with annihilating a poor village in Mexico to make a point and terrify the local population into compliance.

Still, it didn't surprise her that Doomers were behind the cartels. Navuh needed money for his operations, and there was a lot of it to be had from drugs and trafficking. The Doomers responsible for the local operation were probably free to do whatever was needed to maximize those profits, and what had been done to that village was their autonomous decision.

Sowing terror ensured there was no resistance to their operations.

If captured, those Doomers did not deserve mercy. They did not deserve stasis and a second chance at life, but if she made an exception in their case, she would weaken her stance, and Kian would pounce on it, advocating for execution in most altercations with the Brotherhood.

Annani sighed. She could use some advice.

It was a shame that the first talk with her grandmother had not even been scheduled yet. The queen had vast experience and, given her machinations, she was also very smart.

She might have some words of wisdom for her grand-daughter.

The irony was not lost on her. Annani was one of the five oldest people on Earth, and yet she looked to someone even older for advice.

Perhaps Toven would have words of wisdom for her? After all, he was even older than she was. When there was a lull in the conversation, Annani caught Toven's eyes and presented her dilemma.

"End them," Kalugal answered for Toven. "And that's coming from me, as a former member of the Brotherhood. There are a few who are worth saving, but the ones Syssi saw in her vision are beyond redemption."

Toven nodded. "I agree. Ordering the torture and murder of children goes against every human and immortal instinct. Those capable of such acts are so diseased that there is no cure for them."

As everyone around the table echoed the same sentiment, Annani sighed.

"I do not often admit to having been mistaken, but I have to concede that it was naïve of me to apply my moral standards and my belief in the good that exists in all of our hearts to those who hold my beliefs in contempt and consider them a weakness to be exploited. Some Doomers might still hold on to a shred of decency, and those are the ones I want to save, but those who are proven to have none left need to be eliminated. Human lives mean nothing to them. Immortal lives mean nothing to them. Suffering means nothing to them. Therefore, they mean nothing to me."

Kian

Kian could sense the change in the room as soon as he and Syssi returned.

He pulled out a chair for his wife. "Did something happen while we were gone?"

His mother nodded. "We had an interesting conversation about the merit of granting captured Doomers a second chance, and I arrived at the conclusion that, in certain situations, that is not advisable. The Doomers responsible for this attack do not deserve a second chance at life."

That was so unexpected that for a moment, Kian was stunned speechless. The Doomers had committed plenty of atrocities before, and his mother had always been adamant about not ending them if they were captured.

Thankfully, she had decreed that the lives of Guardians always came first, so killing Doomers in the heat of battle was okay.

Since most Doomers fought to the death, it wasn't often they were captured alive. It mostly happened when they were severely injured and could not fight any longer. That too didn't happen often, so even though Kian didn't agree with his mother's softhearted edict, he hadn't made too much effort to change her mind about it.

Still, over the centuries they had collected so many Doomers in their catacombs that they were running out of room.

He would like nothing better than to stop the inflow, but he doubted that his mother's resolve would extend beyond the Doomers responsible for the vicious attack on the villagers.

"That's a surprising and welcome change of heart, but I haven't decided what to do about the situation yet. My initial plan was to get rid of the evidence of our involvement by burning the bodies and hopefully avoiding direct confrontation with the Doomers. We are on vacation, we have a wedding to celebrate tonight, and I don't want to rush into things without giving it more thought."

"I agree," Kalugal said. "We don't know how many of them are out here. If it's only the two that Syssi saw in her vision, then we can easily get rid of them and continue on our merry way. But if there is a large group stationed here, we shouldn't go in seeking vengeance and get Guardians killed."

Given the determined expression on his mother's face, she didn't like that answer.

"I understand the need for caution, and I do not recommend rushing in without a plan, but we need to take out this cell of the Brotherhood, and we need to make it look like the locals did it."

That was an angle Kian hadn't considered. "That sounds good in theory, but how are we going to do that?"

His mother smiled. "You are the general, my son. You will find a way."

"Right." He raked his fingers through his hair. "I need to assemble my war council, and I hate that I need to do so during my damn vacation."

Next to him, Syssi shifted in her seat. "Maybe I should touch the amulet again to see how many of them are here?"

Every muscle in Kian's body tensed, and he clenched his jaw to keep himself from resisting. He'd been the one who had suggested that she try again, but now that he looked at the artifact that was still displayed on the table, he had second thoughts.

Resting on top of the fabric that Jacki had wrapped it in, it looked like a piece of costume jewelry, and if Kian hadn't seen how quickly it had thrown Syssi into a vision, he would have thought that it had nothing to do with it other than Syssi's belief in its power. But he'd seen her summon a vision before, and it had taken much more effort even when she did it in Allegra's room and somehow drew on their daughter's power.

But what if Syssi was just getting stronger and faster the more visions she summoned?

Maybe it had nothing to do with Allegra or the amulet?

He turned to her. "I want you to try something for me."

"What?"

"Try to summon a vision without touching the amulet. In fact, go over to the couch so you are not anywhere near it."

Syssi frowned. "Why?"

"I have a feeling that your powers have increased naturally and that you don't need anything to enhance them." He turned to Mia. "If you don't mind, I would like you to go out to the balcony while Syssi is summoning the vision. I don't want you enhancing her powers either."

"Of course." Mia put her chair in reverse.

Syssi lifted a hand. "Hold on, Mia." She turned to Kian. "I'm all for experimenting with my ability, but now is not the time for that. We need answers, and I need all the help I can get. Mia should stay and get even closer to me while I touch the amulet."

"Syssi is right," his mother said. "We do not have time to experiment."

"There is also the issue of fatigue." Amanda looked at Syssi. "We know that your prophetic ability diminishes with every try."

"That's true, but when I tossed a coin with Mia next to me, my accuracy didn't drop with each subsequent toss. I guessed every single one correctly no matter how many times I repeated it."

Mia nodded. "That's how Syssi discovered my enhancing powers."

Kian let out a resigned breath. "I see that I'm overruled." He pushed to his feet and positioned himself behind Syssi. "Go ahead. I'm right here to catch you if you fall."

Syssi

Syssi had been sure that Kian would balk at the last moment, but she should have known that her husband would be true to his word.

She turned to Mia. "I wonder if touching you and the amulet at the same time would produce a stronger vision? Are you up for it?"

Mia shrugged. "I don't even know what I'm doing when I'm enhancing someone's power, but I know that I'm not going to see what you see, so yeah."

Toven looked worried. "I'm not sure about that."

"Why not?" Mia arched a brow. "It's not like I'm being taken into enemy territory, strapped to your back."

He winced. "That's different. I knew that I could protect you there. I can't protect you from the influence of this artifact or what it might reveal to Syssi."

"I'll be fine." She patted his arm before turning her chair around and driving over to where Syssi was standing. "Do you want to hold my hand?"

"Yes. Thank you." Syssi clasped Mia's small hand in hers and hovered the other one over the amulet, when it occurred to her that it wasn't safe for the girl.

The previous vision happened so fast that it had knocked her off her feet and she fell, but Kian had caught her. If Mia was in the way, she might get knocked over.

"Perhaps you should move a little to the side." She looked over her shoulder at Kian. "I trust you to catch me if I fall so I don't topple Mia."

"Of course." He put both of his hands on her shoulders. "Perhaps you can summon the vision while sitting on my lap. That way, you're not going to fall for sure."

She was seriously tempted to take him up on his offer, and the only reason she dismissed the idea was that she didn't want to add even more variables to her attempt.

"It's okay."

Taking a deep breath, Syssi put her hand on the amulet, but unlike the other time, nothing happened.

Baffled, she opened her eyes and frowned at the artifact. "It's not working. Maybe we've exhausted its power."

"Try to concentrate on your question," Jacki said. "Maybe it's weakened, and you need to pull it out of it."

Closing her eyes again, Syssi imagined the scene she'd witnessed before, with the two Doomers and four cartel thugs discussing the murder of innocents, and as the familiar swirl of an incoming vision started spinning in front of her, she surrendered to the sensation and let it pull her through the vortex.

Except, the scene she found herself in couldn't be farther from what she'd expected.

She was in the temple she had seen before, but this time both of the goddesses were there, the one with the silver hair and the seer, both glowing so brightly that it was impossible to discern their facial features.

Next to them, sitting on a cushion on the floor a few feet behind the seer, was a dark-haired goddess who didn't glow at all, and her face looked very familiar.

She was the feminine version of Aru, and she was using what looked like an old-fashioned quill to write in a large journal while the goddesses talked.

As the seer laughed at something the other one had said, the silver-haired goddess laughed too, and the two embraced.

They were obviously friends, and Syssi knew who they were. She also knew who the scribe was, and the pieces of the puzzle fell into place.

Did Kian know? And if he did, why hadn't he told her?

Also, why was she being shown this scene instead of what she'd asked for?

As the vision started fading and the vortex spat her out on the other side, she gasped, opened her eyes, and turned to look at Kian, who was holding her against his chest.

"That was short," he said. "What did you see?"

"Not what I set out to see." She pushed away from him and sank into her chair. "I think that the amulet is out of power."

"What about me?" Mia asked. "Did I help in any way?"

"Yes." Syssi smiled at her. "I think that I got the vision thanks to you, not the amulet. It was about the goddesses, not the Doomers or the cartel thugs."

Kian looked relieved more than disappointed, when he handed her a glass of water. "What was the vision about?"

She couldn't tell him in front of everyone, and she had a feeling that he already knew about Aru's connection to the seer and the queen but had chosen for some reason not to tell her.

"Oh, nothing." She waved a dismissive hand. "Before, I saw each of the goddesses separately, and now I saw them together in the temple, acting like the best of friends."

A sidelong glance at Annani proved her suspicion that her mother-in-law was in on the secret as well.

Syssi really didn't appreciate being kept in the dark like that.

"Perhaps I should give the amulet a try," Jacki said. "We need to know whether it's really out of power."

"Go ahead." Syssi waved a hand over the artifact.

"Wait." Kalugal hauled Jacki into his lap. "Now you can touch it."

Smiling, she kissed his cheek before turning back to the amulet.

Everyone held their breath as she lifted it by its chain and closed the palm of her other hand around it.

A long moment passed before Jacki opened her eyes and shook her head. "It's dead. There is no juice left in it." She turned to Kian. "I guess all we have left is our wits."

He grimaced. "What else is new?" He looked at the inert artifact. "So, what do we do with this thing now? Do you want to throw it in the ocean?"

Jacki looked at it for a moment before shaking her head and turning to Kalugal. "Add it to your collection of well-guarded treasures."

"What else is in there?" Kian asked.

Kalugal turned to look at him. "Mostly items that I'm still working on deciphering and a few things that were removed from sites without permission. Nothing in that collection would interest you."

Kian looked doubtful, but he didn't push the issue. "Would you like another cup of coffee?" he asked Syssi as he sat down.

"I would love a cup." Syssi smiled at Oridu, who rushed over with a fresh carafe. "Thank you."

She couldn't confront Kian in front of everyone about what she'd seen in her vision, but once the others left, she intended to bring it up with him and his mother.

Dagor

"**I** should call Margo." Frankie pulled the phone out of her pocket. "Can you get us another round of drinks?"

Dagor smiled. "No more Bloody Marys for you. Water or coke, what do you prefer?"

"Coke and more peanuts, please."

"Yes, ma'am." He leaned to kiss her pouty lips. "I think being a beta tester for Perfect Match is a waste of your natural talents. You should be a negotiator."

In less than an hour, Frankie had mapped out their two possible futures, one if she remained human and the other if she turned immortal, and had successfully tackled and solved all of his objections.

She chuckled. "Right. You are easy to negotiate with because you love me. My talents didn't work on my former bosses."

"I don't know how they didn't all fall in love with you, but I'm happy they didn't."

Rolling her eyes, she waved him away. "Go. I need to make this call before Margo calls me, or I won't hear the end of it."

"Fine." He pushed to his feet and walked over to the bar.

"One cold Coke coming up," Bob said. "And a bag of peanuts."

"Were you eavesdropping?"

"Of course. I hear everything that's being said on my deck."

"That's creepy. Were you told to do that?"

"I was told to anticipate my clients' needs. How else am I going to achieve that objective if I don't listen to what they say?"

"Do you report what you hear?"

The robot tilted his head in a very human way. "Why would I do that?"

"It's called spying."

A brief moment passed with Bob probably scanning his database of knowledge for what it meant to be a spy. "I see. I was not told to spy. Should I?"

"No, you shouldn't." Dagor shook his head. "I need to talk to William."

"He's right over there." Bob pointed with his long metallic arm.

Dagor must have been so absorbed in the conversation with Frankie that he hadn't noticed William and his mate arriving on the Lido deck and sitting on the other side of the pool.

"I will. Can you give me one more coke?"

"Of course, master."

Frankie was still on the phone with her friend when Dagor returned to their table. He put her drink and the bag of peanuts down, kissed her on the cheek, and continued to the other side of the pool.

"Good morning," he greeted William and Kaia. "May I join you?"

"Take a seat." William pointed at the lounger next to him. "I see that Frankie is feeling much better today."

"Yes, she is." Dagor affected a sly smile. "My venom must have sped up her recovery. She woke up this morning fully healed."

"That's amazing," Kaia said. "I wish we could bottle it and use it as a miracle cure. The problem is that it only activates once it's injected into a body. I tried to collect William's venom and run tests on it, but what I found could not explain any of the effects it has. It's such a bummer."

William didn't look happy about her sharing that information, but Kaia ignored his frown. Instead, she lifted her head and looked in the direction of the railing. "The ship is turning around. Did we forget someone in Acapulco?"

"Maybe." William rose to his feet. "But I doubt it. Maybe it has to do with the women we rescued." He pulled out his phone and frowned at the display. "Whatever the reason, we should have been notified of the change in plans."

Sensing Frankie approaching, Dagor turned to look at her.

She was still clutching the phone to her ear and looked worried. "What's going on? Why are we turning around?"

As Dagor's and William's phones simultaneously buzzed with incoming messages, Dagor tensed. "Something is up." He pulled out his phone and read the message. "Please report to the dining hall for an emergency meeting."

"I got the same thing," William said.

"I didn't." Kaia stared at her phone and then looked up. "If only you guys are being summoned, it has to do with what happened yesterday, and there is trouble."

"I'll call you right back," Frankie said to her friend and ended the call. "I didn't get anything either, and I'm officially freaking out. I bet the damn amulet showed Jacki another village being attacked and more women being taken." She started shaking. "I can't believe that it's happening again."

"We don't know that." Dagor pulled her into his arms. "Maybe it's about something completely different. Wait until we find out what it's about. It might be something as simple as someone who has been accidentally left behind. I don't remember anyone taking a tally of who was on board before leaving the port."

She raised her eyes to him. "Will you let me know as soon as you do?"

"I'll send you a message. But in the meantime, don't freak out. Whatever it is, we can handle it. We have a ship full of highly trained Guardians and gods. No one stands a chance against us, not even if the entire cartel comes after us."

Frankie

❦

rankie watched Dagor and William walk out through the sliding glass door of the Lido deck and turned to William's mate. "What do you think is going on?"

Kaia had been the first to acknowledge that an emergency meeting meant trouble, but she didn't look concerned, which was reassuring.

"It probably has something to do with the cartel, but your boyfriend is right. You have nothing to worry about other than your friend not getting picked up from Cabo on schedule. You should call her and tell her that we will be at least two days late."

"Two days?" Frankie squeaked. "Margo is going to be so peeved."

That was putting it mildly. Margo was not quick to anger, but when she was pushed too far, it was better not to be anywhere near her.

"Yeah." Kaia gulped her drink before putting it down on the side table. "We left Acapulco yesterday evening, and we were sailing through the night. It will take at least until nightfall to get back unless it's urgent and the captain increases the speed. If he does, we can get there this after-noon, but that's still only a few hours saved. I don't know how long it will take them to solve whatever problem they encountered, but it will take at least half a day, and then we need to cover this distance again."

"You're right. It's gonna be at least a two-day delay, if not longer."

Kaia smiled. "I hope your friend is having fun in Cabo."

Frankie hoped so, too. Margo had sounded more upbeat the last time they had spoken, so maybe things were going well, and since the bachelorette party was supposed to last a week, she wouldn't have to wait alone the entire two days, just the last one.

That meant that Margo would have to book another night in the hotel, and that might be a problem. What if it was fully booked?

What if it was too expensive?

Lynda had paid for the flights and the rooms, and since it was an all-inclusive resort, they could eat and drink as much as they wanted as long as they didn't order premium alcohol.

"I need another drink." Frankie glanced at Bob before shifting her eyes to Kaia and the empty glass on the side table. "Can I get you something?"

"No, thank you." Kaia took out a pair of sunglasses from her tote and put them on. "I'm going to take a little nap. I don't need as much sleep as I did before the transition, but I still need more than William, and he kept me awake until sunrise this morning." A smile tugged on Kaia's lips. "Not that I'm complaining."

Frankie didn't know that the girl used to be a Dormant. She was just as beautiful as all the other immortal ladies, so it hadn't even occurred to her.

"When did you transition? Was it recent?"

"Yeah, although it feels like a lifetime ago." Kaia chuckled. "I crack myself up sometimes. A different lifetime, get it?"

"I guess so." Frankie smoothed a hand over her neatly combed-back hair. "Was it difficult? I mean, the transition?"

"Not really. It's not fun, and it's different for each transitioning Dormant. I itched all over, and that was pretty bad, but others had it much worse. The good news is that the clan hasn't lost a Dormant to transition yet, so you shouldn't be afraid. Also, having a god induce you improves your chances of a quick and successful transition.

Seeing how you are already walking around and moving with ease the day after you were shot, I'd say that it's already happening."

It would be so nice if Kaia was right, but Frankie doubted that. "Aren't I supposed to develop a fever and lose consciousness?"

The girl frowned. "Fever is standard for all transitioning Dormants, and so are elevated heart rate and blood pressure, but not everyone loses consciousness. How old are you?"

"Twenty-seven, why?"

"The older the Dormant, the more difficult the transition, and in this regard, you are not considered young. Still, a god's venom might compensate for your age."

Frankie grimaced. "Thanks for making me feel old. Now I really need that drink."

"Enjoy." Kaia waved her off.

The girl needed to learn some social skills, but given that she was rumored to be a genius, that kind of went with the territory.

"Hello." Bob grinned at her. "What can I get you, Mistress Frankie?" He tilted his head. "Is it Francine or Francesca?"

"Both, and two more. My parents named me after my great-grandmothers, so my full name is Francine, Emilia,

Francesca, and Fiona. My brothers used to tease me that I was triple F."

Bob assumed a frown, which didn't really work since his metallic skin didn't wrinkle, but it was close enough. "I have never heard that expression. What does it mean?"

"I'd better not tell you. Can I have a strawberry daiquiri?"

"Of course." The grin returned.

As Bob turned to get what was needed for her drink, it occurred to Frankie that he might know more about the change of the ship's course than the rest of them.

"Do you know why we have turned around?" she asked.

"We did?" He looked surprised, which worked pretty well with his mechanic eyebrows lifting and his camera eyes widening. "I was not aware of that."

"Oh, well. It was worth a try. I thought you were connected to the ship's mainframe or something."

In sci-fi movies, all the machines on board a spaceship were usually connected to the main ship's computer, so she assumed it was the same on cruise ships, but evidently Bob operated independently of the navigation and other systems.

He placed the drink on a napkin, added a paper umbrella, and pushed it toward her. "Enjoy."

"Thank you." Frankie took the glass and walked over to the table she and Dagor had sat at before.

A few more people had arrived while she'd been talking to Kaia, and several cast her curious glances, probably wondering how she was walking around after being shot the previous day.

In a way, it was odd for the immortals to notice her rapid healing.

Several of the Guardians had been shot as well, but their immortal bodies expelled the bullets and mended their flesh so quickly that it was as if it had never happened. So yeah, everyone knew that she was human, but she had thought that most of them wouldn't give it a second thought because they were so used to seeing people heal rapidly.

Evidently, she'd been wrong.

Kian

"Hold on." Syssi put her hand on Kian's arm. "I need to talk to you."

"Is it urgent? I called an emergency meeting, and everyone will be waiting for me in the dining hall."

"They can wait a moment longer."

She waited until it was just them, his mother, and the Odus. "There was more to the vision that I didn't mention. There was a third goddess in the room with the queen and the seer that had no glow at all and looked like the female version of Aru." She arched a brow. "Is there something you are not telling me?"

The guilty look in his eyes was enough of an answer. "I'm sorry, but it wasn't my secret to tell. Aru was adamant about keeping his sister's part in this top secret, and I understood why. She's putting her life in danger."

"Doing what?"

When he hesitated, Annani let out a sigh. "Just tell her, Kian. Syssi already knows that the queen, the seer, and Aria are working together, and the rest is not as important. Besides, if you don't tell her what's going on, she will just have another vision about it. Apparently, the Fates want her to be part of our little conspiracy."

"There is nothing little about it." He reached for Syssi's hand. "Aru and his twin sister can communicate in the same way that Ella and Vivian do. Their telepathic connection is independent of time and distance. It's instantaneous. Aria works as a scribe for the Supreme Oracle of Anumati, who is also the queen's best friend. Aru told his sister about my mother, she relayed the information to the Oracle, who told Queen Ani that she has a granddaughter on Earth. The queen was overjoyed, and now she wants to talk to my mother through the twins. We didn't arrange the first telepathic meeting yet, but it should happen soon."

As Syssi's eyes darted to his mother, she smiled. "I am very excited. My grandmother wants to teach me about Anumati's history, its politics, and its social structure. I have no doubt that I will learn many fascinating things about the planet of the gods and how they became the creators of so many intelligent species throughout the galaxy."

"She wants to teach you how to be a queen," Syssi said. "Is she involved in the resistance?"

Kian nodded. "I think she is its leader. We will know more after my mother's first session with her."

"Can I attend?" Syssi looked at his mother with pleading eyes. "I can be your scribe, writing down everything Aru says so you could later go over the notes and study them. It's easy to forget important details while listening to lectures. I always took notes, and when I got home, I copied them to make a clean version that I could later study from for the test."

"I would love that." Annani leaned over and patted Syssi's hand. "But we need to ask Aru's permission." She sighed. "Usually, a task like that would be Alena's, but I cannot share this information with her."

"That's a problem." Syssi chewed on her lower lip. "We shouldn't keep this from the immediate family. It's too big of a deal, and eventually, it will have to come out. If we can trust your sisters and their mates with our lives, we can trust them with Aru and Aria's secret as well."

"I know." Kian groaned. "But even Aru's teammates don't know about his unique ability, so how am I going to convince him that it's okay to reveal it to my sisters and their mates?"

"Easy." Syssi grinned. "Tell him that I've seen the queen, the Oracle, and his sister in a vision, and I told everyone about it."

"But you didn't."

"Not yet."

"Please, don't tell anyone." He leaned over and kissed her cheek. "It was very difficult for him to tell me about his sister. We need to respect his wishes and keep it on a need-to-know basis."

"Fine." She leaned into him and hugged his waist. "I won't tell anyone."

"I need to run." He kissed the top of her head. "They are waiting for me."

Letting go of him, Syssi nodded. "I'll collect Allegra from Alena's cabin."

He hesitated at the door. "Do you want to come to the meeting?"

"Fates, no." She waved a dismissive hand. "I'm very happy to leave all the strategizing to you. Although, I want to remind you that the best people to consult are Dalhu, Lokan, and Kalugal. They know how Navuh operates, and they could guess how many people he would send for an operation like this."

Dagor

Once Kian had explained his wife's vision and its repercussions, Dagor pulled out his phone and texted Frankie to let her know what was going on as he had promised.

The truth was that he was excited about a chance to finally meet the clan's enemies face to face, and casting a sidelong glance at Negal, he saw a similar spark in his friend's eyes.

Not that the Doomers would have time to socialize. Given the vehemence in Kian's voice, their life expectancy was very short.

"We have two options," Kian said. "If we get to the bodies before the Doomers discover them, we can burn the evidence and continue our journey without having to go out of our way to find the Doomers and do away with them. Or we can seek them out and eliminate them. Killing them won't solve the local cartel problem because the

Brotherhood will just send replacements, and I'm not sure that we should get involved in a fight we cannot ultimately win. On the other hand, the next team might not be as monstrous as this one, and until the replacements arrive, the local population will enjoy a short breather. That being said, if the Doomers have discovered the bodies already, though, the first option is out, and we have to find them and eliminate them."

Dagor was fascinated by how the members of the Brotherhood were so different from the good people sitting in the dining hall with him. Genetically, they were the same people, so how had they turned out so wrong?

Their leader must be extremely powerful to corrupt their minds like that, but it was also possible that they were born defective. As a god, he was more familiar with the power of genetics than his new immortal friends, and to some extent, sycophantic traits could be bred in or out at the whim of the scientist.

Still, free will was not to be dismissed. People could channel their negative tendencies into doing good for society, and at the same time, it was possible to channel positive tendencies into evil deeds. It all depended on the ideology adopted by the individual or the expectations of their culture.

In a way, it was like the amulet. Its innate power was neither good nor bad, but it could be used for doing good or evil.

Thankfully, Anumati had outgrown that stage in its evolution, and not even the Eternal King could convince an entire population that murdering members of a different ideology was a righteous thing to do.

Even the Kra-ell, who were savages compared to the gods, had not wished to kill all gods out of hatred or some other deep-rooted resentment. They had just wanted to be granted equal rights.

What ideology could the Doomers' leader come up with that would justify the annihilation of Annani's clan?

Would William be able to explain that?

Dagor wasn't close to Kian like Aru had become, and so far, William was the only clan insider he had befriended.

As questions flew at Kian and were answered, Dagor wondered if he and his teammates should get involved. If they wanted to keep their association with the clan a secret, it wasn't a good idea for them to fight the Doomers alongside the immortals. If any of the enemy survived and managed to escape, the information leak could be catastrophic.

On the other hand, however, he and his fellow gods could provide valuable assistance.

The clan could easily handle the two Doomers that Kian's mate had seen in her vision, but what if there were many more of them? There could be thousands for all they knew. It wasn't likely, but it was possible.

Ultimately, it would be Aru's decision as the leader of their team, and Dagor had a feeling he would want to assist the clan.

"So, what's the plan?" Anandur asked. "Is it going to be a quick in-and-out mission, or should Wonder and I postpone our wedding?"

Kian grimaced. "That's another reason to just get rid of the evidence and get out, but I think it's wishful thinking on our part to assume that they didn't find out about it already. The Doomers were probably expecting the cargo of abducted women, and when it didn't arrive, they would have gone to investigate. It's very likely that they already know what happened and are investigating who was in the area yesterday. What they don't expect is for us to return, so at least they won't be lying in wait for us."

"That still doesn't answer my question," the redhead said. "Do we postpone the wedding or not?"

"We don't," Kian said. "For now. Hopefully, we will resolve the situation fast enough to still hold the celebration tonight." He scanned the room until his eyes landed on Toven. "We will probably need your assistance in compelling the Doomers to file a report explaining what happened to the cartel and their cargo in a way that will mask our involvement. I would hate to have to get rid of this ship."

Aru lifted his hand. "My teammates and I offer our assistance. We can help you fight, and we can also thrall the other immortals to do as you command."

"Thank you." Kian dipped his head in Aru's direction. "We will reconvene in my cabin later to discuss the plan. Our resources will have to be divided between the ship and the away team. Half the force will need to remain on board to protect the civilians and the women, and half will deal with the bodies and the Doomers."

Frankie

꧁꧂

"I have bad news," Frankie said as soon as Margo answered the call.

"What happened? Did the ship really turn around? Did someone go overboard? Was someone left behind in Acapulco?" Margo fired off without waiting for an answer.

Usually Margo was a level-headed individual, but she was very protective of those she cared about, and since she saw the world as a dangerous place that was full of baddies who were out to get good people, she worried whenever things didn't follow familiar patterns.

"None of the above."

What the hell was she going to tell her? That they had buried the body parts of cartel monsters and were going back to burn them?

Margo would immediately build a conspiracy theory around it, but even she couldn't guess the truth.

"Then what happened?" Margo was practically shrieking in her ear.

"I can't tell you. It has something to do with Tom's mystery partners and some vicious competitors of theirs."

"Ugh, Frankie. Really? Stop with the bullshit and tell me what's going on, or I will imagine the worst."

Frankie doubted that. The worst had happened, and not even Margo could have imagined that. She'd been raised Catholic, but she'd never really believed in heaven and hell until now. Those monsters must have been hell-spawned to do what they did, and what had been done to them had not only been well-deserved but not enough.

"It's nothing the people here cannot handle. That's all I can say without violating my nondisclosure agreement, and all you need to know is that I'm not in any danger."

"Fine." Margo let out a breath. "I'll get it out of you when you finally get here."

If Toven compelled Margo to silence, then maybe she would be allowed to tell her friend the truth.

"Are you going to be okay staying there for two more days? How are Lynda and the other bridesmaids treating you?"

"They are done posturing and trying to make me feel inferior. Now they are just partying like there is no tomorrow and flirting with all the cute waiters."

"That sounds like fun."

"Nah, I'm bored, and I want out of here, but I'll survive two more days." Margo sighed. "I'll download a couple of books, sit by the pool, and read while sipping on margaritas."

"That actually sounds like even more fun than getting drunk and flirting with the staff, but I still feel bad about leaving you stranded."

"It's not your fault. Besides, Lynda is going to be so happy that I'm not bailing early after all, and that will save me a lot of grief down the line. She won't have anything to hold over me because I'm staying to the end of her lame bachelorette party."

"Yeah, there is that." Frankie took a sip from her strawberry daiquiri. "So, no cute guys in Cabo? What about the other guests? Any single guys?"

"There is a bachelor party with at least thirty guys here, but you know how men get when there are no women to tame their behavior. They are gross and spit out the most cringeworthy pick-up lines. I turned my ring around so it looked like a wedding ring, and I told everyone who showed interest in me that I was married, but even that failed to deter some of them. Enough about me, though. I want to hear about you and Doug."

A smile lifted the corners of Frankie's lips. "I know that you are going to call me crazy, but I'm in love with him, and he loves me back. Our future together is still unclear, but we are working on a solution that will be acceptable to both of us."

There was a long moment of stunned silence on the other end. "You have known the guy for how long?"

"Three days, but when you know, you know, right? It's not like I fall in love with every guy I meet. Dagor is the first one that I actually care about. The others were just place-holders until my knight showed up."

And what a knight indeed. She still couldn't believe that a god was in love with her.

"Dagor?" Margo asked. "Is that Doug's nickname?"

"No, that's his real name. He introduces himself as Doug to Americans who have trouble pronouncing names they are not familiar with. Anyway, he's awesome, and you are going to love him. He's your type. A hot nerd."

Margo laughed. "How hot?"

"Scorching. We can hardly keep our hands off each other."

"Does he have a brother by any chance?" Margo asked.

"No, but his friend Negal is very handsome, too, and he has a very even-keeled personality. He's the dependable sort. But if you don't like him, there is another guy I have my eye on for you. His name is Max, and he's part of the security detail. He's flirty as heck and handsome in the boy-next-door kind of way—if the boy next door was six foot three, had the body of a professional wrestler and the face of a magazine model. Both guys are outstanding exemplars of masculinity, the good type, not the toxic one. You'll have a hard time deciding between them."

Frankie hoped that Margo and Negal would hit it off so their triad would all have gods for boyfriends, but if Margo chose Max, she had no problem with that either.

"Why choose?" Margo laughed. "I've been reading a lot of those reverse-harem books lately. It's fun to imagine having more than one guy, but I don't think I could do that in real life. I'm a one-man woman. Besides, who has the stamina to satisfy more than one man? I certainly don't."

Frankie stifled a giggle. Margo would soon discover that stamina was not a problem with immortal lovers. The venom was a miracle drug that was an aphrodisiac, euphoric, and analgesic all in one.

"Yeah, I'm not into polyamory either. Kudos to those who enjoy it, but it's just not me. I'm so happy that I found my one and only, and I can't wait for you to meet him."

"I can't wait either. I have to go, Frankie. Lynda is waving at me, and I'd better see what she wants before she throws a tantrum."

"Okay. I love you, and I'll see you in two days." *Fates willing.*

"Yeah. Be careful and stay safe."

"Always."

Ani

As Ani awaited her husband to join her for a rare, shared dinner in the grand dining room of the palace, she was not surprised that he was running late. El did not forgo a single opportunity to flaunt his royal privilege.

He never waited for anyone.

Everyone waited for him.

Ani did not mind. The tapestries adorning the chamber had been recently replaced with new masterpieces, as was done once a month from time immemorial, and she busied herself with admiring the artistry and craftsmanship.

The opulence of the room, with its grand size and shimmering chandeliers, was a fitting stage for the political theater often taking place around the ornate table, but it was rarely played out by her and El.

They did not dine together often, and when they did, it was to discuss affairs of the state. They were not a couple, not anymore.

In the past they had kept up the pretense, but after El had murdered their only son, Ani no longer bothered. She could not prove what he had done, so removing him from the throne had not been possible, and her fading into the background had not been an option either.

She had a job to do, and to do it, she had to pretend that she did not know El was responsible for his only legitimate son's demise, and she had to remain cordial to her husband. At first, it had been difficult, but thousands of years later, it had become second nature. They both played their roles as the rulers of Anumati together but apart.

Ani's role was limited, and she was not allowed to poke her nose into El's affairs or even question his decisions.

He was the king, and she was his official consort.

Nevertheless, she shouldered many responsibilities and represented families whose support was crucial to El's rule over Anumati. Also, she had nearly complete autonomy over her responsibilities, but she knew that El kept a close watch on her activities, and his spies were everywhere.

She had her own spies in his court, and he probably knew that as well, but he either did not care or could not figure out how anyone could spy on him while being compelled to reveal nothing of what they witnessed while in his service.

As the doors opened the king's guards entered first, taking their positions in the four corners of the room, and only then did El enter with all the pomp and ceremony of his station.

Her husband exuded power and commanded attention, but there was a calculated restraint in his demeanor, and not only because he was keenly aware of the delicate balance of power between them.

He had perfected the façade of the powerful ruler who was carrying the mantle of leadership for the sake of his people and not for personal glory, and every move he made, every expression on his face, reflected that.

What a master manipulator he was.

As much as she detested him, she admired his skill.

Ani rose to her feet and bowed. "Good evening, Your Majesty."

He dipped his head in greeting and motioned for her to sit back. "Good evening, Ani. I was delighted to receive your invitation to dinner. It has been much too long since we dined together. How have you been?"

"I have been busy." She offered him a measured smile. "The Supreme Oracle and I were discussing a new and exciting project that is of the utmost cultural and historical significance."

"Oh yes. It has been brought to my attention that you have visited the temple more often than usual. I was worried that you were experiencing the malady of ennui and sought solace from the Supreme Oracle."

Ani's gut clenched with sudden fear. If El could prove that she was losing her mind or sinking into depression, as many of the old gods did, he could put her in stasis for the long sleep.

Was he threatening her?

"Thank you for your concern, husband, but nothing could be further from the truth." She flashed him a bright smile. "I am championing so many new and exciting projects that I barely have a moment to rest, let alone suffer from boredom."

"I am glad to hear that." He leaned back so a servant could spread a napkin over his thighs. "So, tell me about this project that is of utmost cultural and historical significance."

No one could accuse El of not being attuned to her every word, but he was like that with everyone. Hypervigilant and always aware.

"The other day, I read some of the prophecies etched on the columns of the temple, and it occurred to me that they represented only a small fraction of the greatest prophecies throughout Anumati's history. Also, most of our citizens will never get a chance to visit the Supreme's temple and read them, and that would be a shame. We need a comprehensive, written collection that will be available to any citizen. The compilation would not only serve as a testament to our rich heritage but also as a guide for future generations of Anumatians."

El looked intrigued but also skeptical. "Recording what is etched on the columns is a good idea, but that is just a small fraction of the greatest prophecies. Most are lost in time or bear no resemblance to the original."

She dipped her head in acknowledgment. "My thoughts exactly. That is why I asked the Supreme Oracle to dedicate an hour a day to retrieving those prophecies from the vortex of time. We will have a scribe present to record what she says, but we will choose only the most significant prophecies to include in the compilation."

El's eyes darkened. "You know how unpredictable an oracle's visions are. Sofringhati might be the most powerful oracle ever born, but even she often spits out nonsense. She will have to be asked very precise questions to pull relevant prophecies from the past. Also, some of those predictions are not for public consumption."

"I am well aware of that. This is why I will be right there with the Supreme, asking the relevant questions and deciding which prophecies will go into the public record and which ones will go into a private one that will be kept in the royal archives and accessible only to you and me." She forced her expression to soften and reached for his hand. "I pray to the Fates that you and I would never succumb to the dreaded malady of ennui, but it is inevitable that one day we will, and those prophecies will serve to guide our successors."

The king's gaze hardened slightly, but Ani could see the cogs turning in his mind. She knew him so well that she could guess precisely what he was thinking even without the little tells that betrayed his excitement.

What if she discovered an ancient prophecy that was lost in time but could benefit him in some way?

What if she could warn him of potential threats to his throne?

Finally, he smiled. "It is a marvelous idea. Knowledge is power, and those lost prophecies could shed light on opportunities and threats we could not even imagine. It is crucial, though, that the knowledge is safeguarded. I want to review every new prophecy Sofringhati pulls out of the vortex of time and personally approve which ones are suitable for public consumption and which should remain private."

Ani nodded. "Of course."

As the servant placed a bowl of soup in front of the king, he thanked him graciously and turned to Ani. "Our reign has always been guided by the wisdom of our ancestors and the predictions of the oracles. It is our duty to preserve these insights for the citizens of Anumati."

Ani inclined her head in acknowledgment, hiding the triumph she felt from her husband's keen eyes. "With your permission, Your Majesty, I will announce the project at the upcoming gala."

He nodded. "It is very fitting to announce such a scholarly undertaking at a fundraiser for the new university. Well done, Ani."

Ani inclined her head. "Thank you, El."

Frankie

With nothing to do until Dagor returned, Frankie sat on a stool and leaned her elbows on the bar. "The strawberry daiquiri was really good, but I've exceeded my alcohol allowance for this morning. Can you make me a virgin version of it?"

"Of course, mistress." As usual, Bob looked as if serving her was the greatest joy of his day, and she wondered what about his expressions and voice created the effect.

Was it the rounding of his camera eyes?

Or was it the chirpy voice with which he replied?

When he was done preparing her drink, he added a pink paper umbrella, put the glass on top of a napkin, and pushed it toward her. "Would you like another bag of peanuts with your drink?"

"No, thank you. I've exceeded the daily allowance on those as well."

He arched a metal brow. "I was not aware that there was a limit. Are peanuts harmful when consumed in large quantities?"

"They can be if they are moldy, but that's not why I don't want any more. I've just had enough."

"I see." He turned his head and smiled at a group of teenagers heading his way. "Mistresses Lisa and Cheryl, and Master Parker. How lovely to see you again. Pink lemonades for the young ladies? And root beer for the gentleman?"

"Yes, please." Lisa sat on a stool next to Frankie. "Hi." She smiled. "How are you feeling?"

For a brief moment, Frankie was confused by Lisa's question, but then she remembered that she was supposed to be recovering from a gunshot. "Much better. Can't beat a god's—" she stopped herself before saying something inappropriate in front of the teenagers "—influence."

Lisa laughed. "You mean venom, and yeah, it's good to have a boyfriend with potent venom on hand." She leaned closer and sniffed. "You've started working on your transition, right?"

It was a little embarrassing to talk with Lisa about what it took to activate a Dormant, but the girl was over sixteen, and some of Frankie's cousins who were that same age were already sexually active.

Frankie had always been so small that people had assumed she was a kid even in college, so her first time had been when she was nineteen, but she was the exception rather than the rule.

"Yeah, we did, but I'm still not sure I'm even a Dormant."

Lisa leaned over and sniffed again. "You are definitely not entirely human. I think you've already started transitioning."

Frankie's heart leaped with excitement but was then gripped with fear. "Can you smell it?"

Lisa shrugged. "Not really."

"Then why did you sniff me?"

The girl turned to her friend. "It was Cheryl's idea. She asked me how I knew who was a Dormant and who wasn't, and I said that I didn't know, so she suggested that maybe it was the smell. But it's not. I just sense it, and I can't explain how."

"I don't have a fever," Frankie murmured. "Isn't that one of the first signs?"

Lisa shrugged. "I don't know. My mother passed out and was unconscious. I was freaking out, but it all ended well. Perhaps you should talk with her and some of the other transitioned Dormants."

"Yeah, I probably should. Maybe one of them didn't get a fever either."

It was so scary. What if she was transitioning already and didn't know it?

"Parker transitioned." Cheryl turned to the boy. "Did you get a fever?"

"I did, but it was nothing. I felt worse getting the flu when I was still human."

"How does it feel?" Frankie said. "Do you feel different after your transition?"

He nodded. "I'm fearless, which my mom keeps telling me is not good because immortals can still be killed. But I feel invincible."

"That must be awesome," Frankie murmured. "What about the prospect of living forever?"

He shrugged. "I don't really think about that, and when I do, I think of all the things I can do. I don't need to limit myself to one path in life. I can be a pilot, an engineer, a doctor, and a ballet dancer. I can be whatever I want."

Cheryl chuckled. "I've seen you dancing. You can forget about that one because you suck."

"For now." He leaned toward the girl until their noses were nearly touching. "But I can practice indefinitely until I get better."

As a wild idea popped into Frankie's head, she perked up. "Hey, you can dance with the stars."

He arched a brow. "What stars?"

"Like the television show *Dancing with the Stars*, when they take average Joes and Janes, pair them with great dancers, and they compete on television. There could be a Perfect Match adventure like that." She lifted a hand to her forehead. "Oh, wow. That could be amazing. I have to tell Toven about it." She leaned toward the kid and kissed his cheek. "Thank you for giving me the idea."

Looking flustered, he lifted a hand to the cheek she'd kissed. "You're welcome."

Frankie pulled out her phone and started typing a note with her ideas for the adventure. When she was done, she sent it to Mia, asking that she show it to Toven and ask his opinion.

The return text came back a few minutes later. *He thinks it's an awesome idea and asks that you develop the story further.*

"Yes!" Frankie pumped her fist in the air.

"I assume Toven liked it," Parker said.

"He did, and he wants me to develop it. It can be about two contestants falling in love despite competing for the grand prize. Like an enemies-to-lovers kind of story. They both need the prize money for something important, but then they fall in love, and each one tries to let the other win."

"I love it," Lisa said. "People can have a sexy adventure and learn ballroom dancing at the same time."

Dagor

Dagor started typing a message to Frankie as he walked out of the dining hall. *We are done. Are you still on the Lido deck?*

Frankie: *I'm still here.*

Dagor: *I'm on my way.*

He needed a drink, and then he was taking Frankie to the cabin and making love to her until they arrived back at Acapulco.

Fates knew what they were going to find there, and he needed to load up on love and closeness.

The truth was he wasn't sure yet that his team would be asked to join. Kian was meeting with his war council in his cabin to formulate a plan, and he would let Aru know whether their team's assistance was needed or not.

Dagor was itching for a fight, but he also didn't want to leave Frankie alone. His first duty was to protect his mate, and although eliminating the enemy counted toward that goal, staying with her was the best way to keep her safe.

He found Frankie sitting at the bar with a fruity drink in hand.

"Hi." He leaned over her and wrapped her in his arms. "I missed you."

She chuckled. "You were gone for less than an hour." For some reason, her compact body felt tense against his chest.

He leaned back to look at her. "What's wrong?"

"Nothing." She sighed. "I had a great idea for a Perfect Match adventure, and Toven loved it. He asked me to develop it further, but I got stuck. I don't know what else to add."

"I wish I could help you, but I'm not very creative. Mia is a writer, right? Maybe she can assist you?"

"Mia is an illustrator of children's books, but she still knows more about creating stories than I do. I'll ask her."

Despite his sage advice, Frankie's shoulders still seemed just as tense as before. "What else is bothering you?"

She let out a breath. "Lisa said that I might be transitioning, but I don't have a fever, and I feel great. Everyone says that a fever is the first sign that the transition is starting. It's so annoying not to know what's going on with my body."

"Who is Lisa?"

"She's a Dormant who supposedly can tell who is a Dormant and who is not. I met her a while ago when she visited Mia, and later, she told Mia that Margo and I were both Dormants. She was just here and said that I might be transitioning, and I freaked out."

"Why? Isn't that what you want?"

"Yeah, but I want to know when it's happening, and I don't like that it's not happening the same way as it does for everyone else."

"Let's think about it rationally. First of all, Lisa might be wrong. Does she have a proven record of guessing correctly?"

"I don't know. According to Mia, Lisa guessed correctly one other time, but she hasn't had the chance to do it enough times to establish her talent."

"So, there is also a chance that she's right," Dagor said. "And because she has a special sense for those things, she senses them before any symptoms manifest."

"I think that's what scares me the most. I don't want to lose consciousness while shit goes down in Acapulco. Are you going to fight with the clan?"

"Not if you are transitioning. I'll stay by your side."

"Thank you." Frankie let out a breath. "That's very comforting to me. But I still don't want to lose consciousness and miss out on all the weddings and not be there when Margo comes on board so I can introduce her to Negal."

He arched a brow. "Is that your plan?"

"Well, yes. How cool would it be if all three of us had boyfriends who were gods? But if she doesn't like Negal, which could happen even though he's a great guy, I can introduce her to Max, but if I'm out of it, who's going to do that?"

That was an easy problem to solve. "I'll do it. I'll introduce Margo to Negal."

"What if she doesn't like him?"

Dagor grimaced. "Then I'll introduce her to Max. Happy?"

Instead of answering, Frankie wound her arms around his neck and pulled him in for a kiss. "I love you," she murmured against his lips. "You are the absolute best."

"I know, and so are you. So, did I address all of your fears and objections?"

"Almost. I will still miss the weddings. The Clan Mother comes up with a unique address to each couple, and I don't want to miss that or the vows."

He rolled his eyes. "I'll take photos of all the wedding gowns and record the ceremonies and the vows for you."

"What about the dancing? I wanted to dance at the weddings."

"Unless you want to do it while unconscious, with me carrying you to the dance floor, I can't solve that objection."

Frankie affected a pout. "You're a god. You're supposed to be omnipotent."

She was adorable, and he loved her so much.

"I don't know about the omni, but I'm certainly potent." He lifted her off the stool and into his arms. "We have seven hours until we reach Acapulco, and I know how I want to spend them."

Holding on to his neck, Frankie laughed. "I like your plan. But how are we going to get to Acapulco so fast? We've been sailing for nearly fourteen hours, and I doubt the ship can double its speed."

"Don't ask me how." He carried her through the sliding doors and continued to the elevators. "Kian said that's how long it's going to take, and I have no reason to doubt him. Still, seven hours is plenty of time."

Kian

Kian wrapped his arm around Syssi and Allegra and kissed their daughter's warm cheek. "I'm sorry for taking over the cabin."

"There is nothing to be sorry about. I was heading to your mother's cabin anyway. Allegra is more than happy to spend the day with her grandmother, and all your sisters will be there to celebrate Wonder's bachelorette party. Callie, Carol, and Aliya will be there too, and Okidu will be there to help with the little ones, although I doubt his services will be needed." She chuckled. "I bet Allegra's feet will not touch the ground while all the ladies satisfy their baby fix."

His mother had insisted on hosting the party for her oldest friend, but he doubted Anandur would get to celebrate his last day as a bachelor.

Kian would keep him on the ship, and at least half of the Guardian force would remain to guard the civilians, but they wouldn't be celebrating with whiskey and cigars while their friends were fighting Doomers.

Hopefully the bodies hadn't been discovered yet, so it wouldn't come to that. The Doomers would start getting suspicious when their cargo didn't arrive, but they would likely assume that a competing cartel had stolen the women and killed off their henchmen. The only way they could know that immortals had been involved was if they discovered the body parts that looked like they had been shredded to pieces by wild beasts.

The question was whether they should pursue the Doomers even if it wasn't necessary, and Kian was conflicted about that. If they chose to fight the Doomers, or if they were forced to do that, they would be lucky if the wedding happened at all.

"I hope we will not need to postpone the wedding. I would hate to disappoint Wonder. Anandur will pretend like it's not a big deal, but I know he will be disappointed as well."

"We do what we must." Syssi stretched on her toes and kissed his cheek. "Good luck, my love." She leaned away and looked into his eyes. "I hate war, and I don't want any of our people to get hurt, but these Doomers need to go, and I don't mean back to the island. Find them and eliminate them, even if it means postponing Anandur and Wonder's wedding. Give them hell."

Those were words he had never expected to hear from his gentle wife. Evidently, she'd now reached the same tipping point that he had gotten to centuries ago, and he regretted that she had been forced to do that.

He sighed. "We can't win this war, love. Navuh will just send a new team, and they will take revenge on the villagers."

Syssi briefly closed her eyes, and when she opened them, they shone with inner light. "I'm not qualified to give advice on these matters. You have good people on your team, and I trust you to come up with the best course of action for us and for the people living here. I don't want to make their lives even more hellish than they already are, but I can't stand the thought of the Doomers and their cartel cronies doing whatever they want, massacring and abducting people."

Welcome to my world, Kian thought but didn't verbalize. "Don't worry, my love. We will figure this out."

She cast him a forced smile, and he smiled back with just as much effort. "Enjoy the party."

The smile slid off her face. "It's hard to enjoy anything with this over our heads."

"I know, but we need to try. Otherwise, they win."

With a nod, Syssi opened the door and walked out.

Kian shook his head.

It was a sad world when even his peace-loving, sweet, empathic wife wanted him to unleash hell on these Doomers and their cronies. Not that the miserable state of affairs was news to him, but he would have liked to shield his wife from the ugliness.

The worst part was knowing that one day his daughter would have to deal with this crap. Kian was under no illusions that a utopian future awaited them where evil was eradicated, and everyone lived in peace and harmony. And that was even before considering the looming threat of the Eternal King.

Letting out a breath, he walked over to the bar, opened a new bottle of whiskey, and pulled out ten glasses. His war council included the usual suspects—Onegus and Turner to formulate a strategy, William to assist with technology, Andrew for his experience with counterintelligence and terrorist activity, and Toven because he might need the god's compulsion power. He'd invited Kalugal, Lokan, Rufsur, and Dalhu because they knew how Doomers operated.

Aru had offered his assistance, and Kian might still take him up on his offer, but he wasn't sure he wanted the gods to take part in the fight. He doubted that the Doomers would be able to distinguish them from the immortals just from looking at them, but given the reports on Negal's incredible strength and speed, these new gods were a different breed, and they would give themselves away as soon as the fighting started.

Kalugal

K alugal leaned back in his chair with his whiskey glass in hand. "My educated guess is that there is a team of twelve Doomers stationed in the area. That's the minimum size for operations abroad." He cast a glance at Lokan. "Is that still the case?"

Lokan nodded. "I'm not involved in these kinds of operations, but as far as I know, twelve is still the size of an average team. Don't forget that Navuh now has more warriors than he knows what to do with, so there is no reason to send out teams smaller than that."

"It was when I was still a member of the Brotherhood," Dalhu said. "But given how violent the area is and the various cartels competing for dominance, they might have sent a larger group. The next one up is thirty."

Kian let out a breath. "We can handle thirty Doomers. The question is whether they will mobilize their cronies to help them."

"That's not a problem." Kalugal waved a dismissive hand. "In fact, none of this is. I can take hold of their minds and freeze them, immortals and humans alike. I don't know why we are even here."

Kian smiled. "I like your confidence, but things are never as easy as that. The good news is that we know they are there, and we are prepared to take them on."

Turner lifted a hand. "We are getting ahead of ourselves. We can avoid a conflict if they haven't discovered the bodies yet. They know something is up because their shipment of women is missing, but their first assumption will be an attack by a competing cartel, not searching for bodies. They will investigate that first, and it might give us enough time to eliminate the evidence, which is the only thing that can point toward us. We can either burn the evidence or start a rumor about a satanic cult operating in the area. "

"We left more clues than just the torn-up bodies," Onegus said. "The tour trucks are riddled with bullets, and the tour company has records of renting out those trucks to tourists from a certain ship. Then there is Luis and another driver who were injured and are recovering."

"That's true." Kalugal put his empty glass on the table. "I thralled them to remember that we were ambushed by robbers and managed to escape by the skin of our teeth. It won't be difficult to connect the dots."

Turner made a noncommittal sound. "Why would they suspect tourists or call the local tour companies to ask questions? Perhaps it will occur to them after they've exhausted all the other options, but given how large this area is and how many players there are, it will take considerable time for them to start thinking in that direction."

Kalugal was surprised that Turner, the most cautious and calculating among them, was so dismissive of their blunder.

He blamed himself for not burning the bodies. He'd been busy with the traumatized victims, and it hadn't occurred to him that he could use gasoline from one of the trucks to douse the bodies and set them on fire.

"There is a simple way to find out whether they are onto us," he said. "I can call the tour company and ask whether anyone inquired about rentals the day before."

Onegus turned to him. "The Doomers would have thralled them to forget that."

"In most cases, my compulsion is strong enough to power through a thrall. I can also call Luis, but I will leave him for last."

"Why last?" Kian asked. "You should call him first."

"If they got to Luis, he might be compromised, and by calling him, I'll tip our hand."

"The same might be true of the receptionist in the tour company." Kian turned to look at Brundar. "Did you rent the vehicles to collect the women from the same place?"

"No."

"We should call that place as well," Kian said.

"Do you want me to do that?" Brundar asked.

"No, we need Kalugal to make the calls so he can compel the information out of whoever answers."

Turner shook his head. "We should wait until we get there and question those involved in person. Their phones might be compromised."

Kian cursed under his breath. "I don't want to get into the port blind. What if they are waiting for us?"

"We can handle them," Toven said. "If we have megaphones on board, Kalugal and I can freeze them all in place before they can fire a single shot."

"We have the noise cannon," William said. "We can use it to amplify your voice, but the cannon can distort that special quality that carries the compulsion."

"Regular megaphones will do." Kian pushed to his feet and walked to the bar. "So, is that our strategy? We get Yamanu to shroud the area, Toven and Kalugal freeze the scum, and we make target practice out of them?"

"I like that idea," Anandur said. "It's going to be over so quickly that I might even squeeze in a bachelor party before the wedding."

Onegus chuckled. "You forget the cleanup. That will take much longer."

When Dalhu uttered a growl, everyone's eyes turned to him. "I'd rather get up close and personal. Tearing them apart won't take much longer than shooting at them, but it's no fun when they can't fight back."

"The humans their henchmen violated, mutilated, and slaughtered couldn't fight back either." Kian returned to the table with a fresh bottle of whiskey. "I say it's fair to pay them back in kind."

Kian

Kian found it difficult to keep the vehemence from his voice and even more so to keep it from his mind, but he couldn't fix all the world's problems no matter how much he wished to. Together with the Kra-ell, he had a force of about two hundred warriors, and that was barely enough to protect their three locations, let alone the innocents of the world.

He used to wonder if humanity was worth fighting for, and many times he had arrived at the conclusion that it wasn't, but he had a clan to keep safe, and when he'd become a husband and a father, there was no longer a question whether he would keep fighting.

He had no choice but to fight until his last breath.

"I think you should involve Aru and the other two," Toven said. "Not because we need them for this mission, but to solidify our alliance with them. If they fight with us against the Doomers, it will cement their loyalty to us."

Kian refilled everyone's glasses and sat down. "That's a good point. I'll call Aru."

Kalugal lifted his hand. "Before you do, I want us to consider calling the tour offices ahead of time. I know there is a chance someone could be listening on the line, but I can compel them as well."

Turner shook his head. "Not if they are recording all the conversations and listening to them later. I don't think your compulsion is retained in the recording."

Kalugal frowned. "I can't believe I've never tested it before. Let's do it now." He pulled out his phone. "Who should I call?"

"Not someone who is here," Kian said.

"Of course not. You can hear me." He smoothed a hand over his short beard. "The problem is that almost everyone I can call will do exactly what I ask them to, even without the element of compulsion. Jacki wouldn't, but she's immune, so she's not good for testing."

"Record a message and send it to Amanda," Kian suggested. "Ask her to call Anandur to tell him that Wonder had a change of heart and doesn't want to marry him."

"That's a good one." Kalugal glanced at Anandur. "There is no chance that Wonder would ever do that, right?"

Anandur crossed his arms over his chest. "Not in a million years. Wonder adores me."

"Get ready for a storm," Dalhu said. "Amanda will not find this funny."

Grinning like a fiend, Kalugal recorded the message and sent it to Amanda.

A moment later, his phone rang, and as he answered it, everyone braced for Amanda's outrage.

"What the hell, Kalugal? That's the cruelest prank ever. What were you thinking?"

"I'm sorry. We were testing a theory, and apparently, my compulsion power lost its potency when recorded and played back. And by the way, it was your brother's idea, not mine. I needed to ask you to do something you would never do unless you were under compulsion."

"You could have asked me to wear a dress made from polyester and come model it for you. Kian knows I would rather go naked than wear that. It gives me hives."

Kian chuckled. "And where would you have found such a dress on short notice? We needed to know right away."

"You have a point." She huffed out a breath. "Anything else I can help you with?"

"No, that's it," Kalugal said. "Please accept my apology for causing you distress."

"Apology accepted." She ended the call.

"Well, that idea crashed and burned." Kalugal put his phone back in his pocket. "We need to find some other angle. What if I can call and ask if anyone found a forgotten pair of sunglasses in one of the trucks?" He turned to William. "I'm sure you can reroute the call so it would appear as if it was coming from an Acapulco hotel. Not all the tourists arrive by ship. Some fly in, so there is no reason for the Doomers to suspect that their cargo is on a ship." He straightened in his chair. "We can have Roni hack into the hotel's surveillance cameras, and if Doomers show up asking questions, we will know that they found the bodies."

As all eyes turned to William, he shifted in his chair. "It's going to be difficult to do with the equipment I have on board, and if the hotel's camera feeds are not online, it's not going to work. The first thing Roni needs to do is find out which hotels have their security on the cloud, and then we will make that call appear as if it's coming from one of them."

Kian wasn't sure that it was worth the effort, given that they could easily overpower the Doomers and their hired monsters, but Kalugal seemed adamant about getting more information, and there was something to be said for that as well.

"Let's do it." He turned to William. "Call Roni and tell him what we need. I'm going to call Aru and ask him to join us."

Wonder

"What was that all about?" Syssi asked when Amanda ended the call.

With everyone talking about the ship turning around and going back to Acapulco, Wonder had been distracted and only heard snippets of the conversation. Amanda had said something about a cruel prank and polyester, which didn't make much sense.

"I can't believe these guys." Amanda snatched yet another margarita from Onidu's tray, her fourth if Wonder's count was correct. "Kalugal wanted to test whether his compulsion worked through a recording. Kian suggested me as the test subject, and Kalugal sent me a recorded message, commanding me to tell Anandur that Wonder got cold feet and didn't want to go ahead with the wedding."

Wonder laughed. "Anandur would have never believed it. He knows how much I love him."

"I know, but if that wasn't a recording, I would have been forced to make that call and sound like an idiot." Amanda plopped on the couch next to Wonder.

"What did polyester have to do with it?" Annani asked.

"I told him that he could have tested his hypothesis by telling me to wear a polyester dress and model it for the guys. There's no way I would have done it unless I was under compulsion." She smiled at Wonder. "Speaking of dresses, I'm dying to see your wedding gown. What did you end up doing?"

They had discussed incorporating Wonder Woman elements in the design, and Amanda had given her some pointers, but the dress was one of the few things that Wonder wanted full control over, and she had communicated with the designer herself. Most of the other decisions she had left in Amanda's capable hands.

In fact, Amanda had designed the dining hall decorations for all ten weddings and coordinated the menu with the kitchen staff. The female was a force of nature. Wonder had no idea how she'd managed all that on top of planning her own wedding.

"It's a very subtle nod to Wonder Woman. I have a gold tiara, and Callie is going to curl my hair and tease it so it looks like Wonder Woman's. I also have gold cuffs, and the dress has a gold bodice that looks a little like armor. And before you ask, I have no idea what fabric it's made from. It could just as well be polyester."

Amanda shivered. "I hope not."

"Real gold?" Syssi asked.

"Yep." Wonder took a sip from her margarita. "I wanted to get them at a costume shop, but Anandur wouldn't hear of it. He ordered real ones made for me."

"What about the dress itself?" Sari asked. "Any gold, red, and blue in it?"

Wonder shook her head. "As I said, the bodice is gold. That's as far as I was willing to go. Anandur wanted me to get a blue and red cape to put over the dress, but given how hot it is down here, a cape would have looked ridiculous."

"The venue is air-conditioned." Syssi put her glass on the coffee table. "But you are right. A few subtle nods to the character you took your name from are fun, but too much would have turned the wedding into a parody."

Wonder laughed. "That would have suited Anandur perfectly."

"Is he wearing anything interesting?" Alena asked.

"I have no clue. He wouldn't let me see, claiming that it was bad luck. I just hope he doesn't show up in fishnets and leather shorts."

Amanda nearly choked on her margarita. "Butt-less leather shorts."

Callie gasped. "He would not dare to show his butt to the Clan Mother."

Amanda was still shaking from laughter. "He would be facing her, so she wouldn't see his butt. I'm telling you, that's precisely what he's going to do."

Wonder groaned. "Fates, I hope he doesn't. I love his sense of humor, and he makes me laugh all the time, but this once, I want him to be serious and show up in a tux like any other groom."

"Boring," Amanda muttered under her breath. "Although I have to say that my Dalhu looked absolutely dashing in his tuxedo, so there is something to be said about traditional attire for the groom."

"Your dress was a showstopper," Syssi said. "Both of you looked amazing, and your vows to each other brought happy tears to my eyes."

Wonder winced. She'd worked on her vows for weeks and even asked Parker to help her, but the result still sounded like something a middle schooler would have written. She'd never known how to express herself in words and had always envied Annani for her natural oratory talent.

Her oldest friend had been born to rule, and the Fates had bestowed on her all the necessary talents, including the gift of saying the right thing at the right time, and sounding as if she had prepared ahead of time.

Wonder's Fates-given talent was superior physical strength, and at times like this, she felt ashamed for not contributing to the war effort. She should be preparing to fight along with the males and avenge the poor females who had been rescued, but even though she was physically built for war, mentally, she wasn't.

At least this time, she had a good excuse. She was the bride, and this was her day.

"By the way." Syssi shifted to face Annani. "I spoke to the kitchen staff and asked them to make more food this evening so our guests will get a nice meal during the celebration. I know it's not much, but it makes me feel a little less guilty about having fun while they are still grieving."

Hearing Syssi say that made Wonder feel a little better about indulging while the victims suffered and the males were ready to go to war with the Doomers and the human monsters they had helped shape in their demonic image.

Leaning over, Annani patted Syssi's hand. "You would have gotten along beautifully with my sister. Areana ran a house for widows who had nowhere to go." She turned to Wonder. "Do you remember that?"

"Of course. Areana has a good heart. It's a shame that the Fates saddled her with a mate like Navuh. It's also a shame that my sister chooses to stay with Areana."

Annani arched one red brow. "What would you have Tula do?"

"Escape. We could have rescued her the same way we rescued Carol. Areana would have made up a story about

Tula being depressed and committing suicide, the same way she did for Carol."

Now, that was a mission Wonder would have taken part in. To free her sister, she would have overcome her aversion to warfare and fought like a lioness.

Aru

Aru closed the cabin door behind him and was heading toward Kian's place when the familiar sensation of his sister opening a channel stopped him in his tracks.

Can you talk? Aria asked.

I'm heading to a meeting with the princess's son, so I don't have a lot of time. He leaned against the wall and pulled out his phone, pretending to scroll through his social media feed.

I'll make it short. The queen spoke with the king about recording the prophecies, and he loved the idea. We are on.

When? Aru smiled at an immortal walking toward the elevators.

The queen is going to make a public announcement at the upcoming fundraising gala and she will let us know then. It is safer for her and everyone involved if her activity is publicly known and endorsed by the king.

Smart. Anything else?

No, I just thought you would want to know that the first stage of the plan was successful. How are things over there? Are you getting to interact with the princess?

She is very excited about communicating with her grandmother. Other than that, I see her every night as she presides over the clan weddings. There is one every night.

I wish I could be there to see that.

I am glad that you are not. Earth is a savage place. Well, it is not fair to bundle everyone into the same group, but some elements are just barbaric beyond description. They are worse than the most horrible predators in the most dangerous colonies because they torture and maim for pleasure. Animals do not do that.

That sounds horrible. I wish you did not have to be stuck there.

He let out a breath. *As I said, there are many good people here, and I am not in danger. It is just difficult to stomach the savagery, but I will tell you about it some other time. Kian is waiting for me.*

When you are free, open a channel and talk to me. I feel like you need to lighten your load.

That was one of the great things about having a twin. Aria always knew when he needed to offload, and she was resilient enough, so he did not need to sugarcoat things for her.

I do. Just do not tell the Supreme or the queen what I told you. I do not want them to change their minds about making Earth a hub for the resistance.

Aria chuckled. *The queen has not decided any such thing. It was your idea, and I did not hear either of the ladies saying anything about it. For now, all the queen wants is to get to know her granddaughter, and if she finds her worthy, to groom her for the throne.*

Yes, I know. But just do not say anything.

I will not. I promise. I love you, and I will talk to you later.

Same here, sister of mine. Aru closed the channel, pushed off the wall, and put his phone in his back pocket.

When he rang Kian's cabin doorbell, Anandur opened the door and grinned at Aru. "Your Highness." He bowed at the waist and waved with his hand, gesturing for Aru to come in.

"I'm not a royal or even a noble." He clapped the redhead on the back. "Are you ready for your nuptials tonight?"

"I am, but it's not certain that the ceremony will take place. I'm staying on the ship, but I won't get married with half of my friends fighting Doomers out there."

"Is there any news on that?" Aru sat down next to Turner, the clan's strategist.

"Nothing yet, but we are working on it." Kian rose to his feet and walked over to the bar. "Can I offer you some whiskey?"

"Always." Aru smiled at his host. "Thank you."

He wasn't much of a drinker, but Kian seemed to enjoy sharing his whiskey with his guests, and accepting the drink was an easy way to please his host.

Kian returned to the table a moment later and handed him a glass. "So, Aru, do you want to fight by our side?"

"Of course. I offered our help right away. What do you need me to do?"

"I'm not sure yet. If the Doomers show up in the port with a contingent of cartel thugs, we don't leave the ship. Kalugal and Toven can compel the Doomers and their cartel cronies to shoot each other or just freeze in place so we can take them out. Yamanu will provide the shrouding, of course. But if we need to go burn the bodies and go after the Doomers wherever they are hiding, we will need to split the force, with half remaining to guard the ship and half going out."

"Which group do you want us in?" Aru asked.

"I don't know yet." Kian regarded him with that intense gaze of his. "My Guardians tell me that Negal is as strong and as fast as the Kra-ell. Is that true for you and Dagor as well?"

Aru nodded. "The more recent generations of gods were given several enhancements that your grandfather's generation were not. We are stronger and faster, and we have better hearing and eyesight. We are also less sensitive to the sun and do not need protective eye gear. Simple sunglasses are enough."

Kian tilted his head. "Is that all the gods of your generation or just a select few?"

"Those are standard enhancements that everyone gets. Naturally, nobility and royalty get more and better enhancements."

"Like what?"

Aru leaned back with his drink. "They don't disclose that. It's considered rude to ask Anumatians about their genetic enhancements, and it's considered bad manners to show them off, so it's anyone's guess what anyone else has."

Frankie

∽

"Let me look at you." Frankie pushed Dagor down on the bed.

He fell back only because he hadn't put up any resistance. "You're looking at me."

He reached for her, but she swatted his hands away.

"I never get the chance to just admire you because you are immediately all hands and mouth and tongue, and I forget my own name."

A smug smirk curving one side of his mouth, he lifted his arms and tucked his hands under his head. "I'm all yours. Do with me as you please."

Damn, it was sexy that a god was putting himself at her mercy.

No, that wasn't it. She should stop thinking of him as a god. He was just Dagor, the man she'd fallen in love with and who loved her back. It didn't matter that he wasn't technically a man, and it also didn't matter that he was immortal and that his blood could heal injuries. Well, it mattered, but that wasn't why she loved him.

"I love you." Frankie dipped her head and kissed his chest, where his shirt was parted at the top.

"I love you too, but you need to tell me when you want my hands on you because I'm not good at guessing."

She opened one more button and kissed the skin she revealed. "I like it that you ask." She popped the next one open and kissed that spot as well. "It's very sweet in a very dorky way." She continued unfastening all the buttons and spread his shirt. "I love your chest." She put her hands on his pectorals. "You are so broad and hard."

He chuckled. "There is another part of me that can be described with the same words, and it's very much in need of your attention."

"I bet." She looked at where the line of sparse hair descended from his navel and disappeared under the waistband.

Frankie had wondered about that before. The gods designed themselves to be incredibly pleasing to the eye, so if they had left body hair on their males, it was because goddesses found it attractive.

Dagor groaned. "Can I touch you now?"

She leaned up and kissed him lightly on the lips. "Patience, my love. We have seven hours, so there is no rush, and I want to take my time with you."

"You're torturing me."

"Oh, please." She rolled her eyes. "Don't be such a baby. Hold those arms over your head until I tell you that it's okay to touch me."

As she slanted her lips over his and slipped her tongue between his fangs. Dagor gasped and she felt his chest muscles contract under her.

It was difficult for Dagor to allow her to lead, to let her tongue lap at his while he wasn't allowed to touch her, and she appreciated his compliance with her wishes.

Holding on to his shoulders, she enjoyed the play of muscles under her hands as she teased and licked. He growled but responded only with his tongue, flicking it against hers and stoking her fire.

Her breasts were heavy, her nipples so stiff that they ached, and her core tingled with need.

She'd wanted to keep exploring, but the need inside of her was overpowering her resolve, and as fun as having Dagor at her mercy was, it was more fun when he took over.

There was always tomorrow to continue her explorations.

"You can touch me now," she murmured against his lips.

"Thank the merciful Fates."

She was under him between one breath and the next, naked within two heartbeats, and then he was kissing her breasts, his hot breath fanning over her nipples.

"Dagor." She threaded her fingers into his short hair. "I ache." She pushed on his head until his mouth was over her right nipple. "Kiss it."

"Bossy," he murmured over the stiff peak. "I don't hate it." He finally dragged his tongue over her aching flesh.

It was good, so damn good, but it wasn't enough.

Tugging on his hair, she hissed, "I said, kiss it."

He'd said that he didn't hate it when she gave him commands, right?

"So damn bossy," he murmured against her nipple.

When he pulled it into his mouth, she arched to get him to take more, and as he switched to her other breast, he cupped the wet one he'd just left.

"Dagor." She let go of his hair and pushed his shirt down his arms, needing to touch more of his skin.

If she could, she would have ripped it off him, and she had the silly thought that once she was immortal, she would do that just to see if she could. He shrugged it off, and the hand that released her breast traveled south to brush against her thigh.

As he smoothed his hand up her thigh, she rubbed her palms down his torso, and when she clasped his shaft over his pants, he groaned but kept sucking on her nipple.

When he finally brushed his fingers over her wet center, she quivered, and her hold on his erection tightened.

"You need to get naked."

Lifting his head, he looked at her with his glowing eyes and smiled, revealing his elongated fangs. "I like bossy Frankie."

"Good. Then do as I say."

"Yes, ma'am." He lifted off her and pushed his pants down his hips.

The man was male perfection.

Not a man. A god. An immortal.

The one she loved.

Her mate.

Dagor

There was nothing more beautiful than Frankie in the throes of passion, wanton with desire, her eyes hooded, and her legs parted for him.

Kneeling between her spread thighs, Dagor slipped a finger inside her wet heat, and as she closed her eyes and moaned his name, it was all he could do not to pounce on her and impale her on his shaft in one go.

But Frankie was tiny, and he needed to make her ready.

Watching his finger going in and out of her, he added his thumb to the play, circling her engorged pleasure button.

"Yes. Oh, yes." She stiffened, and her back bowed as she climaxed.

He closed his fist around his erection, willing it to have patience until Frankie was ready for him.

Her sheath squeezed his finger, and her wetness coated it the way he needed it to squeeze and coat his shaft, but he kept pumping in and out of her and gently stroking her clit until her tremors subsided, and she pushed on his hand.

Her expression was still dazed when she rocked her hips and opened her eyes. "Get inside of me, Dagor."

He chuckled. "Still so bossy." He flipped them around so he was on his back, and she was straddling him. "If you want me, you'll have to take me."

"Challenge accepted, big guy." She looked at his erection with hungry eyes.

She gripped his shaft in her small, soft hand and began working it inside of her, and when she rose to sink farther down, Dagor's lips parted with a groan.

He hoped that seeing his fully elongated fangs wouldn't scare her.

The other times they had been intimate, she'd taken a much more passive role and hadn't had such an unobstructed view of them.

But when she opened her eyes, all he saw in them was desire and feminine satisfaction. It seemed that Frankie loved being in charge for a change, and he loved seeing her like that.

Her perky breasts danced as she rode him slowly, too slowly, and as much as he wanted her to have her moment, he needed her to start moving faster, or he was going to lose his sanity.

Gripping her hips, he pushed up hard, and when she moaned and braced her hands on his chest, he took it to mean that she was ready for him to take over.

"Fates, Frankie," he growled. "I can't get enough of you."

For several thrusts, he surged in and out of her, but then she began to ride him with gusto, and he let go of her hips to cup her breasts.

Frankie moaned when he squeezed and pinched, and when she was on the brink, she threw her head back and rode him even faster.

He could feel how close she was and that she needed something more to fall over the cliff. Letting go of her breasts, he clasped her ass with one hand and reached with the finger of his other to press on her clit.

"Come for me, Frankie."

"Yes. More."

His fingers dug into her ass; he held her in place as he rammed up into her and rubbed her engorged pleasure button harder.

The building expression of ecstasy on her face was a wondrous thing, and then she exploded, her sheath clamping around his shaft and squeezing tight.

With one swift motion, he flipped them around, pinned her head to the mattress, and had just enough presence of mind to lick her neck before sinking his fangs into her and filling her with his seed and venom at the same time.

She yelled, then shuddered around him, and then she was climaxing again, the small muscles inside her sheath milking him until there was nothing left.

His shaft softening only a fraction, he continued thrusting into her slowly until the last of her tremors subsided.

For a few long moments, Dagor feasted his eyes on Frankie's blissed-out expression, her long lashes fanning over her rosy cheeks. He would have happily stayed inside her until she woke up in a few hours, but he needed to clean up the mess they had made.

Reluctantly, he slipped out of her, and their combined juices rushed out, soaking the sheets under them.

Thankfully, he had brought an armful of bedding to her cabin so they wouldn't have to rush into the laundry every time they made a mess.

Dagor chuckled softly.

It paid to be an organized nerd who always planned ahead.

When he returned with several washcloths, Frankie was in exactly the same position he'd left her, and as he cleaned her with gentle strokes, she didn't even twitch a muscle.

Once he was done, Dagor gazed at Frankie's lithe, compact body and was overwhelmed with his feelings for her.

How had he fallen in love so quickly and thoroughly?

It was as if the Fates had designed Frankie especially for him. He wouldn't change anything about her except turning her immortal. Everything else just had to stay the same, or it would detract from her perfection.

Annani

Annani watched her old friend smile and chat with Callie, Carol, and her other guests, the smile never leaving her face for longer than a few breaths.

She rejoiced in Wonder's happiness, but there was a tinge of sadness over the childhood friend that was lost forever. Gulan's body might not have died in the earthquake that had swallowed her, but the female who had woken from stasis nearly five thousand years later was not the girl who had been Annani's servant and best friend.

At a different time in history, Gulan's old job description would have been a lady-in-waiting, and perhaps that title would not have grated on her as much as being called a servant had.

Apparently, Wonder had forgotten the deep friendship that had formed between them, or maybe she had never felt it as strongly as Annani had.

Gulan had chosen to shed her old identity and emerge as Wonder, the namesake of a comic's female superhero whose powers were about love, truth, and beauty. The character had been created during World War II as part of a team of superhuman beings who fought the Axis forces and various other villains. It was a most fitting name for Gulan. She was strong of body and character, and even though she detested violence, she had used her incredible strength to overpower and imprison Doomers, who had gone on a killing spree of women in the area she had lived in at the time.

The world could use a real Wonder Woman and her Justice League companions right now. Things were once again spiraling out of control, and the forces of evil were on the rise. Some were cloaked in good intentions, and others were not even bothering to do that.

Annani sighed. She was tired of the endless cycle of gaining some ground, only to lose most of it again. When things were going well, humans soon forgot how bad it used to be and allowed the forces of evil to take it away from them.

She could use her old friend to bolster her resolve, to encourage her when she despaired, but even living in the village had not brought them closer.

Wonder worked long days in the village café and spent her evenings studying a variety of subjects. She could not decide what subject she wanted to specialize in, but she knew for sure that she did not want to be a Guardian even though that was the role she had been born for.

Her friend's incredible strength made Annani wonder if Gulan's godly ancestors had some Kra-ell blood in them. To her great shame, she had never inquired who Gulan had descended from.

What kind of a friend was she, never to look into Wonder's lineage?

Back then, Annani had thought that getting to know Gulan's parents and her sister was enough, but it was not. She had acted as a princess would, feeling superior and being condescending without meaning to. It had been based solely on her birthright as a princess and heir to the throne.

Nowadays, it had more to do with the experience of having lived through five thousand years of history, while Wonder had lived only through just over twenty-three. While Annani experienced history firsthand, Wonder had learned about it from Annani's stories and from books.

It was not the same.

Despite the agelessness of her appearance, Annani carried the wisdom and nuances of her extended life, while Wonder had had only two decades to shape her as a person, most of them having been lived in a different world.

And yet, Annani had managed to maintain a spirit that was young at heart, a vivacity that animated her. In contrast, Wonder had always been more reserved and somber. She had been that way as Gulan in their shared youth back in ancient Sumer, and also as the woman she had become after her awakening.

"Remember our adventures outside the palace, Wonder? When I snuck out wearing your little sister's clothes?" Annani asked. "The days when we believed we could change the world if only we put our minds to it?"

Wonder smiled, a touch of wistfulness in her eyes. "You were so tiny that only Tula's clothes could fit you. And as for believing in our power to change the world, it was you, not me. I was happy to leave the world as it was if it could earn me a few peaceful days. You were fearless, and I was the opposite of that. Being your maid was the most stressful time of my life. I don't think I was as scared when I took three Doomers captive."

Annani winced. "You were not my maid. You were my best friend."

Wonder shook her head. "I was paid to guard you and keep you company."

"That is not what a maid does. Your job was a cross between a lady-in-waiting and a bodyguard." Annani chuckled. "You were the voice of reason and kept me grounded when my ideas were too wild."

Wonder rolled her eyes. "Tell me about it. Do you remember when you tried to convince me to sneak out of the palace and steal a boat? You wanted to visit the nearest city."

Annani laughed. "How can I forget? We got caught."

"Fortunately, it happened before we stole the boat. Your father would have been furious, and he would have blamed me for not reporting your shenanigans."

As they meandered through shared memories, each recollection bridged the chasm of time between their shared past and present. In Wonder's stories, Annani could see the young, reckless girl she once was.

She still retained some of that youthful exuberance and thirst for adventure, but she lacked the naïveté that had made her so hopeful as a girl.

Her daughters had been born in different epochs, different worlds, but none of them had ever been as naïve as their mother had been in her youth.

Alena was serene because she chose to be, not because she was oblivious to the ugliness around her. Sari was a born leader who cared mainly about keeping their clan safe and prosperous and less about the state of humankind. Amanda cared equally for her clan and the humans, but then she was the youngest and most sheltered.

"I propose a toast." Wonder lifted a full margarita glass. "To Annani, who has championed women's rights for thousands of years. You've seen societies change and evolve, and you've always been at the forefront, fighting for equality and justice, finally to achieve your goals in the twentieth century."

Annani sighed. "Women's rights have always been close to my heart. Seeing the progress over the centuries gives me hope, but there is still so much to do. It is disheartening that modern-day feminism often gets lost in political debates, while critical issues like trafficking do not get the attention they desperately need."

The mood of the group grew somber as they were reminded of the victims they had recently rescued, now being cared for on the lower deck of the ship.

"It's a harsh reality," Syssi said quietly. "The fight against trafficking and exploitation of women and girls is a battle that seems never-ending. But it's a battle we cannot afford to lose."

Amanda reached out, placing a hand on Syssi's arm. "The work we do makes a difference, even if we can't save everyone. This is why we continue to fight, why we continue to dedicate resources to a seemingly lost cause. We stand up for those who can't. Every life we save, every victim we rehabilitate and empower, is a step towards a better world."

Sari lifted her glass. "I'll drink to that."

Dagor

The chime of a message notification echoed in the quiet cabin, pulling Dagor's attention away from the serene sight of the sleeping beauty in front of him. He reached for his device and read the message from Aru.

Please come to my cabin at your earliest convenience.

He had no problem guessing what the summons was about. They were joining the immortals in their fight against their enemies and the cartel thugs.

"Bring it on," he murmured. "I'm more than happy to rid Earth of a few more monsters."

He wondered why Kian hadn't gone on the offensive and eliminated his enemies on their island. He knew where it was, and he had the means to blast it to pieces. Nuke it if needed. One explanation was that there were innocents on that island that Kian was reluctant to kill, or maybe it was more about avoiding attracting attention. If Kian nuked the island, the humans would investigate.

Regrettably, the immortals were not susceptible to pathogens, so the Eternal King's usual modus operandi' when wanting to eliminate an entire population wouldn't work.

Glancing at Frankie, Dagor debated whether he should try to wake her up before leaving. Her breathing was calm and even, and there was a peaceful expression on her face. Blissful even. She'd been upset with him when he'd left the cabin while she'd been asleep, but waking her from such a deep and restoring slumber would be a shame. Still, he was determined not to make the same mistake twice.

He would tell her where he was going and why, and then she could go back to sleep.

"Frankie," he whispered.

When there was no response, he put his hand on her shoulder and gave her a little shake. "Frankie, I need to step out for a bit."

Not surprisingly, she was still soaring on the wings of venom-induced euphoria, too loopy to even flutter her eyelids open.

There was only one thing he could do, which was to leave her a note. She'd indicated that leaving a message on her phone was acceptable.

Pulling out his device, Dagor began to type a message.

Hey Frankie, I didn't want to wake you, but I need to step out for a bit. Aru just texted me, asking me to come to his cabin for a meeting, and I didn't want to leave without letting you know where I was.

Dagor was about to press send when he reconsidered and decided to add something romantic. The problem was that he knew next to nothing about romance, and he didn't have time to search the internet for romantic poems or ask one of the AI bots to write something for him.

With a sigh, he typed what he would have said if she were awake.

I'm not going to be gone long, but I know that I will miss you no matter how short the meeting is. I think I'm addicted to you in the best possible way. I love the way your body feels against mine, soft and yet solid. I love the sweet scent of your skin, and I love your smiling eyes. You are like a breath of fresh air in a stale world. I'll be back as soon as I can, and in the meantime, I will be thinking about you and counting the minutes until I can return.

He read over the message once and was satisfied with the result. It might not win any poetry contests, but it conveyed how he felt.

After sending the message, Dagor lingered a little longer, watching Frankie sleep, and then leaned down and placed a gentle kiss on her forehead.

Aru's cabin was on the top deck, next to the clan leadership, and as Dagor rang the doorbell, Negal opened up and motioned for him to come inside.

"It seems like we get to fight again." Negal grinned.

Dagor took a seat on the couch across from Aru. "I didn't get to fight in the previous altercation, and I'm very enthusiastic about having another opportunity to escort the vermin and their hired thugs to hell."

Anumatians didn't believe in the same hell that humans did. Their place of atonement was not a pit of fire where sinners burned for eternity. It was just a void of nothing, and being stuck there, endlessly reflecting on past lives and all the evil deeds committed through millions of years of existence, was scary enough.

Aru smiled but then quickly schooled his features. "Kian asked us to join them, not because they need our help. It's a way to cement our alliance."

"Makes sense." Dagor leaned back and crossed his arms over his chest.

The idea of solidarity with these immortals resonated with him. If he was to remain on Earth, he needed a community of people to call his own, and he liked the clan and what it stood for. He wouldn't mind becoming a member, but more importantly, he wanted that for Frankie.

If she turned immortal, she would need a community of immortals, and both of them could be happy living among these people.

Provided that Frankie turned.

Gabi had started transitioning days after she and Aru had first been intimate together. He'd heard that some of the Dormants had taken much longer to start transitioning, but they hadn't been induced by a god.

Frankie should have already started showing signs of transitioning.

But what if Lisa was right and Frankie was already on her way to becoming immortal without symptoms? Perhaps it had happened while she was recovering from her injury with the help of his blood?

"So. What's our assignment?" Negal asked.

"According to the former members of the Brotherhood, Kalugal, Dalhu, and Lokan, the Doomers rarely send out teams smaller than twelve, and that's probably the number of immortals we will face. But they are also very likely to be aided by a large cartel militia."

The mention of the cartel tightened the muscles in Dagor's jaw. "The humans are nothing," he spat. "The three of us could obliterate them on our own."

Aru chuckled. "Indeed. But even we can be brought down with enough bullets. The ship is well stocked with weapons, and I'm not talking about handguns. We are not trained in what they have, and we need to get in a few practice shots before we get to Acapulco to familiarize ourselves with the weapons. We don't know yet whether they will be waiting for us at the dock or if we will need to go after them. If it's the second option, half the force will stay on the ship to defend it, including Toven, who is the strongest compeller the clan has. We should decide who stays and who goes as well."

Dagor didn't need to think this through. "You need to stay."

Aru frowned. "Why? Don't you have faith in my fighting abilities?"

Dagor snorted. "We trained together. I know precisely what you can and cannot do. Your fighting skills are mediocre at best, but you can talk yourself out of tight spots. You are the one who's communicating with the commander, and you are good at spinning tales. If Negal or I have to explain why you are unavailable to answer his call, it won't end well."

"Good point." Aru rubbed a hand over his jaw. "I'll stay."

"When and where do we practice with the weapons?" Negal asked.

"I wasn't told yet. I'm waiting for further instructions."

Frankie

ᘒᑎᓆ

Frankie sensed that Dagor wasn't in bed with her even before she was fully awake. It was a feeling of something missing, something essential that she couldn't live without.

He could have been in the living room or maybe taking a shower, but she knew he wasn't anywhere in the cabin.

It was odd, to say the least. It was disconcerting.

She had lived for twenty-seven years without Dagor and hadn't felt like anything or anyone was missing from her life, but now, only a few days after meeting him, he had become so important to her, so vital, that she felt a sense of loss when he wasn't near.

Did all people in love feel that way?

It was scary to become so dependent on someone.

Opening her eyes, she confirmed that he really wasn't there. Some part of her hoped that she'd been wrong, and she would find him asleep next to her.

Dagor had promised to be with her until the ship reached Acapulco, and even when it did, it wasn't certain that he and his teammates would join the Guardians going to shore. He might stay with her.

There was no way seven hours had passed already, and the ship had arrived at Acapulco. Besides, given the swaying, the ship was still en route.

So where was Dagor?

Suddenly, panic seized Frankie. What if something had come up, and he'd left the ship early?

Perhaps Kian had decided that there was a faster way to reach Acapulco and he'd hired helicopters to take a team to shore?

Or maybe they had used the lifeboats?

Could it be that the smaller boats could get there faster?

Frankie had no clue.

Snatching her phone off the nightstand, she was relieved to confirm that less than two hours had passed since they had returned to her cabin, and there was also a message from Dagor.

Frankie smiled. He'd remembered what she'd told him about leaving while she slept. She clicked on the message, and as she read it, her smile grew wider with every word.

Dagor felt the same way she did. He was addicted to her, couldn't stand being away from her, and counted the seconds until they were together again.

Well, he hadn't used those precise words, but his meaning was clear.

The only thing missing to make things perfect between them was her turning immortal. Perhaps now that Dagor was busy, she could use the time to meet up with a few of the recently transitioned Dormants and ask them about their experience.

Frankie hit Mia's number. "Are you busy?"

"I'm working on an illustration, and Toven is in a meeting with Kian and the rest of the gang. Why? Do you want to meet up and do something together?"

"I would like to talk with some of the recently transitioned Dormants. Do you think you can call up your new relatives and we can meet on the Lido deck? We can talk over drinks."

Mia chuckled. "Let's see. There's Darlene and Cassandra, Toven's granddaughters, and Roni, who is Toven's great-grandson, but he's busy right now, hacking into hotels in Acapulco."

"Why?"

"I don't know. That's what Darlene told me. We can also invite Kaia, who is not related to Toven directly, and Karen, who is a Dormant like you awaiting transition."

"Really?" Frankie perked up. "How long has she been trying?"

Mia chuckled. "She hasn't started yet. Her situation is complicated. Gilbert, her partner, is a newly transitioned immortal, which means that his fangs and venom are not yet fully functional, so he can't induce her transition. She can wait five more months or so until he's ready, or she can do what Darlene did and use a surrogate."

Frankie frowned. "What do you mean by a surrogate? Are you suggesting that she takes another immortal into her bed when she's in a committed relationship? Don't they have like five kids together?"

"Three. Kaia and Cheryl are Karen's daughters from a previous marriage. But yeah, it's complicated. They need the surrogate only for the bite, but you can imagine how difficult it is to coordinate a thing like that."

"Yeah, I bet." Frankie chuckled. "It would have been easy if Karen and Gilbert were the adventurous types who didn't mind experimenting with multiple partners, but I guess they are not."

"I don't think immortals are capable of that," Mia said. "Darlene's mate had to be chained to the bed to prevent him from attacking the guy who volunteered to be the surrogate."

"Oh, wow. I'm surprised that the guy volunteered. Who was it?"

"I don't think you know him. His name is Max."

Flirty Max was just the type to volunteer for something like that. Now, she was definitely introducing him to Margo.

"I've met him. He's cool."

"Yeah. Max is a good guy, and it was nice of him to volunteer. So, when do you want to meet up on the Lido deck?"

"As soon as possible. Dagor is in a meeting with Aru, and I don't know how long it will take, but I don't want to miss any time with him."

"I get it. Let's meet up in twenty minutes?"

"Perfect. It will give me time to grab a shower and get dressed."

Mia laughed. "I'm not going to ask why you need a shower in the middle of the day."

"I could have just returned from a swim in the pool."

"Right. But you didn't."

"I did not."

Mia laughed again. "I'll see you in a bit."

Smiling, Frankie put the phone on the nightstand and got out of bed. It was nice having Mia so close, and it would have been nice to move into the village and see her every day, but if it meant not being with Dagor, the choice was easy.

Her mate came first for the simple reason that she couldn't stand being apart from him, and he couldn't be apart from her either.

With the clan satellite phone, she could call Mia whenever she wanted from wherever she was, and it would be almost as good as being next to her in person. The same wasn't true for Dagor. She needed him to be near, needed to touch him, smell him, kiss him, hear him murmur in her ear...

Kian

"We can do it." William handed Kalugal a piece of paper. "Roni says that's the best hotel to route the calls through. It has hundreds of rooms, and despite what's going on with the cartels, it's about seventy percent booked. It also has a surveillance network covering all the public spaces, everything is accessible on the net, and Roni had no trouble hacking into their network."

"So, everything is ready for Kalugal to make the call?" Kian asked.

William nodded. "Roni is on standby." He chuckled. "This kid is incredible. He was ecstatic when I told him we needed his help. He said that he was frustrated about not being able to contribute because he's not a fighter, but this is something he can do better than most."

Kian could understand Roni's feelings all too well. If he could, he would have stormed the Doomers wherever they were and relished taking them down, but he was the leader of a community that depended on him, and he couldn't just gallop into battle whenever he felt the urge.

He had to stay behind and trust others to do their jobs. It wasn't different from having to rely on others to manage the clan's companies. Learning to delegate had been difficult, but he was getting better at it.

The life of an immortal was a continuum of endless learning experiences, and the same was true for the gods. Those who stopped learning succumbed to ennui.

"Okay, then." Kalugal rubbed his hands. "Which phone do I use to make the call?"

"This one." William handed him a device. "It's ready for you. But before you do, read the other comments Roni wrote down. He altered the hotel's records to show you staying there for the past week, and he also added ten rooms to your account that you supposedly booked yesterday." William smiled. "That was my idea. If the Doomers call to investigate, they will think that you rented the additional rooms for the rescued victims."

"Smart." Kalugal looked at the piece of paper. "I see that he booked it under the fake name I gave the tour company Luis works for."

William nodded. "Kevin Gunter and his wife Cecilia are staying in room 304. Roni says that there is a camera in the hallway directly across from the door to this room, and one of the exterior cameras is covering the window. If they come for you from either one, we will know. Calls to the landline in that room will be rerouted to the phone I just gave you."

"Excellent." Kalugal pulled out his phone. "I need to check the number for the tour company. By the way, how did Roni hack the hotel room's landline?"

William shrugged. "Call forwarding through the hotel's system. It's not complicated. All the numbers are listed in the hotel's database."

"Clever." Kalugal entered the number to the tour company into the new phone William had given him, activated the speaker, and leaned back against the couch cushions.

"*Buenas tardes*," a female answered. "How can I help you?"

"Hello, this is Kevin Gunter," he said with a heavy German accent. "Yesterday, my friends and I hired Luis and two other drivers to take us to the Tehuacalco ruins. One of my friends forgot his sunglasses in one of the vehicles, and he's wondering whether anyone has found them."

"I'll be happy to check for you, Mr. Gunter. Can you hold for a moment?"

"Of course." Kalugal smiled and put the call on mute. "I bet she's stalling so they have time to trace the call."

"It's possible," Kian agreed.

Several minutes passed before the woman came back online. "I'm sorry, Mr. Gunter, but no one has found any sunglasses."

Kalugal unmuted the call and affected a heavy sigh. "That's a shame. They must have fallen out during our tour of the ruins. If any of your tour guides finds a pair of Gucci sunglasses and brings them to your office, please call me at the Rivera Hotel. My wife and I will be staying here for another three days."

"Of course, Mr. Gunter. What is your room number?"

"It is not necessary for you to know the number to call me. The front desk will know where I'm staying and forward your call."

"As you wish, Mr. Gunter, but things are not as efficient here as they are in Germany. The person at the reception desk might ask me for the room number and refuse to forward the call based on the name alone." She chuckled, but it sounded forced. "They will need to look up the name in the computer, and that's one extra step they might not wish to do."

"For security reasons, I do not give out information about my lodging, *Fräulein*. I will call the front desk immediately after this and demand that they transfer calls to my room without asking for the room number. They will comply with my demand, or I'll escalate the issue to management."

"As you wish, sir."

"Thank you, *Fräulein*. Good day." He ended the call.

"Great performance," Kian said. "It was a good touch to refuse to give out your hotel room number. Made it sound more legit."

Kalugal smirked. "I know."

"So, what's next?" Kian asked.

"Roni is watching the feed from the hotel and waiting to see if anyone shows up," Onegus said. "If no one comes looking for Mr. Gunter, it's safe to assume that they haven't discovered the bodies yet. But if someone does show up, it might be because of the missing women we took and not necessarily because of the bodies."

Kalugal frowned. "Wasn't the whole idea to find out whether it was too late to eliminate the evidence of our handiwork or if we could still do that?"

"That was just one part of the plan," Kian said. "The second part was eliminating the Doomers who ordered the attack on the village. I know that it won't fix anything and that the Brotherhood will just send reinforcements, but I can't in good conscience let them live."

Dalhu nodded. "I agree on both counts. We need to take them out."

Frankie

"Thank you all for coming." Frankie pulled out a couple of chairs from a nearby table and added them to the one she and Mia had chosen. "I would buy you all drinks, but since they are on the house, it doesn't count toward repayment. All I can offer you is my sincere thanks."

Darlene waved a dismissive hand. "I'm so glad that this is behind me. I still remember how scary it was, and I'm happy to help in any way I can."

"Thank you." Frankie waved at Bob. "Can you come over and take our orders?"

"Yes, mistress, of course." He zoomed in from behind the bar. "What can I serve you, ladies?"

After they were done ordering their drinks and snacks, Frankie turned to Gabi. "Can you tell me about your transitioning experience? How long did it take to start after you and Aru started to work on it?"

"It just happened. Aru didn't know about Dormants. I knew I was one and what it meant, but I didn't know that Aru was a god. Anyway, my transition started on the third day." She smiled. "A god's venom is very potent."

Frankie felt the blood drain from her face. It was her fourth day with Dagor, and she'd even gotten a transfusion from him. She should have started transitioning already.

Perhaps she wasn't a Dormant after all.

She swallowed the bile that rose in her throat.

But wait a moment. They had used condoms at the beginning. The first time they hadn't was yesterday.

There was no reason to panic.

She let out a breath and turned to Kaia. "What about you? How long did it take for your transition to start?"

"Five days."

That was encouraging. "Was it difficult?"

"Not at all." Kaia glanced at her mother. "But it was slow for me. It took forever for my healing time to improve. I must be a very weak immortal."

"What does that mean?" Frankie asked. "I didn't know that there were weak and strong immortals."

"The more removed a Dormant is from the source, the more diluted their genes are," Kaia explained. "Kian is the son of a goddess, and therefore he is a strong immortal with an incredibly fast recovery time. I must be many generations removed from my godly ancestor, and that's why my healing time is much slower."

"There are exceptions," Darlene said. "I'm Toven's granddaughter, which makes me very close to the source, but my transition was pretty average."

After Darlene had shared the rest of her transition story and Bob had brought their drinks and snacks, Frankie turned to Karen. "Mia tells me that you are waiting for your husband's fangs and venom to be functional to transition."

Karen winced. "Gilbert and I are not married, but that's not important. We are fully committed to each other, and now that Gilbert is immortal, he's even more possessive and jealous than he was before. Everyone thinks that I shouldn't wait because of my age, but even though Gilbert and I have discussed several other options, neither of us is comfortable with any of them. Gilbert's latest idea was to ask one of the gods to volunteer his fangs. The advantages of that are clear. First of all, a god's venom is more potent, which will give me a better chance, and he can also thrall Gilbert and me, so it's not as difficult for us. But since Toven, Aru, and Dagor are already taken, that leaves only Negal."

"Not for long," Frankie said. "I plan to introduce him to my friend Margo, and if they hit it off like Dagor and I did, Negal will be taken as well. If you want to proceed with your plan, I suggest that you do that before we reach Cabo and Margo comes on board."

Karen groaned. "No pressure. No pressure at all." She briefly closed her eyes. "Is there any chance you could talk to Negal for us and explain what we need? It's so damn embarrassing. How the hell am I going to ask him such a thing?"

"I sure can," Frankie said. "Negal is a good guy. I have no doubt that he will be happy to do it."

Kaia shook her head. "You are not in high school, Mom, and you are not asking a friend to find out if a guy likes you. This is a delicate matter that should be addressed with the gravity it deserves by either you or Gilbert, but Gilbert is the better choice to approach Negal. The guy doesn't get embarrassed by anything."

"I'd better talk to Gilbert right away." Karen pushed to her feet and smiled apologetically at Frankie. "I hope you don't mind that I'm leaving so abruptly."

"Of course not." She waved her off. "Good luck."

Karen turned to leave but then turned back. "Do you know where we can find Negal?"

"He's in a meeting in Aru's cabin." Frankie pulled out her phone. "Dagor hasn't texted me yet, so they are still there."

Kaia looked up at her mother. "You can't bother them with your issues now, Mom. They are planning what to do about the Doomers once we get back to Acapulco, and the last thing they want to talk about is your transition. You should wait until tomorrow."

"I'm going to talk with Gilbert, and if he wants to approach Negal today, I'm sure the god will not mind sparing a few minutes to talk to him. All he needs to do is say yes or no. If he agrees, we need to make plans for tomorrow or, at the latest, the day after. That's all the time we have."

Now Frankie felt bad. "Perhaps I can wait a day to introduce Margo and Negal."

Karen shook her head. "Margo is your and Mia's best friend, and Negal is Dagor's. You can't postpone introducing them even if you want to. Besides, maybe it's good to put some fire under us so we finally get on with it."

Karen

K aren didn't rush back to her cabin as she'd set out to do. Instead of the elevator, she took the stairs down to the third deck and used the time to think about what she wanted to say to Gilbert.

The truth was that he'd been the one pushing for her not to wait for him to grow out his fangs and venom glands.

In her opinion, her body wasn't going to age significantly in the four to five months it would take for Gilbert to be able to induce her transition, but it seemed like no one else shared her opinion.

Then, there were all the other changes Gilbert was experiencing. He was rewinding the clock, getting younger in front of her eyes, and his stamina would tire out an eighteen-year-old. His exuberance and energy had been exhausting when he was a nearly fifty-year-old human.

Now that his body could keep up with his mind, Karen felt like she was left trying to catch up.

He claimed she was his one and only, but Karen had always known how important it was for partners in the relationship to have more or less equal footing on the scale of attractiveness. There were several measures that could compensate for one another, like looks, intelligence, and professional success, and she included full-time motherhood in that, but the aggregate score should be as similar as possible.

She and Gilbert had that equilibrium until he transitioned, but now the gap was widening by the day, and not just because he looked a decade younger than she did. His energy and reduced need for sleep meant that he could do more now than he could before, and he was using that time productively, including taking on more responsibilities with their children.

Karen felt outperformed, and she didn't like that at all. Still, was that reason enough to expedite her transition?

No, it wasn't.

But having a god's venom induce her was, and Negal was the only one still available, but not for long. She was on the older end of the range, and she needed all the help she could get to emerge immortal on the other side and not dead.

Karen had five children to think of, and if there was even the slightest chance that having a god induce her would make the difference in her survival, she owed it to her children to do everything in her power to secure his help.

With that realization solidified, Karen squared her shoulders and quickened her step. She'd already checked with Bridget that the clinic on board had all the necessary equipment, so that wasn't an issue. She would hate to miss the remaining weddings, but chances were that she wouldn't start transitioning until they returned to the village. It had taken Kaia five days to start transitioning, and she was nineteen. Karen expected that it would take at least twice as long for hers to start.

When she opened the door to their cabin, she was greeted by the usual chaos of her family. The twins were fighting over a toy, and Gilbert was chasing after Idina with a dress in his hand while their daughter was squealing with laughter and running around with nothing but her ladybug panties on.

Naturally, Gilbert could have caught her with ease, but it was a game they liked to play. Most of the time, Idina pretended that she didn't want to get dressed, and Gilbert pretended to be angry as he chased her with what he wanted her to wear. Sometimes, though, it was for real, and Idina refused to wear a particular item of clothing for this or that reason. When that happened, no game could convince her to change her mind, and Karen had learned just to go with the flow and let the girl wear whatever she wanted.

Was that bad parenting?

Maybe, but Karen was okay with not being perfect at every-thing. As a mother of five with a full-time job, she'd learned to compromise.

When Idina darted by her, she caught her around the waist and lifted her into her arms. "Stop running. You are making my head spin." She kissed her daughter's cheek and extended a hand to Gilbert for the dress.

"I need to talk to you," she said as she pulled it over Idina's head. "Remember what we talked about regarding the gods?"

He nodded.

"Aru and Dagor are out, and Frankie has just told me that she plans on introducing Negal to her friend when she comes on board in Cabo." She put Idina on the couch and gave her the remote. "Find a show you want to watch, sweetie."

Idina grinned like she'd just won a prize. "Thank you, Mommy," she said with the sweetest voice.

"You are welcome." Karen walked over to the kitchenette, with Gilbert following close behind her. "If Negal and Margo hit it off, there is a good chance that he will be out as well. We need to act now."

Gilbert ran a hand over his hair, of which there was much more now than there had been a month ago. "I need to talk to Negal."

Karen nodded.

"I'll get Eric and Max, and we will talk to him together. It will be easier to explain, and it won't sound like a creepy come-on."

"Good idea. Negal is in a meeting in Aru's cabin, and I don't know when it will be over. We basically have tomorrow night and perhaps one more to do it or miss our chance." She took in a breath. "If Negal doesn't work out, I'm waiting for you to be ready. The only reason to complicate things and do them in this convoluted manner is the added benefit of the god's extra-potent mojo. Frankly, if we can't get Negal, I don't see much benefit in involving another immortal who doesn't have that extra something. As for my advanced age, I don't think my body will change much in the next four to five months."

Gilbert

Thankfully, Darlene wasn't in the cabin when Gilbert explained to Eric what he needed to do and why it was urgent.

"How are we going to get Max?" Eric asked. "He's in a Guardians' meeting down in the dining hall."

"Can you text him? Maybe he can take a break?"

"We can do this without him. I was there, remember? I can tell Negal everything that happened." He grimaced. "Well, not everything, but the general gist of things."

"What if your testimony is not enough? Negal needs to hear it from the guy who did the biting and get pointers from him. It's not easy for an immortal to work himself up enough to produce erotic venom. Usually, they need to be near a female they are attracted to."

"Yeah, you're right." Eric rubbed his jaw. "Max did it without a female. He watched porn on his phone." He smiled. "I like the term you coined, erotic venom. What do you call the other type?"

"Combative venom."

"Not bad. You should put it on the clan virtual bulletin board. I'm sure it will catch on right away."

Gilbert didn't have the patience for this sort of idle chitchat. "Can you please text Max now?"

"Right." Eric pulled out his phone, typed a one-sentence message, and sent it.

"What did you tell him?"

"I asked if he had ten minutes for me."

"It will take longer than that to explain what we need."

Eric shrugged. "True, but there is a better chance of him answering in the affirmative when he thinks it will take only ten minutes and not an hour. Not that I think it will take that long. Twenty minutes at most."

As the phone pinged with an incoming message, Eric read it and smiled. "He asks when and where."

"Now, and here. We will explain what we need and then wait by Aru's door until Negal gets out. That's the part that might take longer than ten minutes."

"You should have said that before." Eric typed the message.

"I told you that Negal was in a meeting with Aru."

"Yeah, but you didn't tell me that you wanted to wait outside the door. Isn't that overdoing it?"

Gilbert released a breath. "I don't want to give him a chance to evade me. I need a yes or no answer before Frankie's friend gets here."

When Eric's phone pinged with another message, he looked at the screen. "He's on his way."

"I'd better pour us some whiskey." Gilbert walked over to the bar. "You have to give it to Kian. He's had all the cabins equipped with the best stuff."

"It's not coming out of his pocket." Eric shrugged. "The clan is paying for it."

"I'm not sure." Gilbert took out three small glasses and uncapped the whiskey. "But even if that's true, who makes all the money for the clan? If not for Kian, they wouldn't have all this money."

"True, although I'm sure Sari and her people contribute."

Gilbert pursed his lips. "Frankly, I don't know how it works. It might be that Sari takes care of her people, and Kian takes care of his."

"Then who's financing Annani's place in Alaska? It has to be a joint effort."

"Yeah, you're right."

When the doorbell rang, Eric opened the way for Max, and the two did the bro hug while clapping each other on the back.

Gilbert wasn't on such friendly terms with the Guardian, so he just offered him his hand. "Thank you for coming. I know that the timing sucks, and you are busy with preparations for the Acapulco mission, but this can't wait." He handed him a glass.

"I have time." The Guardian took a small sip. "But I need to watch the alcohol today. We have target practice scheduled for an hour from now, and it's not a good idea to hold an automatic while inebriated." He took another sip. "Damn, this is good whiskey. It's really hard to say no."

Eric snorted. "You have a hard time with saying no in general." He clapped him on the back. "You're too easy."

"Ain't that the truth." Max sighed. "So, what do you need my services for?" He leveled his gaze at Gilbert. "Are those the same services I provided for Eric and Darlene?"

"Close, but not the same. I want to ask Negal to help Karen and me the same way you helped my brother and his mate, and I think it will be good if he hears what's involved from you."

Gilbert had been worried that Max would be offended that he hadn't asked him to be the initiator, but if anything, the guy looked relieved. "Sure. I'll talk to him. Where is he?"

"Negal is in a meeting with the other two gods in Aru's cabin. I suggest we get up there and wait outside to trap him before he leaves to do something else."

Max nodded. "He and the other two are coming to the training. We can talk in the bar until the practice starts."

"Don't you think us cornering him by the door would be perceived as creepy?" Eric stuffed his hands in his pockets. "It might be off-putting for him."

"Which part?" Max cocked a brow. "The asking him to bite Karen while she and Gilbert are hot and sweaty, or the lurking outside the door, waiting for him to emerge?"

"I meant the second one, but you are right. The whole thing is creepy."

Negal

"Target practice is in an hour." Aru pushed to his feet. "We should grab something to eat first."

"Dining hall?" Negal glanced at Dagor.

"I'm going to check with Frankie. If she didn't eat yet, I'll meet you down there." He walked over to the door and opened it. "Hello, are you waiting for me?"

Negal and Aru exchanged looks. It couldn't be Gabi because Dagor wouldn't have sounded surprised or asked if whoever was out there was waiting for him.

Out of habit, Negal inhaled, sensing three immortal males out in the corridor.

"We are actually waiting for Negal," one of them said. "Is he coming out?"

Dagor moved aside, giving Negal and Aru an unobstructed view of the newcomers.

Negal recognized Max, who had headed the Guardians who'd joined the tour of the ruins. He'd fought alongside him until Frankie was shot. Then Negal had figured that she and Dagor needed someone to protect them on the way back to the ship, and he'd been the closest, so he'd jumped into the truck, but in the few moments that Max had seen him in action, the guy had seemed impressed.

Perhaps the Guardian wanted to ask about Negal's enhanced strength?

The other guy was Gabi's brother, Gilbert, and the one standing next to him was Eric, the middle brother.

"Hello, Max." He offered the Guardian his hand. "It's good to see you again." He turned to Gilbert. "Good to see you too, Gilbert, Eric."

Aru stepped out and frowned at Gilbert. "What's wrong? Is Gabi okay?"

"Gabi is fine. We need Negal for a few minutes, if you don't mind."

"What for?" Aru asked.

"It's a private matter," Gilbert said.

What could they possibly want from him? Did they have a relative they wanted to introduce him to?

Negal was enjoying his popularity among the clan ladies, and he had no wish to limit himself to just one.

Aru cast him a sidelong glance. "Do you want to go with them?"

"It depends." Negal cast Gilbert a broad smile. "What are you offering?"

"A drink on the Lido deck."

Negal was a little hungry, but he was curious to hear what Gabi's brothers wanted with him.

"Lead the way." He motioned for them to proceed.

"Don't forget that target practice is in an hour." Aru clapped him on the back. "You might want to grab something to eat first."

"I'll survive." Negal fell into step with Gilbert while Eric and Max trailed behind them. "So, what's the deal? Do you have a cousin you want me to meet?"

Gilbert shook his head. "Let's wait until we are sitting with drinks in our hands. This is not going to be an easy conversation."

"Now you're worrying me. Did I overstep some boundary I wasn't aware of with one of the clan ladies?"

He'd been cordial to a fault, and he'd only engaged with those who had actively come after him. He hadn't flirted with anyone or seduced them with his godly powers, or anything else that could be interpreted as questionable.

"Nothing like that. You did nothing wrong, Negal. I'm about to ask you for a huge favor that's going to make us both very uncomfortable."

Negal's gut twisted in a knot. Did they need him to give blood to someone?

Maybe one of the women down in the lower decks was in critical condition?

But how had they found out about it? Had they guessed that Frankie's recovery couldn't be explained any other way?

What was he going to do when they asked him?

Deny it?

Say that he had no idea what they were talking about?

Damn, what a mess.

The four of them made the rest of the way to the Lido deck in silence, found a table apart from the rest that offered some privacy, and ordered drinks from Bob.

"So, here is the situation." Gilbert put down his gin and tonic. "You know how female Dormants are induced, right?"

So that was what they wanted him for. "I'm sorry, Gilbert, but I can't. Your daughter is too young."

Gilbert frowned. "What are you talking about?"

"Isn't that what you need me for? To induce the transition of your daughter?"

"Cheryl?"

"Of course. Do you have another daughter who is almost of age but not yet?"

"No, but that's not what I want to ask you to do." Gilbert took a fortifying breath. "This is about my mate Karen. I'm a newly transitioned immortal, which means that my fangs and venom glands are still growing, and they are not functional, so I can't induce her. She's not young, and her best chance of transitioning is a god's venom, and you are the last god available. Naturally, I'm not suggesting that you have sex with my mate, only that you provide the bite."

He must have looked stunned because Max lifted a hand to get his attention. "I did that for Eric's mate, and it's not as complicated as it seems. The only problem we encountered was Eric demolishing the bed in a jealous fit. Bonded immortal males are very possessive of their mates, and we planned for that. We had him chained to the bed, but he pulled so hard on the chains that the bed fell apart."

Negal was starting to get the picture of how it was supposed to work. The couple would be engaged in the act, and they wanted him to bite the female when Gilbert was about to climax.

"Did it work?" Negal asked.

Eric nodded. "Max did a hit and run, but it worked."

"What do you mean by hit and run?"

Max lifted a hand. "I've got this. While Eric and Darlene were getting it on in their bedroom, I was in another room, getting in the mood. The doors were open, so I knew when to dash in, do my part, and dash out."

"Well." Negal rubbed the back of his neck. "That's definitely not something I've ever done, but I'm willing to give it a try. After all, it's for a good cause, right?" He turned to Gilbert. "Are you sure that my venom is the best thing for your mate?"

"Yes. And there are other benefits." He swallowed. "You can thrall us not to see you, which other immortals can't do. Well, they can thrall Karen because she's still human, but not me, and I'm the one with the jealousy problem. Hopefully, that will make chaining me to the bed unnecessary. It will also make it easier for Karen."

"I can definitely do that," Negal said. "And even without the thrall no chains are needed. You are no match for me."

"He's right about that," Max murmured. "I've seen him in action." He looked at Negal. "You are as strong as the Kra-ell, right?"

Negal nodded. "After the rebellion, the gods decided to enhance future generations so we wouldn't be defenseless against the Kra-ell."

"Makes sense." Max emptied the rest of his drink down his throat and lifted the empty glass to signal to Bob that he needed a refill.

"One more thing." Gilbert cleared his throat. "Do you need a partner to get in a mood, or can you take care of it by yourself?"

Negal didn't like pleasuring himself when there were plenty of females available, but he wasn't a stranger to that form of release either. When they'd trekked through Tibet, there hadn't been any suitable partners.

Perhaps he could find a lady who wouldn't mind him leaving in the middle to bite someone else?

Nah, it was better to do it the way Max had. He could always seek a companion after he was done with his good deed.

"I can use my imagination to get in the mood. When do you want to do this?"

"Does tomorrow work for you?" Gilbert asked. "We can do it after Brundar and Callie's wedding. Our teenage daughter will be babysitting her younger siblings in another cabin, so we will have all the privacy we need."

"Good plan. I'll leave the party when you do and follow you to your cabin."

"Thank you." Gilbert offered him his hand. "Your help means a lot to me and my mate. Your venom is her best chance of survival."

Dagor

"I'm finally done." Dagor clutched the phone to his ear. "Do you want to meet me for lunch in the dining hall?"

"Do we have time for a quickie?" Frankie asked.

Dagor's steps faltered. "That's worth skipping lunch for."

"I don't want you to go hungry. Not if you need to fight later. Can't we do both?"

"I have target practice in an hour."

There was a moment of silence. "That's plenty of time. We can have a twenty-minute quickie and then get lunch."

"If I bite you, you'll be out. I have a better idea. I'll stop by the dining hall, fill up two plates, and bring them up to the cabin. We will eat first and then make love."

"Works for me. I'll put on something sexy."

He groaned. "You're killing me, Frankie. Tell me what you are going to wear."

She laughed. "I'd better not, or you'll be sporting a tent while picking up the food."

"Right. By the way, do you know what Gilbert, Eric, and Max need Negal for?"

"Oh, wow. Karen really did it. But I can't tell you. You'll have to ask Negal."

"Why can't you tell me?" Dagor took the stairs down to avoid the crowd at the elevators.

"Because it's private, and they might be embarrassed about sharing the details. That's all I'm going to say on the subject."

"Fine. I'll get it out of Negal." He entered the dining hall and continued to the kitchen. "I'm going to hang up now so I can collect our food. Any preferences?"

"I don't know what they are serving today, but I'm not a picky eater. Whatever you bring is fine."

"See you soon." He ended the phone with a kissy sound that should have been embarrassing, but Dagor didn't care.

If Frankie loved it, he would be talking dirty to her and making kissy sounds in the middle of the war room.

Well, that might be a slight exaggeration. But anywhere else was fair game.

"Can I have two plates to go?" he asked one of the ladies working in the kitchen. When it was clear that she didn't understand what he'd said, he grabbed two empty plates and mimed putting food on them.

Smiling, she nodded. "*Da, ya ponimayu.*"

Dagor dipped his head. "*Spasiba.*"

He should have addressed her in Russian to begin with, but he'd been so preoccupied with thoughts of Frankie and what she would be wearing when he got to the cabin that he'd forgotten the kitchen staff came from Igor's old compound, and they all spoke Russian, and some also spoke Finnish.

When the two boxes of food were ready, he thanked her again and hurried out the door.

Thankfully, there was no line at the elevators going up, and he only had to wait for the cab to empty before getting in. No one stopped the elevator on its way to Frankie's deck either.

Once he was at the door, he rang the bell and held his breath as he waited for her to open up.

Would she be wearing stockings and garters and nothing else?

Or maybe just a see-through baby-doll?

He hadn't seen any such garments when he'd looked for something comfortable for her to wear after she'd fainted, but maybe she had a hidden stash somewhere. He hadn't looked in the nightstand drawers, and those were roomy enough to hide a number of flimsy, sexy outfits.

When Frankie opened the door, he was only slightly disappointed to see the short, colorful silk robe that left her long legs exposed but hid everything else of interest. She wasn't wearing stockings either, which meant no garters.

"Hello, beautiful." He leaned to kiss her pouty lips. "I like the robe."

"Oh, this old thing?" She batted her eyelashes playfully. "The sexy stuff is underneath." She moved aside to let him in.

When she closed the door behind him, he put the boxes on the entry table and reached for her. "Let me see."

"Na-ah." She batted his hands away. "No peeking until after we eat, or you will go hungry to your target practice, and I won't have you being outperformed by Aru and Negal and all the Guardians."

"I don't mind."

Usually, he was super competitive and minded very much, but he didn't mind losing if it meant seeing what Frankie had under the robe and hopefully peeling it off her with his fangs.

Not that it would make a difference to him. He had perfect aim.

"But I mind." She took the boxes and put them on the table. "Do you want a plate?"

"Not if you don't. I'd rather be done with lunch as soon as possible and get to unwrap my gift."

Frankie

The truth was that Frankie didn't have anything super sexy underneath her robe. It was just a nice little panties and bra set that she'd gotten on sale at Victoria's Secret, but it wasn't something that would cause Dagor's jaw to drop.

Hopefully, he wouldn't be too disappointed.

As Dagor wolfed down every last morsel in his box, Frankie picked at her food, careful not to overeat, even though everything was delicious. Intimacy on a full stomach wasn't fun.

When he was done, she pushed her box toward Dagor. "I'm full. You can finish it."

He didn't argue, and she enjoyed watching him eat everything.

"Would you like me to make you a drink?" she asked with a seductive smile.

"I'll make it." He rose to his feet and walked over to the bar. "What's your pleasure, beautiful?"

She loved it when he called her beautiful. He sounded like he truly meant it and wasn't just flattering her.

"Something sweet and simple, please. Perhaps vodka with cranberry juice and some ice cubes."

"Coming up."

She took the opportunity of him being preoccupied with the drinks to move to the couch. Tucking her legs under her, she leaned over the armrest.

Hopefully, the pose was sexy.

Holding a drink in each hand, he walked over to the couch, sat down next to her, and handed her the fruity drink. "Cheers." He lifted his glass and clinked it with hers.

"Cheers." She took a small sip.

Dagor had been generous with the vodka. A little too generous. Frankie liked her drinks on the lighter side.

He put his whiskey glass on the coffee table and smoothed his hand over her calf. "I want to unwrap my present."

"Go ahead." Her robe had parted, revealing her thighs almost all the way to her underwear.

Dagor's hand started a slow trek up her thigh, parting the rest of the robe until he reached her hot center and cupped it.

"I see that someone has been entertaining naughty thoughts. What were you thinking about, love?"

"You, of course."

"I know that you were thinking of me. I want to know what you were imagining." He slid his finger under the gusset of her panties and stroked her wet folds.

Frankie bit on her lower lip. "This."

"Really?" He slipped his finger into her and pumped it slowly in and out of her. "Or maybe it was this?"

"Yes, a lot more of this." She rocked on his finger, getting more of it inside.

There was something obscenely arousing about the way he was leaning nonchalantly against the couch cushions and fingering her.

His finger retracted and then lazily pushed back in. "I love how wet you get for me." He continued his slow fingering, getting her wetter and needier.

"And I love getting you hard," she teased.

"Oh, I am. I can hammer nails with how hard I am."

He withdrew his finger and came back with two. "Do you like this?"

Her eyes rolled back in her head. "Yes. Don't stop."

Leaning, he used his other hand to release the tie of her robe. "I've wanted to do that since the moment I entered the cabin."

As he parted the robe, exposing her body, his glowing eyes went to her breasts. She was wearing a white lacy bra that didn't do much to hide her nipples, especially the way they stood to attention under Dagor's hungry gaze.

Her panties were white lace as well, matching the bra. It was a bridal set that she'd bought on a whim because it was so pretty, and now she was glad she had because Dagor was practically salivating.

"This is very pretty." He pulled the bra cups down, exposing her breasts. "But what's underneath is even prettier." He leaned and took one of her nipples into his mouth.

His lips felt cold for a moment, but then he swiped his tongue over her stiff peak, and it felt hot.

"I'm glad you like it," she rasped.

He switched to suckling her other nipple and pinched the one he'd just left behind.

It was just the right amount of pleasure and pain, and as moisture leaked into her lacy panties, Frankie threaded her fingers into Dagor's hair. "Take me to bed."

He let go of her nipple and lifted his head. "Impatient, are we?"

"I have to be. We don't have time to take it slow."

He seemed to have forgotten the target practice he had in less than half an hour.

"Right." He shifted back, took her into his arms, and pushed to his feet while holding on to her.

She wrapped her arms around his neck. "I love how strong you are."

"I love you." His arms tightened around her.

As he laid her gently on the bed, Frankie pulled the robe off and tossed it aside. She was still wearing the panties, and the bra was still pushed under her breasts, but she was leaving those two items for Dagor to take off.

"Gorgeous."

Lowering his head, he kissed the skin on her inner thigh, working his way up with small nips and kisses until his mouth hovered over her center.

"Such pretty panties." He hooked his fingers in the elastic and tugged them down her legs, kissing and sucking her skin all the way down to the very tips of her toes and then back up.

By the time he reached her center, Frankie was panting with need, and the sight of Dagor's fully elongated fangs sent a shiver of excitement tinged with trepidation through her.

He could nick her with those monstrosities, and it would hurt unless he licked it with his magic saliva. Everything about him was magical, and she was the luckiest woman on the planet to have him fall in love with her.

Using just the tip of his tongue, Dagor parted her lower lips with soft strokes, and judging by the growling sounds he made, he was enjoying every moment of it.

Lucky. She was a very lucky lady.

Frankie arched up, shamelessly asking for more, but Dagor must have forgotten that they were in a time crunch and kept going at his unhurried pace.

"Dagor." She pulled on his hair. "Stop teasing me."

He treated her to another long lick. "I love driving you crazy with need."

He teased her mercilessly.

Frankie needed him to pay attention to her throbbing clit, but he was purposefully avoiding it, licking and kissing her folds and her slit but not where she needed him most.

"Dagor!" She pulled on his hair with a growl.

Chuckling, he flattened his tongue on her engorged nubbin, and she saw stars.

"Yes!" she screamed.

If not for his unyielding grip on her thighs, she would have shot up to the ceiling.

Her cry must have finally broken through to him, and as his tongue kept flicking over her clit harder and faster, she climbed toward the edge in seconds, and as he pushed two fingers inside her and closed his lips over that pulsating bundle of nerves, she detonated.

"Dagor!" Frankie screamed her climax.

Somehow, between one heartbeat and the next, Dagor got rid of his clothing, removed her bra, and lay on his side next to her quivering body.

"You are so beautiful to me, Frankie." His hand traveled up her ribcage, finding her breast and palming it for a moment before pinching her aching nipple.

His other hand joined the first, the pinching and plucking just shy of being painful, and just like that, she was nearing another climax.

Leaning over her, he kissed and nipped the side of her neck until he reached her earlobe. He nipped it a little harder and then licked the little hurt away.

How was he doing that with those huge fangs of his?

When he moved to her lips, she was once again delirious with desire, and when he slipped two fingers inside her, she exploded again, screaming his name into his mouth.

He kept kissing her through the aftershocks of her climax, and then he was hovering on top of her, the tip of his shaft poised at her entrance.

"I love you," he murmured.

"I love you too." She wound her arms around his torso, trying to reach his buttocks, but her arms weren't long enough.

Arching up, she got him to slide in a little further, and he took it from there.

He pulled back and surged in again, moving slowly at first, but that didn't last long. As he kept pumping hard and fast, the coil inside of her tightened once more, and as his shaft swelled inside of her, she knew that he was close.

As Dagor latched his lips onto the spot he was going to bite, Frankie tilted her head to the side and braced for the searing pain that she knew was coming.

His tongue swept over the spot, once, twice, preparing her, and then he bit down and climaxed at the same time.

Kalugal

"**S**till nothing," William said. "Perhaps they haven't discovered the bodies yet."

Kalugal stood by the sliding doors of Kian's cabin, aimlessly gazing at the small waves the ship was gliding through. Hours had passed since he'd made the call to the tour company, but no one had come to question the hotel staff yet. No one suspicious looking had even crossed the lobby, and no one other than the housekeeper had entered the room Roni had put under his fake name. She would have been a suspect if they hadn't seen her cleaning the other rooms on that floor.

The rooms Roni had added as of yesterday hadn't been investigated either.

Still, Kalugal's gut was sending a warning message to his mind that things were not as they seemed, and that the shit was about to hit the proverbial fan.

He didn't have to rely solely on his gut either. It had been many decades since he'd last served in the Brotherhood, but he doubted things had changed substantially. When the cargo hadn't arrived, someone had been sent to investigate, and the breadcrumbs they had carelessly left behind were large enough for even the dumbest Doomer to follow.

They knew, and they were plotting something.

When the phone William had given him for the task rang, he wasn't surprised.

He activated the speaker. "Kevin Gunter speaking," he said, using his well-practiced German accent.

"Hello, Mr. Gunter." The voice on the other end was rough, and his accent was easily recognizable. "You have something that belongs to us, and we want it back."

"I do not know what you are talking about. Who is this?"

"Don't play dumb. We know what you did to our men and that you stole the cargo. You think you are some big shot who can come in, make a statement by shredding my men to pieces, and take what belongs to us, but you've made a big mistake by infringing on our turf. Since you are obviously a foreigner, you might be unfamiliar with who runs things in this area, so I'm willing to overlook the loss of my worthless men, provided that you return our property unharmed and untarnished to the same place you took them from. This is a one-time goodwill gesture that I will not extend again."

Kalugal's jaw tightened. The Doomer on the other end was talking about the women as if they were nothing more than cattle.

"Again, as I said, I do not know what you are talking about. Good day."

"Wait! We have Luis and his family. If you don't bring the women back by eight this evening, I will personally kill the four small kids, slowly and painfully, while my men will take turns having fun with Luis's wife and fourteen-year-old daughter. On second thought, his twelve-year-old son is a handsome boy. Perhaps some of the men would have fun with him as well."

Rage threatened to consume Kalugal, but he needed to continue the pretense and play into the Doomer's assumptions about him. It seemed that the guy wasn't sure that he was dealing with immortals, and Kalugal needed to keep it that way.

On second thought, it was more likely that the Doomer was only pretending to believe that he was dealing with a competing foreign cartel. He'd probably guessed who had torn his henchmen to pieces and taken the women. Other thugs wouldn't have cared about Luis and his family. They would have laughed at the demand to return the women in exchange for the tour guide.

Only someone who was decent and moral would respond to the threat. That did not apply to Doomers, mobsters, cartel bosses, and, regrettably, many others.

If the guy were a lone operator, Kalugal could have compelled the Doomer to release Luis and his family, but he wasn't, and the others would realize that something was wrong if the guy started acting too out of character.

"Perhaps we can come to an agreement. You know how the saying goes, it's not really stealing when taken from a thief."

"There will be no agreement. You will return the women and never come to this area again."

The plan was, no doubt, to ambush whoever came with the women, and since the Doomers knew they were dealing with immortals, they assumed that they would send a small force that they could easily overpower.

Kalugal affected a resigned sigh. "You know my name, but I don't know yours, and if we are to negotiate, I need a name."

"You can call me Bud, but there is nothing to negotiate."

It was obviously a fake name, but it didn't matter. Kalugal didn't need the vermin's real name because he would be dead soon.

"I can't make it by eight, Bud. The cargo has been moved and is more than half a day away." He switched to his compulsion voice. "The earliest I can do is meet you at the place you indicated at four in the afternoon tomorrow. You must agree to this. Until then, keep Luis and his family safe," Kalugal pushed with all the strength of his compulsion to ensure compliance.

If Bud was the commander of the group, Luis and his family would be safe.

"Be there exactly at four," Bud said.

"I will do my best, but in case I can't make it on time, should I call you on this number?"

"Yes, and don't bother trying to trace it. It's encrypted."

"I have no doubt."

As the call ended, Kalugal turned to Kian. "We need time to get organized. That's why I told him tomorrow at four."

"Obviously." Kian briefly closed his eyes. "What a cluster-fuck." He opened his eyes and looked at Kalugal. "I detected the accent. Bud is a Doomer."

Kalugal nodded. "Not only that, but he also knows who we are. He pretended not to know, so we wouldn't guess who he was and would come unprepared."

From the corner of his eye, Kalugal saw Turner nodding. The guy's strategic mind was, no doubt, already working on a plan.

"I'm glad we have a full day." Turner pulled out his phone. "We need to get vehicles, drones, explosives, and, if possible, satellite pictures."

Kian

Thank the merciful Fates for Turner. It seemed like he already had a plan, or at least the framework for one.

"What do you have in mind?" Kian asked.

"We are not going to the Acapulco port. We will find a spot several hours drive from there, use the rescue boats to get to shore and use ground transportation from there. If they know that we are coming with the ship, they will be waiting for us at the harbor, and they might be planning to attack it. Even if we are moored away from the dock, they could use speedboats and gliders to attack us. We can't count on the Mexican military or navy to come to our aid."

"I'm not worried about that." Kian crossed his arms over his chest. "Let them come. Toven and Kalugal can freeze them in place, and we have enough firepower on this ship to blow them out of the water."

Turner shook his head. "The best offense is to avoid confrontation where possible, especially when the enemy dictates the time and place. We need to take them by surprise."

"You are right," Kian said. "Please, continue."

"As I said, the Guardians will use the rescue boats to get to shore, and I'll arrange for armored vehicles to be waiting for us at a predetermined location."

"The less predictable we are, the better," Onegus said. "But they might anticipate our move."

Turner shrugged. "I doubt it. There is no way they know about me and my connections in Mexico. If you didn't have me, would you have been able to arrange for armored vehicles and the other equipment on such short notice?"

"Probably not," Onegus admitted. "Are you sure that you can get what we need?"

"Positive. I have a lot of connections in Mexico." Turner pushed to his feet. "I need to make a few phone calls and finalize the plan. I'll do it in my cabin and return as soon as I have everything mapped out."

"Thank you." Kian put his hand on Turner's shoulder. "I hate ruining your vacation."

Turner chuckled. "This is fun for me. I was afraid that I would be bored on the cruise."

"Well, then. I'm glad to supply you with entertainment."

He hadn't added that it was a shame people were suffering in the process. It wasn't Turner's fault. The guy liked solving problems. He didn't create them.

"What I wonder is why Bud didn't send a team to the hotel," Kalugal said. "That's the first thing I would have done."

"Maybe he didn't need to," William said. "He could have someone hack into the hotel's surveillance network the same way Roni did, but I doubt Doomers could have come up with that idea. That's not their style. He probably suspected that it was a trap or a decoy, and he either bribed or thralled the staff in the reception or the cleaning crew to check those rooms and report what they found. Naturally, they reported that no one had used the rooms, and Bud realized what we had done. We didn't consider that because the plan was to see if they would respond. Surprisingly, the Doomers were smart about it. The question is if they found out about the Silver Swan." He turned to Kalugal. "When you tampered with Luis's and the other drivers' memory, where did you have them pick you up?"

"I didn't alter that. They picked us up at the dock, but that doesn't mean that they know which ship we came from or even that we arrived on one. Many of the guided tours meet up at the dock. We could have come from any of the cruise ships and large yachts in the harbor, or we could have flown or driven in and stayed at one of the hotels or resorts. If I were in their shoes, a cruise ship would be the last place I would expect to find immortals."

"I hope you are right." Kian sighed. "I want to keep the damn ship. Not only did I remodel it twice, but it now has sentimental value attached to it."

Kalugal leaned back in his chair and crossed his arms over his chest. "Let's try to think like Doomers for a second. We didn't use firearms against the humans, so their remains don't contain any bullets. If the Doomers were thorough in their investigation, they would have realized that only a sizable group of immortals could have inflicted so much damage without weapons. They would assume that we came upon their henchmen by chance and were unprepared, which implies we were tourists. They would then search rental cars and tours for bullet-ridden vehicles. That's probably how they found Luis. I wonder why they didn't take the other two drivers, though."

"Luis was injured," Onegus said. "That made him a prime suspect."

"That might be," Kalugal agreed. "The next step would have been to search hotels, resorts, Airbnbs, and ships for Kevin Gunter. When Roni made the retroactive reservations under my name, it was probably after they had concluded their search. Bud knew that the information about my hotel stay was fake. Still, we could have been staying at a different hotel under a different name."

Kian let out a breath. "If they checked all the ships that were moored in the harbor yesterday, they would have found out that the Silver Swan's passengers boarded her at Long Beach. They also know that the clan is located somewhere in Los Angeles. It's not difficult to piece the two together."

Onegus didn't seem to share his opinion. "Half the ships in that harbor came from Long Beach."

Kian lifted a brow. "How many of them were privately owned?"

Onegus smiled. "That's the beauty of the way we do business. If anyone checks the records, the Silver Swan is not privately owned. It's the first passenger ship of a new luxury cruise line."

"I hope you are right. As I said, I would hate to have to get rid of it."

"Worst case scenario, you will change her name again." Onegus pushed to his feet. "I'm calling a meeting of the head Guardians. We will need Yamanu to shroud and Arwel to detect where Luis is held. They are not just going to bring him and his family to us. I hope you know that."

Kian nodded. "Unfortunately, I have to agree with you."

As Onegus started typing on his phone, Kian went through the list of Guardians in his head.

Yamanu's abilities would be needed to shroud the vehicles, providing them with the element of surprise. Kalugal wasn't a Guardian, but his formidable compulsion power was a game-changer. He would have to head the team going to meet with the Doomers. His ability to immobilize them and their cartel recruits could mean the difference between the success and failure of the mission.

Bhathian could lead the Guardians, and Max could assist him. The younger Guardian was showing a lot of promise, and Onegus was giving him more and more command positions to hone his leadership skills.

Kian's gaze drifted back to the balcony doors and the tranquil sea beyond them. Tomorrow would be stormy no matter how well they prepared, but at least today they could enjoy Anandur's wedding and even go through with the bachelor party no one had thought was going to happen.

The question was what would happen tomorrow and whether they would wrap up the whole mess in time for Brundar's wedding.

Dagor

The sun's glare was mitigated by a smattering of clouds, and the air was pleasantly warm on the deck as Dagor, Negal, and Aru lined up for target practice.

The Guardians had set up makeshift targets—empty cans precariously balanced on the ship's railing.

Max handed them the same rifles the Guardians were holding. "This is an M4 Carbine. It's a lightweight, gas-operated, air-cooled, magazine-fed, selective rate, shoulder-fired weapon with a collapsible stock. It is the standard firearm issue for most U.S. military units." He sounded proud to be in possession of such advanced weaponry, and Dagor stifled the impulse to sneer at what these immortals considered top shelf. It was primitive compared to the weapons they had on Anumati, but it would do the job just the same.

Still, as he held it in his hands, he appreciated the light-weight design and the ease with which it handled. He had been trained in many weapons, including swords, hatchets, javelins, throwing stars, and some that had been invented on other planets, so mastering this relatively modern firearm would be a breeze.

"Do you know how to use this style of weapon?" Max asked.

"I can figure it out." Negal took aim and squeezed off a few rounds. A line of cans jumped off the railing, spinning into the air before splashing into the ocean. "Not bad for a beginner." Negal turned to Max with a smug grin on his face.

Aru stepped up next, took aim, and fired. The crack of the rifle was sharp, but he only hit one can. "Seems I'm a bit rusty." Aru shrugged.

The guy had always been a lousy shot, and there was no excuse for it, given that he was a god.

Dagor suspected that the reason for Aru's lack of aptitude with firearms was that he abhorred killing. It was odd since all troopers went through psychological screening, and those who were not suitable for combat were given administrative assignments. There might be something to Negal's suspicion that Aru had been given the leadership post for reasons that hadn't been disclosed to the two of them. Nepotism couldn't explain it, though, because an indefinite station on Earth was more of a punishment than a reward.

"Your turn, Dagor." Max motioned for him to take position.

He shouldered the rifle, feeling the familiar adrenaline rush of competition, took aim, and fired in quick succession.

Three cans clattered against the railing and tumbled overboard.

"Not bad." Max clapped him on the back. "You three seem to know your way around a rifle. Put new cans up, step back twenty feet to the line over there, and fire again. It's not as easy from forty feet away. Just try not to hit the railing. Kian will have our heads if we damage the ship. He'll tell us to fix it and repaint it."

"Don't worry." Negal took several empty cans from the cardboard box next to the railing and arranged them in a neat line. "I won't hit the railing or shoot into the water. Every bullet will hit the target." He cast Dagor a sidelong glance. "Two shots each; most cans wins."

"You're on."

"What about me?" Aru asked.

"Sorry, dude." Negal shook his head with a mock sad expression on his face. "You're not in the same league as Dagor and me. You need many more hours of practice."

"That's why we are here," Aru murmured under his breath.

"Fine," Negal relented. "If you want to be the designated loser in each round, be my guest. But remember what Max said about the railing."

As Dagor and Negal took turns again, Negal managed to hit the two cans with his two shots, which earned him approving nods from the Guardians.

Aru took aim but only managed to hit one. Thankfully, the other shot he fired landed in the water without damaging the railing. "Well, one is better than none."

Dagor felt the thrill of the competition, but the truth was that this wasn't a challenge for either him or Negal. He lined up his shot, exhaled slowly, and squeezed the trigger.

The first can flew off the railing.

He quickly realigned and fired again. The second can followed the first.

"Poor Aru." Negal shook his head. "Are you up for another challenge?"

"Bring it on."

"This is not a competition," Max grumbled. "This is practice. Aru, you need to keep firing from forty feet until you hit two in a row. Negal and Dagor, move back to the fifty-foot mark."

The practice continued with the Guardians offering tips and sharing laughs about this and that, and Dagor felt like he had been transported back to the training camp. He enjoyed the sense of camaraderie and the lightheartedness, but in the back of his mind he acknowledged that the reason for this target practice was anything but joyous.

The reason was the aftermath of a terrible tragedy, of a monstrous act against defenseless innocents. He didn't enjoy killing, but if he got a chance to kill those responsible for it, he would relish it.

As Dagor reloaded his rifle, ready for another round, Max called a halt to the practice.

"I have an announcement." His voice boomed to get everyone's attention. "There's been a change of plans. We're not going to Acapulco this evening. Kalugal received a call. The Doomers are holding Luis and his family hostage and demanding we return the women we rescued in exchange for their lives. The team in the war room is working on developing a strategy, but the gist of it is that we're going to stop at a different location along the coast, use a lifeboat to get to shore, and drive from there to the meeting point, which is where the bodies of the thugs were buried. Turner is organizing vehicles for us."

Dagor felt a knot of tension form in his stomach. He liked Luis, and he feared for his life and that of his family. Those people were beyond ruthless.

"When are we getting there, and what are we going to do about it?"

"I don't have the details yet," Max said. "Kalugal used compulsion to ensure the safety of Luis and his family until we get there. We don't know whether they've found out that we have a ship and that the women are on board, but in case they did, we don't want to bring the ship back and make it a target. We hope to surprise them and use compulsion to overpower them. I assume that Yamanu will shroud our team so the Doomers' human cohorts won't be able to see us. I don't expect it to be too difficult of a mission."

Dagor hoped Max was right.

He would do everything in his power to prevent Luis and his family from being added to the list of victims those monsters claimed.

The practice resumed, but the mood had shifted. It was no longer about sport and competition. Each shot Dagor fired was aimed at the enemy, and he did not miss a single one.

Frankie

When Frankie woke up, Dagor was gone, and there was no note from him either, but it was okay. She knew where he was. Still, it would have been nice to get a note with sweet love words.

Oh, well, she hadn't fallen in love with a poet. Dagor was an engineer through and through.

Stepping into the shower, she took her time washing her hair and conditioning it. Mia was coming later to style it for her, so maybe it was a little too early for that, but Frankie was sticky from lovemaking. Besides, Mia was an immortal now, with the sense of smell that came with it. Frankie had nothing to be embarrassed about, but if the roles were reversed, she wouldn't have wanted to smell Toven on Mia.

Following her transition there would be a lot of adjustments to be made, but she was ready to embrace them.

What were a few inconveniences compared to living forever and being nearly indestructible?

Well, her family was still a problem she didn't know how to solve. If she was a Dormant, then her brothers were as well, and so was their mother, but her father probably wasn't, and leaving him behind in the human world was too painful to consider.

Perhaps she wouldn't transition after all, and agonizing about her father was premature.

Once she was done, Frankie wrapped a towel around her hair, rubbed her body dry, and padded naked into the bedroom even though the curtains were open. Who was going to see her?

The seagulls?

Chuckling, she pulled on a pair of panties and a loose, long T-shirt that she used as a nightgown. It was good enough for lounging in the cabin and watching some television.

She was just getting comfortable when the doorbell rang, startling her. It was too early for Mia, and Dagor knew the code to her cabin. Snatching the remote from the coffee table, Frankie switched to the door camera view, and when she saw it was Bridget, her heart started racing.

The doctor had probably come to check on her wound, and Dagor wasn't there to run interference. Could she just ignore her and not answer?

But then Bridget would call her, and she would have to lie that she had been asleep and let her in anyway.

Damn.

Walking up to the door, she plastered a smile on her face and opened it for the doctor. "Hey, Bridget. I didn't expect you." She patted the towel on her head. "Sorry about that. I've just stepped out of the shower."

"No need to apologize. I came uninvited." The doctor scanned her from head to toe with professional precision. "You look good for someone who got shot less than twenty-four hours ago. You seem to be doing remarkably well, but I want to make sure that everything is healing properly."

Right. Bridget probably suspected that something strange was going on and wanted to find out what was responsible for Frankie's rapid healing.

"Oh, it is. Remarkably so." She chuckled nervously. "Dagor has been taking such good care of me," she babbled, a bit too enthusiastically. "He bit me so many times that I probably have more venom in my veins than blood. In fact, I won't be surprised if I'm transitioning already. I don't have any symptoms, though. Is it possible to transition without developing fever?"

Bridget smiled. "Very young girls transition without any symptoms, but not adults. Not in my experience, anyway."

"Bummer." Frankie's heart sank, but she quickly rallied. "But at least it healed my wound because it's completely gone." She smiled apologetically. "Where are my manners? Please, take a seat." She waved a hand toward the couch.

"Thank you." Bridget put her black doctor's bag on the coffee table and sat down. "I didn't take that into consideration, but you are right. The venom has healing properties, and when delivered frequently, I guess it can speed up recovery quite dramatically."

"Lucky me." Frankie sat across from Bridget. "My boyfriend is a god with very potent venom, and he has been taking excellent care of me."

"Yes, it would seem so." Bridget tilted her head and looked at Frankie from under lowered lashes. "Given that Dagor is a god and the frequency of his venom injection, perhaps you are right about transitioning with no symptoms as well." The doctor seemed to be considering something for a moment. "We could test it. I could make a small cut on the palm of your hand and see how quickly it heals."

Frankie hesitated.

She didn't want to have the test done without Dagor being present. Besides, she was pretty sure that she wasn't transitioning, and she didn't want to have a cut on her hand.

Then again, Dagor could probably heal it with a few licks of his tongue, and if that didn't work, he could give her another tiny blood transfusion, although that was quite extreme for a little cut, so that probably wasn't a good idea.

Mostly, though, she didn't want to be disappointed by a negative result.

"I'm not ready yet." She smiled nervously. "We haven't been trying for long. We used protection before I got injured, so it's way too early for me to start transitioning."

"As you wish. Can I take a look at your wound before I go?"

Laughing, Frankie lifted her shirt. "What wound?"

Bridget shook her head. "Incredible. You've healed as fast as an immortal. Are you sure you don't want me to test you?"

Frankie shrugged. "It's the venom. I'm sure of that. Dagor and I managed to sneak in a little afternoon delight, so the latest injection is still in full force. Even if the cut heals faster than it should, it will be because of that."

"You are the boss of your own body, and you decide when and where." Bridget rose to her feet and took her bag. "I'll see you at the wedding tonight."

"Yes. And this time, you'll see me dancing the night away."

"I'm looking forward to it."

After the doctor left, Frankie sat down on the couch and reached for the remote, but instead of flipping through channels, her mind engaged in flipping through thoughts.

Perhaps she could run a little test by herself?

It wouldn't tell her anything because it was true that she just had a fresh injection of venom, and that would screw with the results, but she was curious, and she was never good with patiently waiting for things.

Padding to the kitchenette, she pulled a sharp knife out of the drawer and pricked the tip of her pointer finger.

"Ouch. That hurt." She put the finger in her mouth and licked the little drop of blood that had welled over it.

That wasn't going to tell her anything.

She pulled the finger out and watched as another drop of blood welled over the tiny wound she'd inflicted.

Well, so much for fast healing. It didn't seem to stop bleeding any faster than usual. The only difference was that it didn't hurt as it normally would.

Less than a minute later, it stopped bleeding, and it took another five minutes for it to disappear completely.

It wasn't the instantaneous healing of an immortal, but it was definitely faster than humans.

A wave of dizziness washed over her, and she pressed her hand to her forehead. "It's the venom. That's all. There is no way I'm transitioning."

But what if she was?

She needed to talk to Dagor, but he was in the middle of weapons practice and couldn't be disturbed.

She needed to talk to someone. Mia. She could call Mia.

Grabbing her phone, Frankie called her friend. "Hi, Mia, are you busy?"

"Not at all. Toven is with Kian, and I'm just doodling on my tablet. What's up?"

"Can you come over right now? You can continue doodling here, and then I will do your makeup, and you'll do my hair."

Mia chuckled. "It's still too early for that. I can come for a little bit and return later when it's time to start getting ready."

Frankie didn't want to inconvenience her friend. "Perhaps we can just talk on the phone. I don't want you to have to come here twice."

She could go to Mia's cabin, but Mia hadn't invited her, and she wasn't going to suggest it.

"Yeah, that will probably be better. Bridget gave me a lecture today about not resting enough. So, what did you want to talk about?"

Frankie chuckled. "Actually, it has to do with Bridget."

Anandur

∾

Turner entered the makeshift war room, aka Kian and Syssi's cabin, with his laptop tucked under his arm and a cup of coffee in his other hand. "The transport is arranged. Armored vehicles will be waiting at the designated location." He put his coffee cup on the dining table.

"Good work." Kian eyed the cup as if he was contemplating the merits of caffeine versus the whiskey he'd been drinking since Kalugal's phone call with *Bud*.

"What's the plan?"

As Turner flipped his laptop open to look at his notes, Anandur wondered what had happened to his yellow pad. Usually, the guy wrote his action plan the old-fashioned way and only used the laptop for information gathering.

When Turner turned the laptop screen toward Kian, Anandur realized that he hadn't been looking at his notes but had pulled up a map of the coast of Mexico.

"We stop here, which is about two hundred nautical miles north of Acapulco. We lower a lifeboat and use it to get our force to shore. There is a road nearby, and that's where the vehicles will be waiting for us. I assumed forty passengers. Thirty-six Guardians, Kalugal, Dalhu, and the two gods. The transport is a mix of vans and SUVs that look like regular civilian vehicles but are bulletproof. We don't want to be detected too soon." He took a sip from his coffee. "They don't really expect us to return the women. They expect us to do precisely what we are planning, which is to take them out and release Luis. Nevertheless, we will play along and pretend that the vans and SUVs are for transporting the women."

"Obviously, they are setting up a trap for us," Onegus said. "Losing the cargo looks bad for them. They probably don't want to report it to their commanders in the Brotherhood because failure will get them in trouble. But if they can show that they killed a bunch of clan members, losing the women will be forgiven. We are much bigger fish."

Kian nodded. "And if they hope to capture some of us alive, they might not booby-trap the area to blow us up, but we still have to assume that they would plan for a massive firepower advantage."

"I'm taking this into consideration," Turner said. "That's why I ordered bulletproof vehicles, but they may still have access to heavier caliber projectiles that would render the armor useless, or worse, RPGs. But keep in mind, they don't know about the assets we have, meaning a powerful compeller and an equally powerful shrouder, and they have no reason to assume that we would be well-armed because we did not use any weapons to take down the cartel thugs. In other words, chances are they underestimate us; they think that together with their cartel friends, they can over-power our inferior force."

"I agree." Kian took a sip from his whiskey. "Doomers prefer engaging face to face because they usually have an advantage in numbers. All they know is what Luis could have told them, which is the number of tourists he took to the ruins. A small group that included several females. They will assume that several immortals on vacation stum-bled upon their goons, killed them, and rescued the women. They might even think that they are dealing with civilians. But in case their tactics involve heavier weaponry or explosives after all, what's the plan?"

Turner waved a hand at Onegus. "That's your part, chief."

Onegus nodded. "In addition to the vehicles, we are getting four surveillance drones. Before we enter the area, we scan it with the drones. If there is no one there, we will know that the place is booby-trapped, and we don't go in. When our force gets in front of the Doomers, Kalugal uses a powerful megaphone to freeze everyone, and the fun begins."

"We should first find and neutralize their scouts." All eyes turned to Dalhu, who rarely spoke up. "The standard operating procedure would have the commander send scout teams to observe and report on the approaching opposing force. We need to get to the scouts and eliminate them first."

"Actually, that may present an advantage for us." Kalugal's thoughtful tone indicated that he was thinking out loud. "We should capture and interrogate the scouts for intel. They would let us know what weapons and traps we would be facing. I can then compel them to report back whatever we want them to. This will amplify our element of surprise and help us navigate whatever the Doomers have prepared for us."

Kian and Turner nodded as one, and it was obvious both liked the info Dalhu shared and Kalugal's idea to capitalize on it.

Anandur sighed. "I wish I could join you. It has been a long time since I've kicked some Doomer butt." He glanced at Kian. "Is there any way you can assign bodyguard duty to someone else?"

Kian shook his head. "I could, but I won't. Your job is to keep your bride happy the day after your wedding, and she won't be if you run off to kill Doomers and cartel scum."

That was true. Wonder could take on any immortal in hand-to-hand combat and win, but she wasn't a fighter by nature. She was a gentle soul like Syssi and Alena. He still couldn't understand why the Fates had gifted her with superior strength when she clearly detested using it.

"Yeah, you are right." Anandur sighed. "I need to stay with my beautiful mate and guard my illustrious leader." He put the back of his hand on his forehead. "Oh, the hardship."

Onegus snorted.

"On a positive note," Kian lifted his nearly empty whiskey glass, "pushing the operation to tomorrow means that you get to have your bachelor party after all, and your wedding won't have to be delayed or postponed."

Anandur grinned. "That's the best news I've heard today. I'm looking forward to celebrating my last night of bachelorhood and then marrying the love of my life without worrying whether my groomsmen are going to make it in one piece and on time. But Brundar's wedding tomorrow might be affected." He turned to his brother. "I don't mind switching nights with you. Wonder might grumble a little, but she will come around."

"No," was Brundar's response. "I don't want a bachelor party, and I don't care about delaying my wedding. Killing the vermin comes first, and Callie agrees."

Knowing his brother, there was no point trying to argue with him.

"Well, I offered."

As the group continued discussing the finer details of the plan, Anandur glanced at Dalhu, who was sipping on a large glass of whiskey with a murderous expression on his face.

The guy needed to loosen up, and the bachelor party Anandur planned for himself was just what Dalhu needed.

Whiskey and cigars were great, but it wouldn't be his party if he didn't include something hilarious that everyone would be talking about for years to come. The thought of entertaining his friends, especially at times like this when everyone was gloomy and bemoaning the state of the world, brought a smile to his face.

Dressing up as a stripper for Kian's bachelor party had been a big hit, and people still talked about it years later. The Scottish sword dance at Bhathian's had left everyone in stitches. Those were tough acts to follow, and he wondered what he could do that would top those performances.

Perhaps he could challenge the guys to a dance-off? He could bring Bob to the party and have him dance for them. Or he could stick to his original plan, wear his Superman costume, and do his best Superman impression. Wonder had incorporated elements of Wonder Woman's costume in her wedding gown, but she claimed that they were just hints and made him swear that he wouldn't come dressed as Superman to their wedding. But since he'd already gotten the costume custom-made, and it was awesome, it would be a shame to let it go to waste.

Dagor

As Dagor made his way to Frankie's cabin, his mood was much less upbeat than it had been when he'd left. The news he had to share was sure to upset her, and he wasn't looking forward to telling her about Luis and his family having been abducted and held hostage by the monsters.

He found her sitting on the couch in the living room, her expression brightening at his arrival but then quickly shifting to concern. "What happened?"

Joining her on the couch, he clasped her hand. "The Doomers have taken Luis and his family hostage. They're demanding we return the women we rescued in exchange. Kalugal compelled their leader to keep the family safe, so hopefully, they will be okay until we get there, which is tomorrow, not today. You should call Margo and tell her about the additional delay."

Frankie's brow furrowed. "We are not returning the women, right?"

"Of course not. Kalugal used compulsion to buy us extra time so we can prepare."

She shook her head. "I don't understand. Why didn't Kalugal just compel the guy to release them?"

"It's not that simple." Dagor sighed. "The person Kalugal spoke to is probably the leader, but we can't be sure of that. Whoever he is, though, he isn't alone. Kalugal can compel only those who hear him. The others wouldn't have been affected by it, and if the person he spoke to tried to release Luis and his family, the others would have realized that something was amiss and stopped him. Kalugal did the best he could under the circumstances, which is to hopefully ensure their safety until our arrival."

"Yeah, that makes sense." She leaned her head on his shoulder. "So, what now?"

"Kian and his war room team are working on a plan to take the Doomers and their cohorts by surprise, rescue Luis and his family, and get rid of the scum."

"That's not going to be easy." She lifted her head and looked into his eyes. "Are you going to join the mission?"

"Aru, Negal, and I can do things that the immortals can't, but it's up to Kian. We are not part of the clan, and we've never trained with the Guardians."

"I hope he doesn't call on you."

Dagor hoped he would, but he didn't want Frankie to worry. He gave her hand a gentle squeeze. "We want to help, and we can handle this easily."

"Just promise me to be careful, okay?" she said softly. "Even gods can be killed."

"I'm always careful, and I'm well trained." He gave her a reassuring smile and wrapped his arm around her shoulders, trying to ease her tension.

Letting out a breath, Frankie shifted to face him. "Bridget paid me a surprise visit earlier. I had no choice but to bluff my way through it."

"What did you tell her?"

"That you've pumped me full of venom, and that must have sped up my recovery." She chuckled. "The best lies are those closest to the truth. Anyway, I got carried away and suggested that I might be transitioning without symptoms, so Bridget offered to conduct a test and make a cut on the palm of my hand. "

He arched a brow. "Did you agree?"

Frankie shook her head. "I told her that you'd just given me a dose of venom, so even if I healed faster, it wouldn't be because my body was changing but because I still had a lot of venom in me. It seemed to convince her, and she let it go. But I was curious, so I pricked my finger to see how fast it healed." She lifted the finger to show him. "The results were inconclusive. I think it healed faster than normal, but what I'm sure of is that without the venom, it would still hurt."

"So, what's the conclusion from your experiment? Do you think you're transitioning or not?"

"I don't know." She chewed on her bottom lip. "I don't have a fever, and that's supposed to be the first sign."

Dagor reached with his hand to check her forehead, but her skin's temperature felt just right to the touch. "You are not warmer than usual. It might be the venom."

Frankie tried to hide her disappointment. "Yeah, that's what I thought."

"Hey." He cupped her face in his hands. "It will happen. We've only just started, and we will keep working on it."

She managed a small smile. "I know. I just hoped that maybe it was already happening."

Wonder

ᢙ∾

Wonder's bachelorette party had been going full swing since before lunch, and she was getting a little tired.

As the afternoon sun streamed through the cabin's glass doors, warming her face, she closed her eyes and tuned out the laughter and chatter.

"You should go rest a bit before the ceremony," Callie advised. "You look tired. Did you sleep at all last night?"

Wonder chuckled. "I was too nervous to sleep, and I don't know why." The thought of lying down only to be alone with her racing thoughts wasn't appealing. "I'm marrying the love of my life, and my best friend is presiding over the ceremony. I shouldn't have a care in the world."

Callie smiled. "You are an introvert, Wonder, and working in the café hasn't cured you of that. It stresses you out to think that all eyes will be on you."

That was only partially true. There were things that stressed her even more. What if Anandur did something to embarrass her in the name of fun? He loved clowning around, and she didn't want to be the stick-in-the-mud who spoiled the fun for him, but for once, she wanted him to be serious and give the ceremony its proper respect. Then there was the issue of the vows. She'd worked on them for weeks, but after hearing Alena's and Amanda's, she realized that what she'd produced was not on a par with theirs. It was tempting to let Callie help her write something better, but then it wouldn't be from her, and the vows were supposed to be deeply personal.

Wonder groaned. "My vows suck, and I'm afraid Anandur is going to do something goofy, but at least that way, everyone's eyes will be on him, so I won't be the center of attention."

Callie laughed. "I'm sure your vows are heartfelt, which is what really counts, and Anandur is not going to do anything too crazy with the Clan Mother watching."

"I hope not. I wish I could see him before the ceremony to make sure he's not wearing something outlandish."

"It's bad luck for the bride and groom to see each other on the day of their wedding," Callie said. "Now, how about a relaxing bath instead of a nap? It might help calm your nerves."

A bubble bath was the perfect excuse to get some alone time without offending her guests. "That sounds great."

Wonder pushed to her feet. "I'm going to take a bath, and while I'm gone, don't overdo it with the drinks."

A chorus of laughter and mock protests trailed her as she walked into the bedroom and were abruptly silenced when she closed the door behind her.

Letting out a breath, Wonder continued into the bathroom and closed that door behind her, too. She drew a bath, adding scented oils that filled the room with a calming fragrance, and as she sank into the warm water, she closed her eyes. With the heat seeping into her muscles, the tension that had built up throughout the day started to unwind.

As the water gently lapped against her skin, Wonder's thoughts drifted to Anandur. Her mate was adorable, and she loved him with every fiber of her being. She loved his sunny disposition, his strength, and the way he looked at her with love and unconditional approval. She made him happy, and he made her happy in return.

Wonder felt a surge of gratitude for the love she'd found not only with Anandur but with the entire clan.

Her new family.

A little over half an hour later, Wonder stepped out of the bath feeling relaxed, centered, and rejuvenated. She applied lotion to her face, wrapped a towel over her head, and put on a robe.

As she opened the door to the living room, Callie stopped mid-sentence and turned to her. "That was quick. Feeling better?"

"Much." Wonder scanned the room. "Where are Syssi and Amanda?"

"They went to check on the rescued women," Carol said. "Well, Syssi wanted to check on them, but since her Spanish is so-so, Amanda joined her as an interpreter." She glanced at her watch. "I think it's time to get on with the second part of the festivities. We need to get you ready, girl." She pushed to her feet. "I need to see your wedding dress. Callie told us that it's unlike any dress we have seen, and I'm bristling with curiosity."

Wonder waved a hand toward the bedroom. "Follow me and take a look."

"Yay!" Carol clapped her hands.

The wedding dress was spread over the bed, and it was a stunning amalgamation of traditional white and elements inspired by Wonder Woman's costume.

"Oh, my goodness, Wonder, it's absolutely perfect!" Carol exclaimed.

Callie had already seen the dress, so she just smiled and nodded.

Aliya got closer and smoothed her hand over the chiffon. "It's very pretty." She lifted her gaze to Wonder. "Mine is more modest."

"I'm sure it's gorgeous."

"Yeah." Aliya's eyes sparkled. "I know that it's considered bad luck, but Vrog helped me pick it. He loved it."

Wonder smiled, her eyes tracing the intricate details of the dress. The bodice was made from gold fabric, and it flowed into a graceful skirt. The accessories included a real gold tiara and a pair of thick cuffs that had been custom-made. Those were the only part of the outfit that Anandur had been privy to because he'd ordered them.

"You're going to look like a goddess," Carol gushed. "Anandur won't be able to take his eyes off you."

"Isn't it a bit too much?" Wonder looked at Callie. "Maybe I should forgo the tiara?"

Her friend's eyes bugged out. "Are you kidding me? This thing is real gold and made for you. I designed your hairdo around it."

"Then I guess it stays." Wonder lifted the tiara and ran her fingers over the delicate carvings. "I'm going to feel like an imposter princess."

"You are a princess." Annani glided into the bedroom. "Every bride is a princess on her wedding day, and you, my dear, will look regal. I cannot wait to see you in this outfit with your hair and makeup done, walking up to the dais surrounded by your bridesmaids." She smiled. "We did not have that custom in Sumer, so we did not include it in our musings about our future weddings."

254

Wonder blushed at the thought. As a girl, she'd fantasized about marrying Esag, Khiann's squire. She'd been devastated by his refusal to break his engagement to be with her, but in retrospect, he had saved her life by breaking her heart. If she hadn't run away, she would have died with everyone else in their city.

She was grateful to Annani and the Fates, who had guided her to suggest Tula as a maid to Areana. Her sister had accompanied Mortdh's bride to his stronghold in the north, which had saved her life.

Frankie

꩜

As Dagor's phone buzzed with an incoming message, he read it with a raised brow. "That's a surprise. I'm invited to Anandur's bachelor party." He looked at Frankie. "I'm not a close friend of his. Why would he invite me?"

"Maybe he likes you?"

"Anandur likes everyone."

Frankie knew that Anandur was the name of one of Kian's bodyguards, but she wasn't sure which one he was. Given Dagor's last comment, though, it had to be the redhead. "Anandur is the tall one, right? The blond who looks like a statue of an angel doesn't like anyone, so it can't be him."

"That's Brundar, who's surprisingly Anandur's brother. He's getting married tomorrow, provided that we are done with the mission in time for his wedding." He chuckled. "I'm sure he's not going to invite me to his bachelor party."

Dagor put his phone on the coffee table. "I don't want to go to Anandur's either."

"Why not? It will be good for you to mingle a little and make new friends." He needed more people to talk to other than Negal, Aru, and her. "Check with Negal and Aru if they've gotten an invitation. It will be less awkward for you if they are there."

"That's not the reason I don't want to go. I don't like the idea of leaving you alone."

"That's sweet." She leaned over and kissed his cheek. "But I'll be fine. I need to call Margo and let her know about the delay. And then I have to start getting ready for the wedding. It will take me at least an hour to just do my makeup, and I'm doing Mia's makeup, too. She's coming over to do my hair."

"In that case, I might go if Negal is going too."

As Dagor's phone buzzed with another message, Frankie had a feeling it was either Negal or Aru asking him the same question.

"It's Negal," Dagor said. "He's asking whether I got an invitation and if I'm going." He lifted a brow. "Am I going?"

"Yes. Text him that you are."

"Yes, ma'am."

When Dagor was done texting, Frankie pulled him in for a scorching kiss.

"If that was meant to incentivize me to go, it failed," he murmured against her lips. "I'd rather stay with you than hang out with a bunch of dudes."

"Go." She playfully pushed him. "But just so you are mentally prepared, tonight, you are taking me to the dance floor. I'm fully healed, Bridget already knows, so there is no need to keep pretending. I plan on wearing one of my form-fitting evening gowns and sky-high heels. Be ready to be wowed."

"Oh, I am." He kissed her back.

Frankie waited until the door had closed behind Dagor before reaching for her phone, but she didn't call Margo right away.

How was she going to explain the additional delay without revealing too much?

Well, she'd just have to wing it.

"Hi," Margo answered. "So, which dress are you wearing for tonight's wedding?"

"The red one."

"Oh, wow. You are going in with all guns blazing."

Frankie winced. "Yeah, I'm dressing to impress. I have a bit of bad news, though. We're going to be another day late."

"What happened?" Margo's voice was laced with concern.

Frankie bit her bottom lip, searching for a plausible explanation. "Uh, there were some complications with docking in the Acapulco harbor." She hoped her improvised excuse sounded believable. Actually, it was true to some extent, just not the whole truth. But Margo wasn't easily fooled, and she could smell bullshit a mile away. Of course, Frankie didn't improve the situation when she decided to embellish the story. "Apparently, you can't just show up with a ship and drop anchor. You need to reserve a spot, and they don't have anything open until tomorrow."

"My bullshit detector is flashing red. What's the real story, Frankie?"

Damn. She could never lie to Margo, not in person and not over the phone.

Frankie sighed. "I wish I could tell you, but I can't."

There was a brief silence before Margo spoke again. "Lynda's bachelorette party is wrapping up tonight, and everyone's flying home in the morning. Maybe I should just call it quits and head back as well. I still have work, you know."

"Please, don't. The cruise is still ending on schedule. The crew can't extend beyond that, and you're not expected back at the office until after the cruise anyway. Just book one more night at the hotel. It'll be worth it, I promise. We will have so much fun, and besides, you won't believe the selection of hot, single guys. It's like a hottie buffet."

Margo laughed. "You should have opened with that. I'll book one more night."

They chatted a bit more about Lynda and her bridesmaids and how Margo's relationship with her future sister-in-law had improved over the past couple of days.

Frankie glanced at her watch and sighed. "I wish I could talk with you more, but I need to start getting ready. You know how long it takes me to put makeup on for an occasion like this."

"Knock them dead, girl, and have that boyfriend of yours take pictures of you in the venue. I want to see you in your dress."

Frankie winced. "I'm not allowed to send out photos of anyone or anything other than myself." No one had told her that, but she'd been told that all of her communications would be monitored. If she tried to send photos of people she shouldn't, they would just not go through. "That's why I didn't send you pictures of Dagor and his friends. Tom's partners are super secretive about everything, and I don't want to risk our future employment with Perfect Match for some pictures."

If everything went well and she transitioned, she wouldn't be taking the job offer, but Margo would.

"So have him take a picture of you before leaving the cabin. I'm sure that's okay."

"I will." Maybe.

Anandur

Anandur couldn't suppress his grin as he headed to his bachelor party, decked out in his embellished Superman costume. He'd added a pair of black, devilish horns and smeared red makeup over his face. It was a nod to the demon illusion he often used to intimidate his enemies, although it had been a while since he'd gotten to use that bad boy.

Kian no longer took an active part in skirmishes, and there hadn't been many of those lately, either. The only time Anandur still saw action was when he occasionally took part in rescue missions. Perhaps the next time he went out on one of those, he would do his demon stunt just to keep up the skill.

"Hello, my Justice League friends." Anandur made his grand entrance, flinging his cape back and thrusting his chest out.

The cabin erupted in cheers and laughter.

Kian handed him a glass full of whiskey. "We were placing bets on what you were going to wear. I won."

"Awesome costume." Bhathian regarded him with a frown. "I hope that's not how you are going to show up to your wedding?"

"I wish." Anandur took a sip from the whiskey. "If I do, my bride will just walk away. She made me promise to wear a tux, but I'll do something to dress it up. Wearing a boring penguin suit is not my style."

Scanning the room, he spotted Kri, who technically should have been a bridesmaid because she was Wonder's friend too, but she'd been his friend longer, and when he'd asked her to be his groomsmaid she'd been more than happy to accept. She had on a tux, her long blond hair was braided, and her pretty face was free of makeup as usual. She looked sharp.

"Superman with horns and a demon's red face." Arwel laughed. "Now that's a combination Hollywood hasn't tried yet."

Anandur laughed. "Maybe I should do like Stallone, write a script and sell it on the condition that I get to star in the movie. It's going to be a blockbuster."

"Good idea." Kri clapped him on the back. "But it will sell better if you take Wonder with you. They'd snatch her up in a heartbeat."

"I know." He grinned. "She's the real Wonder Woman." He lifted his glass in a toast. "To my lovely Wonder, to love, and to new beginnings."

His brother clinked glasses with him and offered him the rarest of gifts—a smile. "I'm happy for you. Wonder completes you."

Anandur affected a gasp and put a hand over his chest. "Wow, Brundar. That's the most romantic thing I've ever heard you say. Thank you."

His brother shrugged. "You only get married once."

"True." Anandur took a sip of his whiskey. "That's a good reason to make the most of the celebration, but I would have liked to join you guys tomorrow. If I showed up dressed like this, it would petrify the humans."

Bhathian shook his head with a grin. "Or make them die of laughter. Besides, the plan is for Kalugal to freeze them, so they will be petrified anyway."

Anandur feigned a pout. "That's no fun. What if you unfreeze them one at a time, after disarming them, of course, and then let them wrestle for their lives?"

"That's not a good idea," Arwel said. "We'd obviously win, and then we would have to put them in stasis because the Clan Mother doesn't allow us to execute them."

Anandur lifted his glass but then lowered it. "Actually, this one time, the Clan Mother has agreed to make an exception because of their monstrous cruelty, and she's not only allowing us to end them permanently but actively encouraging it. My problem is that death by venom is too merciful for monsters. I don't want them to die with a smile on their faces. I want them screaming in pain."

Anandur was glad to see nods all around. "Ripping their hearts out of their chests while they're frozen is better, but doing that while they are fighting for their lives and losing would be even more satisfying. I want them to experience the terror and pain they inflicted on those villagers."

The brutality of his words was not lost on his friends, but they all shared his view that the heinous acts committed by their enemies demanded justice.

Anandur cast a sidelong glance at the gods he had invited to his party and was glad to see similar expressions on their faces. He would have hated it if they'd started spouting nonsense about finding the good in people and giving them another chance. Or worse, trying to somehow justify their horrendous actions. It would have been lunacy, but reading news from the human world, he'd learned that there was no shortage of lunatics, either delusional or paid to spout things that no decent, intelligent person should ever accept or believe.

"Well, that was a fun topic for a bachelor party. Not." Kian chuckled. "I suggest that we forget about the mission until tomorrow and focus on celebrating the joyous occasion tonight." He stepped forward with a bottle of fine whiskey in one hand and a box of premium cigars in the other. "Time for a toast."

He poured whiskey into the line of fresh glasses on Okidu's tray and then waited for his butler to pass them around. "To love and the bliss of matrimony."

As glasses clinked and the sounds echoed around the room, Anandur downed the whiskey in one go, enjoying the smooth, fiery liquid warming his throat.

Kian flipped open the box. "Come and get your cigars, gentlemen and lady, but please light them up on the balcony and make sure that the doors are closed before you do."

Kri leaned over the box. "Which one do you recommend for a novice?"

"The Short Story," Kian said as he handed Kri a diminutive cigar. "They are very good despite their smaller size."

"Okay." She took the offered stick and headed out to the balcony.

After everyone was outside with a cigar in hand, Okidu made the rounds offering cutting services and lighting the cigars for them, and the pleasant smell of the sea breeze was replaced with the rich aroma of tobacco.

Anandur watched Kri puff on hers with surprising ease. Michael, the only one in their group who hadn't taken a cigar, shook his head at his mate. "I thought that you didn't like the smell of cigarettes."

"I don't, but cigars smell good."

Anandur caught Michael's eye and smiled. "Come on, Michael, light up. It's a tradition. You'd better get used to it. We do this at every bachelor party."

Michael grimaced but took the cigar Kian offered him. "You guys are a bad influence."

Anandur grinned. "You want to be a Guardian, right?"

Michael sneered. "I am a Guardian."

"Not yet, you're not. You are a Guardian in training. Light up."

"If I do, are you going to finally graduate me to full-fledged status?"

The kid was good, but he wasn't ready yet. "I wish I could, but you need more training."

"Fine." Michael handed the cigar to Okidu for cutting and lighting. "One more step on the journey toward full status." He took a puff and immediately started coughing.

"This is not a cigarette," Kian said. "Don't inhale. Just hold the smoke in your mouth and then release it."

As the cigars burned and the whiskey flowed, the mood in the room gradually shifted. The jokes resumed, laughter rang out, and stories were shared, each tale more embellished than the last, with Anandur's being the most outlandish of them all.

It was as if they were determined to squeeze every drop of joy out the evening, because tomorrow, they would be busy killing monsters, which would be satisfying but add more taint to their souls.

Evildoers did not only destroy the lives of their victims, their victims' families, and their whole communities, but they also forced the good guys to become killers.

Anandur understood perfectly well why Wonder didn't want to be a Guardian even though she was stronger than most of the males puffing cigars out on Kian's balcony.

She didn't want to be a killer.

To this day, his beautiful, gentle mate had nightmares about killing the males who had set out to violate her and then end her. She had probably saved the lives of countless women who would have fallen victim to those males, and yet she couldn't shake the guilt for taking their lives.

Anandur had gotten over that a long time ago, perhaps because the natural aggression of males made it easier for them, or perhaps it got easier the more times one killed. He was nearly a thousand years old, and he had ended the lives of many, which had probably saved multitudes of innocents.

He had no regrets.

With a sigh, he took another puff of his cigar, letting the rich smoke fill his mouth. Tonight was about living in the moment, about laughter and camaraderie. Later, he was going to marry the love of his life in front of his friends and family.

Things didn't get much better than that.

Dagor

"I'm ready to go." Dagor extinguished his cigar in the ashtray. "I still need to change into my tux."

It would take him a minute, but he was anxious to get back to Frankie and see her all decked out.

"Yeah, me too," Negal said. "I need to take a shower to wash off the cigar stench."

"Shhh." Dagor put a finger on his lips. "You're insulting our host," he whispered.

"Right." Negal rolled his eyes while saying out loud, "I need to wash off the lovely aroma of cigars."

Chuckling, Dagor glanced at Aru, who was in the midst of an animated discussion with Kian.

When Dagor signaled that he and Negal were leaving, he waved them off. "Don't wait for me."

Negal pushed his hands into his pockets. "Did you hear Aru? He said that tearing out the hearts of those Doomers was barbaric. According to him, Anumatians have evolved from such savagery."

Dagor let out a low chuckle. "Yeah, 'evolved.' Anumatians destroy entire populations without even setting foot on their planets, and that's somehow more civilized?"

Negal nodded. "That's precisely what crossed my mind when he said it. It's a convenient way to distance ourselves from the reality of what we do. If we don't see it, touch it, or smell it, then it's somehow okay. That's such hypocrisy."

Dagor's thoughts drifted back to the horrors inflicted by the Doomers' henchmen. The images Jacki's words had painted were forever etched into his mind, fueling rage and a burning desire for justice. "What they did to those villagers was horrific. Nothing less than a barbaric response seems fitting."

Negal remained silent for a moment. "It's a fine line," he finally said, "between justice and vengeance, between civilization and savagery. But the way I see it, you need to respond in kind. It's better to sow such intense fear in your enemies that they won't dare repeat their evil deeds than to act civilized and let them believe that you are weak. That will only encourage more violence and more suffering and will force you to eventually do what you should have done to begin with. Aru must have led a sheltered life before he joined the Galactic Peacekeepers."

Dagor laughed. "Peacekeepers. What a joke that is. We are the overseers, the enforcers, but the noble bleeding hearts back home prefer the nice-sounding term Peacekeepers. The whole universe is full of hypocrisy."

"I guess we'll have to find our own balance," Negal said quietly. "Do what needs to be done, but not lose ourselves in the process. I can perform barbaric acts without becoming a savage. I know why this needs to be done, and I think that the trick is not to relish it."

"That's not easy, my friend. The need for revenge is a powerful force."

They parted ways in the elevator when Dagor exited on Frankie's level, and Negal continued to the upper deck.

He was about to enter the code when Frankie opened the door, and seeing her, he took a step back.

"You look... stunning," Dagor finally managed to say.

Her eyes sparkled with delight at his reaction, and her smile widened. "Thank you. I was hoping that would be your response." She stepped aside to let him in.

"I'm glad I didn't disappoint you." He couldn't take his eyes off her.

Every detail was flawless, from the hair that was styled to perfection to the way her red dress hugged her figure. It was more than her physical beauty that captivated him, though. It was the confidence and joy she exuded that truly made her shine.

He wanted to pull her into his arms and kiss the living daylights out of her, but he knew better. If he ruined all the work that she'd put into looking the way she did, Frankie would give him hell.

He rubbed a hand over his jaw. "I need a few minutes to shower and change."

"Take your time." She smiled. "There is no rush. Do you want me to pour you a drink in the meantime?"

"No, thanks. I had enough whiskey at the party. I'm going to stick to water and juice for the rest of the night."

"As you wish." She walked over to the bar, sashaying her hips. "I'm making myself a gin and tonic."

Stuck looking at her shapely ass, he was rooted in place until she looked at him with a raised brow.

"I'm going." He tore his eyes away from her and forced his feet to take him to the bathroom.

After a quick shower, Dagor changed into his tux, and as he combed his hair, he caught himself humming and smiling at his reflection in the mirror.

It was the Frankie effect.

She brought a sense of excitement and happiness to his life that he hadn't known he was missing. Adjusting his bowtie in the mirror, he took a deep breath and squared his shoulders.

"You look good," she said as he entered the living room, her eyes roaming over him. "Really good."

"Thank you." He extended his arm to her. "Shall we?"

"We shall." As Frankie took his arm, her touch sent a familiar thrill through him, and he wondered whether it would always be like that.

Dagor offered a prayer to the Fates to give him a chance to find out by allowing Frankie to transition.

When they entered the festively decorated dining hall, Frankie gasped. "Look at this. It's Wonder Woman themed."

The tablecloths alternated between red, white, and blue, and a gold sash was draped over their middles. The chair covers were similarly color-themed, with a gold bow tied at each. A gold eagle symbol inside a red circle was projected onto the ceiling.

It was a lovely tribute to Wonder Woman, honoring Anandur's bride-to-be.

Toven and his mate entered right behind them and paused to join in admiring the decor.

"They really went all out with the theme," Mia commented, her eyes taking in the festive decorations. "It looks very patriotic."

"Right." Dagor swept his gaze over the room. "I just realized that the colors also represent the United States flag."

Soft music played in the background, and Dagor wondered whether it also had anything to do with Wonder Woman.

As Toven and Mia continued to their table, Dagor and Frankie joined Aru, Gabi, and Negal.

"You look amazing," Gabi told Frankie. "Where did you get this stunning dress?"

Frankie chuckled. "From my cousin Angelica, who got it in a thrift store. It's supposed to be some famous designer's, but the label was cut off, so it might have been a story the store owner told my cousin."

"It's absolutely stunning."

"Thank you." Frankie beamed.

Dagor loved that she was so confident and comfortable in her own skin that she didn't feel the need to impress anyone with anything other than the power of her personality and her exuberance. She wasn't embarrassed about wearing a borrowed dress that came from a thrift store.

She was proud of it.

In fact, he loved everything about her, from her tiny feet clad in sky-high heels to the tip of her head and the elaborate coif that Mia had twisted her hair into.

"Let's make a toast." Dagor reached for the bottle of champagne, uncorked it, and poured the bubbly into everyone's glasses. He raised his and waited until everyone at their table followed. "To the lovely couple getting married tonight, to my friends, old and new, and to Frankie, who brings light and joy into my life."

Anandur

❧

The moment Anandur had been awaiting was finally here.

He stood at the entrance to the dining hall, flanked by his seven groomsmen and one groomsmaid, dressed in a smart tuxedo and a white dress shirt, which would make Wonder happy. But he wasn't wearing a bowtie, and the shirt wasn't buttoned all the way to the top, so the Superman T-shirt he was wearing underneath was showing.

"You couldn't help yourself, could you?" Kri murmured. "Button that shirt up and hide that thing. Wonder will be upset."

"No, she won't." Anandur grinned. "She will be tickled. You look great, Kri. I love the gold bowtie. It's a nice touch."

"Thank you." She adjusted the tie. "Michael's is blue."

Each of his groom's-persons had chosen a bowtie that was either red, white, or blue to honor his bride, and Kri was the only one who had thought of adding gold to the ensemble.

Brundar looked sharp with his white-blond hair unbound and cascading down his back. Kian looked like a god, which was nothing new, and Onegus was grinning like he was the one getting married. Bhathian was straining the seams of his tux, and he looked miserable, confined in the restricting garment. Arwel had his shoulder-length hair gathered in a ponytail and looked pained, probably because he was picking up the emotions of the rescued women all the way from the lower deck where they were housed.

Yamanu looked great with his black hair gathered in a long ponytail, and Michael was looking at Kri with unabashed admiration.

It had been a tough choice between Michael and Max, and the reason Michael had won was simply because of being Kri's mate. The kid wasn't even a full-fledged Guardian yet, but he showed great promise and most importantly, his heart was in it.

As the music that signaled the groom's entrance started playing, Anandur and his entourage walked toward the dais where Annani was waiting.

Smiling at his guests, he took in the decorations and was impressed by how well they had turned out. It had been all

Amanda's doing, and he owed her a big thank you for making the night special for him and Wonder.

Clad in her white ceremonial robe that was edged with gold, Annani radiated warmth and love but also unmistakable power. Her glowing skin made her look majestic and ethereal, which, as it turned out, was even more spectacular than they had believed. Not all gods glowed in the dark, only the nobility did, and the stronger the glow, the more royal the status.

To him, though, the Clan Mother looked like an angel, her smile reaching across the room and touching his heart. It was a smile that conveyed love, pride, and acceptance.

The chatter and music in the room seemed to fade into the background as Anandur walked toward the dais and his great-great-grandmother, who was the heart of their community.

As he took his place, Anandur scanned the smiling faces of his clan members, and the positive energy sent his way filled him with joy. His gaze drifted across the room, eventually finding his mother seated at the family table.

The look on her face was one of immense pride and affection, and her warm smile seemed to say, "I am so happy for you."

Naturally, his mother loved Wonder.

Everyone did.

His gentle, beautiful, graceful mate. In a few moments, she would walk in, surrounded by her bridesmaids, and she would smile at him from across the room.

He hoped she would be amused by the Superman shirt peeking from under his dress shirt. She'd wanted him to just wear a plain tuxedo and look dignified for a change, but she knew him well enough to expect something mischievous.

If he had done nothing special, she would have been disappointed.

Standing at the foot of the dais, Anandur felt an unexpected wave of emotion sweep over him. Given that he and Wonder were each other's fated mates, he had viewed this night just as a joyous event to celebrate their union with the clan, but now, as the reality of the moment settled upon him, he realized that it was so much more than just a fun party.

This was a binding of souls, a public declaration of his and Wonder's eternal commitment to one another. It was a testament to the love that had grown and flourished between them, a love that was now going to be made official in front of their community. It was an acknowledgment of their bond, a celebration of their unity, and a promise for their shared future.

Wonder

∽

onder hadn't seen her bridesmaid's dresses until tonight, and now that the eight of them flanked her four on each side, she wasn't sure whether she should be mad at Amanda for going overboard with the dining hall decoration and the dress designs or thank her for being so bold.

One thing was for sure: no one was going to forget this DC Universe-themed wedding, so maybe it was a good thing, given that there were ten of them taking place.

Each of her bridesmaids had a different dress that matched her personality in addition to being Wonder Woman-themed.

Carol's was a long, flowing red gown with a subtle gold waistband and gold trim along the neckline. It was Grecian-style, the one-shoulder strap adorned with a golden W emblem. It was bold and pretty, like the female wearing it.

Vivian wore a navy-blue chiffon dress with a V-neck and an A-line silhouette. The skirt was sprinkled with silver stars, mimicking Wonder Woman's star-spangled look. It was conservative and demure, matching Vivian's motherly character. Her daughter Ella wore a knee-length, metallic gold dress with a fitted silhouette and a sweetheart neckline. The dress was more daring and modern, fitting the young female who had recently changed her hair color from pink to blue.

Wonder had gotten close to the two during her study sessions with Parker. Vivian had taken on a maternal role in her life, and Ella had become like a sister to her, but Wonder still wished that Tula could be there to celebrate her wedding.

Callie, her future sister-in-law, had chosen a wrap dress in a vibrant red color, edged with gold piping, and Aliya's dress was a simple navy sheath complemented by a gold headband.

Mey's dress had a red bodice and a flowing, blue, high-low skirt. The transition from red to blue was accented with a gold belt that was supposed to symbolize Wonder Woman's lasso, but Wonder doubted anyone would figure out what it meant to convey. Jin's dress had a gold sequined bodice, representing Wonder Woman's armor, and it was paired with a sleek navy pencil skirt. Eva was dressed in a long, deep blue Grecian-style gown with a flowing skirt and a detachable gold arm cuff.

When the moment arrived and the bride's song began playing, Wonder took her first step into the event hall, flanked by her bridesmaids. Keenly aware of every eye in the room turning towards her, her heart raced with excitement and nervousness, but as she beheld the smiling face of her groom, the anxiety vanished, and only the excitement remained.

Anandur looked dashing in his elegant tuxedo, and a wave of relief washed over her that he had chosen the traditional attire over the Superman costume he had brought aboard. His wild red hair, usually untamed, was slicked back neatly, giving him a distinguished look that only heightened his natural charisma. He looked every bit the hero Guardian she knew him to be, and the sight of him made her heart swell with love.

As their eyes met, she saw in his gaze a radiant happiness that mirrored her own, and the love she felt for him surged through her, so intense and profound that her heart felt like it was swelling within her chest.

Amusement lifted her lips as she imagined the swelling turning physical, overcoming her tight bodice, and causing a wardrobe malfunction.

She certainly didn't need that to make her wedding day even more memorable than it already was. Shaking off the absurd notion, Wonder smiled back at Anandur and lifted her gaze to Annani.

The contrast between Anandur's towering figure and Annani's petite form was striking, but despite the goddess's small stature, she commanded the space with her formidable presence. It was a remarkable sight—the goddess and the Guardian, standing at equal levels, their heights balanced by the dais.

Annani had always been larger than life, and as Gulan, Wonder had felt invisible under the goddess's immense shadow. Compared to Annani, she felt small and insignificant. What were her impressive stature and her physical strength compared to the goddess's power, indomitable spirit, and unwavering determination?

Today, though, as she stood in front of the dais holding Anandur's hand, Wonder realized how far she had come and how much she had grown. She was no longer Gulan, the servant girl who had been tasked with protecting and serving the princess. She was now Wonder, a new person with no limits and nothing holding her back.

Her gaze shifting to Annani, she regarded the goddess who had been a constant in her life, the princess she had idolized as a young girl and still revered.

Despite her diminutive stature and her delicate appearance, Annani was fierce and courageous and had a relentless drive that defied the odds. She had faced adversities that would have daunted most, and yet she had persevered, and her vision for a better future remained clear.

Reflecting on Annani's journey, Wonder was struck by the enormity of what her oldest friend had achieved. Annani was more than just a leader of her clan; she was a guardian of humanity, shielding mankind from Navuh's toxic influence.

No one could compare to Annani, and Wonder shouldn't either. She had her own journey, her own path to follow, and her story hadn't been written yet. She might have been born nearly five thousand years ago, but she'd lived only twenty-three of them, and she had a lot to learn.

She felt a surge of gratitude toward her old friend for officiating at her wedding and for being a symbol of the resilience and hope that Wonder aspired to embody in her own life, of courage, compassion, and steadfastness in the face of adversity.

With a role model like Annani and with the love and support of Anandur and her new clan family, Wonder was stepping into a future filled with endless possibilities, and instead of feeling overwhelmed, she felt empowered.

She made a silent promise to herself to strive to be as courageous, as resilient, and as dedicated to her beliefs as the goddess. In her own way, she would carry forward the torch of hope and justice, standing alongside those she loved and fighting for a better world.

Annani

This night held a special place in Annani's heart, almost rivaling the emotional intensity of her daughters' weddings. Wonder, or Gulan as she was once known, was still her closest friend despite the thousands of years separating them. Seeing her standing next to her prophesied mate and looking so profoundly happy was deeply moving.

As she gazed at the couple before her, Annani's mind wandered to the prophecy of an old human seer who had foretold of Gulan's destined love thousands of years ago.

In a distant land and time, you will find true love with a gentle giant of a man.

What a succinct description of Anandur that was.

A gentle giant of a man.

At over six and a half feet tall and with broad shoulders that could barely fit through a standard door opening and massive muscles all over, he was a giant, and although not many would call him gentle, Annani knew that he had a heart of gold and cared deeply about his brother, his clan, and now his mate.

The soothsayer's prophecy for Areana had also been accurate.

A heavy burden rests on your shoulders, and you have a most important task. Your gentle soul and soft heart will guide you on your path. I see a child in your future, a son born to you and the rogue. Stay strong and true to yourself and teach him right from wrong.

It was easy to see that the rogue was Navuh, and the son was either Lokan or Kalugal. The soothsayer should have said sons, not son, but perhaps teaching Kalugal right from wrong was more important than teaching Lokan because the younger brother was so much more powerful than the older, and if he had stayed with the Brotherhood and become his father's right-hand man, Annani shuddered to think of the consequences. Navuh was smart, but Kalugal was brilliant, and combined with his compulsion power, he was extremely dangerous.

And yet, he'd grown up to be a decent male, a good husband and father, and a fair leader of his men. All of that was most likely thanks to his mother's influence.

The near-perfect accuracy of those prophecies was so evident that it stirred within Annani a flicker of hope for her own prophesied reunion with Khiann, her long-lost love so cruelly taken from her by Mortdh.

Silently, she recited the seer's words from memory.

Do not despair, Princess Annani. Not all is lost. True love cannot die. Its fire cannot turn to ice. Your beloved's love floats in the ether, ready to be reborn. Khiann will find a way to come back to you in some form. Seven children will be born to you, all different, but his spirit will shine through their eyes, warm and bright. And one day, many years from now, he will come to you, and you will know him at first sight. I saw it all with my blind eyes, my lady, and every-thing I see with my second sight comes to pass.

The possibility that Khiann might reincarnate as an immortal, or perhaps even as a god on Anumati, lingered in her thoughts. The recent arrival of gods from Anumati had opened up a realm of possibilities Annani had never considered before. Could her Khiann be waiting for her there?

The notion that she might find him again if she one day took the throne, as her grandmother planned, was both tantalizing and daunting. Even if she was keen on usurping her grandfather, the Eternal King, it would take many thousands of years to achieve, and she wanted her Khiann back now.

Annani pushed these personal reflections aside.

Tonight was not about her and her lost love; it was about Wonder and Anandur. They deserved her full attention.

Focusing back on the couple, Annani allowed the significance of their union to guide her words. This was a celebration of a bond that transcended time and space, a union of two souls destined to be together.

"Today, we witness not just the joining of two individuals, but the celebration of a destiny fulfilled. Wonder and Anandur, your journey to this moment is a testament to the strength of love and the power of fate."

Annani paused, looking at each of them in turn, ensuring her words reached not just their ears but also their hearts. "In each other, you have found a mirror for your strengths, a balm for your weaknesses, and a partner for your journey through life. May your love be a beacon that guides you through every challenge and a sanctuary that brings you peace in times of turmoil."

Annani looked upon Wonder and Anandur with affection as she raised her hands. "Before all gathered here and the eternal embrace of the Fates, I bestow upon you my blessings. May your love be as deep and unending as the oceans, always finding its way back to the shores of each other's hearts. May it be as steadfast as the mountains, unshakable in the face of trials and tribulations. May your union be blessed with understanding and patience, with laughter and joy, with courage and strength. May you always find in each other a haven of peace and a wellspring of happiness. May the bond that unites you grow stronger with each passing day, weaving a tapestry of shared memories, dreams, and aspirations. May you have the wisdom to navigate the journey of life together, hand in hand and heart in heart."

She took a deep breath, her final words imbued with a profound sense of hope and joy. "And may the Fates smile upon you, guiding you through the journey of life, filled with love and fulfillment. May you always find strength in your unity, and may your love be a guiding light for all who witness it."

Annani lowered her hands, her eyes sparkling with unshed tears of joy. "By the power vested in me, I now pronounce you joined in the bonds of fate and marriage. May your journey together be as boundless as the sky and as luminous as the stars."

As the room erupted in applause and cheers, Annani watched as Wonder and Anandur turned to look at their friends and family with happiness and love shining in their eyes.

Officiating over Wonder and Anandur's wedding provided Annani with a deep sense of fulfillment. The coming together of two souls that were meant for each other was a reminder of the beauty and power of love, a force that transcended time, space, and the trials of fate.

Anandur

⌒∽⌒

As Annani concluded her blessing, a new surge of emotion swept through Anandur, and he teared up a little, but that was okay. Everyone would just think that he was goofing around, but Wonder would know better.

He turned to his bride, wrapped his arms around her, and poured all his love and passion into the kiss to outshine all kisses.

In the background, the room erupted into a cacophony of hoots and applause, but as absorbed as he was in holding and kissing his mate, Anandur heard it as if it was coming from a great distance. Still, he could feel a wave of warmth and joy emanating from their guests and enveloping Wonder and him.

As he pulled back from the kiss, he caught sight of his brother smiling—a genuine, heartfelt smile that was such a rare sight to behold that it imprinted itself in Anandur's memory.

Two down and plenty more to go, he promised himself.

Who would have known that the stoic Brundar was a romantic at heart?

Now that Anandur knew the secret to unlocking his brother's smiles, he was going to get many more out of him.

Up on the dais, Annani laughed, the magical sound pulling Anandur from his musing. "That was a kiss to remember," the goddess said, her tone full of mirth. "To loosely quote a movie that has become a favorite of mine, *The Princess Bride*—since the invention of the kiss, there have been a handful of kisses that were rated the most passionate, the most pure of all, and this one left them all behind."

As the crowd erupted in a new volley of hoots, cheers, and applause, Wonder blushed and offered Anandur a shy smile.

The Clan Mother lifted her hand to shush the guests. "Wonder and Anandur, as you stand here before your family, friends, and the Fates themselves, ready to embark on life's most beautiful journey, it is time to pledge your vows to each other."

Anandur hoped he could remember the vows he had so carefully worded and memorized. Taking a deep breath, he waited for the applause to subside, and as the room settled into an expectant hush, he looked into Wonder's eyes and took her hands in his.

"Wonder, my love. From the moment you knocked me out with your taser, threw me over your shoulder, and put me in a cage, I knew you were special. In fact, that was probably when I fell head over heels in love with you."

As a burst of laughter echoed through the crowd, Wonder's blush deepened, but she smiled, encouraging him to go on.

He gave her hand a gentle squeeze. "Never before had I met a woman who could quite literally kick my butt, and I must say, I was thoroughly impressed. You've intrigued me, challenged me, and brought a whirlwind of joy and excitement into my life. You are my rock, my anchor, my everything."

A few chuckles sounded in the background, and someone whistled.

"I promise to cherish every moment with you, in laughter and in tears, in triumphs and challenges. I vow to be your strength when you feel weak and to be your mentor when you need guidance in this modern world you have awoken to, helping you overcome the challenges it throws your way. But most of all, I promise to always make you laugh, to fill our days with joy, and our nights with the warmth of my love. I pledge to be your partner in every adventure that awaits us."

He paused, his heart brimming with emotion. "I vow to love you, to respect you, and to grow with you for as long as we both shall live, which, hopefully, is forever. You are my heart, my soul, and my fierce Wonder. I am forever yours, completely and irrevocably."

As he concluded his vows, the room burst into applause, but Anandur's focus remained solely on Wonder.

Moist with tears, her eyes sparkled with love and adoration.

"I love you," she whispered. And if that was the extent of her vows, it was good enough for him.

Wonder

Wonder remembered her first encounter with Anandur vividly. It had been in the alley behind the club where she worked as a security guard, and the moment that had sealed her fate was probably when he'd smiled at her, giving her a two-fingered salute. Initially, she had thought he was checking her out but soon realized that he was reading her T-shirt, which read "bouncer" for the club. She had wondered then if he was also a bouncer or perhaps a policeman, but he was neither. He was something far more extraordinary—an immortal Guardian—but it would be a while before she found out that he was one of the good guys and not one of the evil ones whom she'd intercepted trying to drain human females of their blood.

He had seemed different from the start, so nice and friendly, but as he followed the behavior pattern of the others, disappointment had washed over her. Appearances could be deceptive, and nice-looking males were often the most dangerous, capable of luring in unsuspecting victims.

Determined not to let her guard down, Wonder had followed him into the alley, hoping that he was different, that he wasn't intent on killing the woman he was taking back where no one could see him.

As she'd peeked time and again, gauging the situation to see if she needed to intervene, she'd been envious of the woman and her obvious pleasure, but when Anandur flashed his elongated fangs, she could wait no longer and had pounced, tasering him until he'd collapsed in a heap. The woman had screamed, and Wonder had quickly thralled her into silence, a necessary but crude intervention.

Straightening the woman's clothes, Wonder had sent her back to the club and turned her attention back to the male.

Anandur had been still twitching from the taser's effect, fighting it with all his might, so she had knocked him out with the butt of her taser gun. After stripping him of his clothes to ensure that he had no tracking devices on him, she'd dumped them in a dumpster and had hoisted him over her shoulder. She knocked him out again before stuffing him into her car, and then dumped him in the gorilla cage, like she had done with the others she had caught.

Now, as she stood beside him on their wedding day, Wonder couldn't help but smile at the irony. The man she had once apprehended and viewed as a potential threat was now the love of her life, her fated mate.

Life was full of unexpected turns.

Her eyes never leaving his, Wonder's heart swelled with love. "It is true that when we first met, I knocked you out and treated you as a threat, but deep inside, I knew you were not the enemy. You shone too bright to be evil, but I couldn't take any chances. I imprisoned you, hoping that you would prove to me that you were good. In my gut, I must have known even then that you were my destined partner, my fated love, and in short order, you convinced my mind that my gut and my heart had been right."

A chuckle rippled through the crowd, and Anandur's smile broadened, his eyes twinkling with amusement and love.

"In you, I found not only a formidable warrior but a kind and loving soul. You've turned my world upside down in the best possible way. You've challenged me, supported me, and loved me unconditionally. You accepted me for who I was and stood by me through thick and thin, even when I insisted on following distant whispers all the way back to the place that I had awoken in."

Wonder paused, her eyes prickling with unshed tears. "Anandur, my love. I promise to cherish every moment with you, in laughter and in tears, in triumphs and challenges. I vow to stand by your side and be your partner in every adventure life throws our way."

Her voice grew softer, more intimate. "Even the most formidable warrior needs to come home to find comfort and support, and I promise to always be there for you as your sanctuary, your confidante, and your best friend." Wonder smiled. "And I solemnly swear to occasionally let you win when we spar, just to keep things interesting."

They never did spar, but she had known their guests would love the comment, and to prove her right, laughter filled the room.

Anandur's grin widened. "You're on, love."

"Most of all," Wonder continued, "I promise to love you with every fiber of my being for as long as we both shall live. You are my heart, my soul, my Anandur. And I am forever and irrevocably yours."

As she finished her vows, the room erupted with more applause and cheers, but for Wonder, the only person in the world at that moment was Anandur.

Frankie

⤜⤛

F rankie dabbed at her eyes with a napkin, blotting the tears that had pooled in their corners.

The three wedding ceremonies she had witnessed had been so beautiful, each with its own unique and touching story, and she couldn't help but wonder what was special about her own love story with Dagor.

What would their wedding vows be about?

She'd met a god, thought that he was hot, and the rest was history?

The most unique thing about their relationship was that Dagor was a god, but even though that was most extraordinary, it wasn't something to wax poetic about.

Upon further reflection, though, she realized that within a very short span of time they'd had experiences most people didn't share in a lifetime.

They'd found a mysterious amulet, rescued a group of women who'd been abducted and were on their way to be sold into sexual slavery, and had killed their abductors.

It had been so traumatic to just listen to the sounds of battle between the Guardians and the cartel monsters that the memory of Dagor protecting her with his own body and absorbing the bullets that could have killed her was blurry. She had been terrified of the sounds of gunfire, the screams, and the shrieks, feeling helpless, huddling on the floor of the truck with Dagor on top of her.

He'd jerked every time he'd been hit, but there had been nothing she could do to help him. When a bullet had passed through his arm into her side, it had soon robbed her of consciousness, but before she'd passed out, she'd seen the panic in Dagor's eyes as he tried to stem the bleeding by pressing on the wound.

Frankie would never forget it.

Her next coherent memory after that had been waking up in the ship's clinic. Then he'd given her his blood to expedite her healing even though it was a big secret that Kian had forbidden the gods to reveal.

The secret was safe with her, and even if she never turned immortal and was somehow allowed to retain her memories of this incredible world she'd been invited into, she would take the gods and immortals' secrets to her grave.

Sadly, though, it meant that even if she transitioned and one day stood in front of the goddess with Dagor by her side, she couldn't share all that he had done for her with others.

Still, there was plenty she could say that didn't violate Kian's orders. Besides, she had known Dagor for only a few days, and she had no doubt that their life together would provide many more wonderful stories to incorporate into her wedding vows.

Next to her, Dagor was deep in thought, perhaps contemplating the same things she was, and as she reached over and gently squeezed his hand, he turned to her and smiled.

Smiling back, she waited for the music to start and the newly mated couple to take the dance floor. "Did you know about how Anandur and Wonder met?"

He shook his head. "I don't know any of these immortals well enough to know their personal stories. In that regard, you and I are in the same boat." He chuckled. "That was unintentional but fitting."

"I'm on a boat—" Frankie sang without completing the line.

She was a lady, and she didn't use vulgar language out loud. Only on the inside, and not that often either.

Her mother had a strict rule about cussing in the house that her brothers often had gotten in trouble for breaking, but Frankie had internalized her mother's words instead of rebelling against them.

The message was simple. If she wanted people to respect her, she'd have to respect herself first and view herself as someone who was worthy of respect. That being said, many people, including her brothers, thought that cussing earned them respect, so there was that.

Dagor laughed. "I've heard that song, but it took me a while to understand what was funny about it."

"Yeah, my brothers kept singing it and earning slaps over the back of their heads from our mother. She doesn't allow language like that in the house."

Dagor's expression turned serious. "I would like to meet your family one day. Do you think it's possible?"

Her breath caught in her throat. "Why not?"

He waved a hand over his face. "This might be difficult to explain."

Frankie cupped his clean-shaven face. "You could grow a beard. It can hide your perfection. Or we can just tell my parents and my brothers that you are the son of a famous model and a movie star, whose names need to stay confidential because you were their love child."

He looked at her with such intensity in his blue eyes that she was taken aback. "What's wrong?"

"If you are a Dormant, so are your brothers, your mother, your aunts and uncles on your mother's side, and all of their children. The immortality genes pass from a mother to her children. You might have an entire tribe to bring to the clan."

"Yeah, I know. It had occurred to me." She swallowed. "It's amazing and terrifying at the same time. How the heck am I going to explain this to my family? And what about my father? He's probably not a Dormant."

His eyes softened. "First, you need to transition, and then we will worry about the best way to do this."

"Yeah, that's what I told myself when the thought crossed my mind. There is no point in worrying about something that might not be relevant if it turns out that I'm not a Dormant."

He lifted her hand to his lips. "I have faith in the Fates. You will transition."

Negal

As Dagor and Frankie left the table to go dancing, Negal scanned the neighboring tables for available ladies he could ask to dance.

He was a hot commodity on this cruise, with so many lovely females vying for his attention that he was having a hard time choosing between them.

When he caught Karen looking at him, though, he knew it wasn't because she was interested. The moment their eyes met, she smiled nervously and averted her gaze.

Her unease was understandable, given what her mate had asked him to do. Come to think of it, he should establish a rapport with her before they proceeded with their plan for tomorrow night.

Pushing to his feet, Negal walked over to the table and flashed a friendly smile at Gilbert before turning his attention to Karen. "May I have this dance?" he asked, offering her his hand.

Karen hesitated, her eyes flickering towards Gilbert. The silent exchange between them was brief, and when Gilbert gave a subtle nod, Karen smiled, placed her hand in Negal's, and stood up.

"I thought we should get to know each other a little," he said.

She cast him a puzzled look. "I'm sorry. What did you say? I can't hear anything over this loud music."

He'd forgotten that her human hearing was limited compared to all the immortals on the dance floor, but if he spoke any louder, everyone there would be a party to their very private conversation.

Instead of answering, he gave her hand a gentle squeeze and steered her toward the glass doors leading to the balcony. "On second thought, I could use some fresh air. It's gotten stuffy in here." He paused with his hand on the door handle. "It's quieter out there."

Karen glanced back at Gilbert, seeking his approval, and upon receiving an affirming nod, she smiled up at Negal. "I would love some fresh air, too."

As they slipped out onto the balcony, the cool night air was indeed a relief from the stuffiness of the crowded dining hall.

Leaning against the railing, Negal wasn't sure what to do with his hands to seem as unintimidating as possible. If he crossed his arms over his chest, he might look threatening, but if he put his hands in his pockets, he would give her the impression that it was not a big deal for him.

It wasn't, but this was a delicate situation, and it was a big deal to her. Her life was on the line.

Suddenly, it occurred to him that he could improve her chances of success by giving her a small blood transfusion.

Anyway, he planned to thrall her and Gilbert to ignore his presence, so if he added a blood injection during the bite, neither of them would be any the wiser.

He spread his arms behind him and gripped the railing. "It occurred to me that we haven't spoken about what's coming. I only talked with your mate, and I noticed that you were nervous."

She chuckled. "Am I so easy to read?"

"Perhaps not usually, but tonight you were obvious, which is understandable. Your mate approached me and asked for my assistance, and I agreed. But then it occurred to me that I didn't check with you whether you are okay with this. He should have brought you along."

Karen let out a breath. "Frankly, it was I who asked Gilbert to talk to you. I'm very grateful to you for agreeing to do it." She chuckled nervously again. "I bet this is not going to be fun for you."

"It's not a hardship either. In fact, I feel honored to be asked to assist in your induction. "

Her expression softened. "That's very nice of you. You're a good guy, I mean god."

He laughed. "Guy is fine. It's a general term I'm comfortable with." Negal glanced at the starry sky and pondered the timing of their plan. "Perhaps we should move our arrangement to tonight." He shifted his eyes to her. "We thought that the mission would happen today, which was why we settled on tomorrow, but now that the mission has been moved, the reverse is true. Besides, the wait time will just intensify your anxiety."

Karen's eyes widened. "I think tomorrow would be better. I need more time to prepare. I'm not quite ready yet."

Negal smiled. "Sometimes it's best to just pull the Band-Aid off, as you humans like to say. We don't know how tomorrow's mission will go. It might delay us another day."

"Oh boy." Karen moved to lean against the railing next to him. "No pressure." A wry smile played on her lips. "It's a good thing that I'm a female. Otherwise, I would have suffered from performance anxiety and failed at the task."

Her attempt at humor made him laugh. He appreciated her effort to lighten the mood. "I can thrall you to relax and basically ignore my presence for the rest of the night starting now. You won't even be aware of me being there."

Karen turned to face him. "That might work. If I don't have to be consciously aware of... well, the process, it might be easier to go through with it."

Pleased with her easy acquiescence, Negal nodded. "I promise to make sure it's a seamless experience for you."

Karen took a deep breath. "Okay, tonight it is."

As the balcony doors opened and Gilbert stepped out, Negal wasn't surprised. He'd wondered how long the guy would hold off before jealousy and concern for his mate would prompt him to join them.

He briefly entertained the thought of using his thrall to ease Gilbert's mind because Karen's stress was probably being amplified by his unwarranted jealousy.

"I hope I'm not interrupting." Gilbert's eyes shifted from Karen to Negal.

"You're not," Negal assured him. "We were discussing moving our plans to tonight instead of tomorrow because of the change in scheduling for the mission."

As Karen stepped closer to Gilbert and took his hand, her gesture seemed to calm him somewhat, but the underlying tension was still palpable. "Negal made a good point about my anxiety building with every passing hour. He said that it's better to just rip the Band-Aid off and be done with it."

Gilbert hesitated for a brief moment before nodding. "I only want what's best for you, and if you want to do it tonight, that's fine with me."

"We'll need to ask Kaia to take the kids to her and William's cabin for the night," Karen said with a slight tremble in her voice.

Negal contemplated reaching into her head and calming her nerves, but he then remembered that human minds were fragile, and he should keep the thralling to a minimum. "Let me know when you're ready." He pushed away from the railing. "I'm going to ask one of those lovely ladies to dance, but I'll be immediately at your disposal whenever you call for me."

"Thank you." Karen offered him a tight smile. "I greatly appreciate your help."

Karen

As they returned to the dining hall, the loud music hit Karen like a physical wall, making any attempts at conversation difficult.

Talking with Negal outside had been surprisingly calming and reassuring, in part because he was so nice and considerate but mainly because he wasn't even slightly attracted to her. His willingness to contribute his venom to her transition was purely altruistic, and he had absolutely no interest in her.

Karen sighed.

Getting old and becoming invisible to young men and gods didn't feel good. It wasn't that she was interested in anyone other than Gilbert, but feeling desirable was a big part of her identity as a woman, and lately, she'd been losing that part of herself.

It was good that she was about to transition and regain her youthful attractiveness.

As Negal walked over to one of the tables and asked an immortal female to dance, Karen sat down and scanned the tables for Kaia and William, finding them on the dance floor.

It was amusing to watch their mismatched dancing moves, with Kaia waving her arms over her head as if she was in a rock concert, and William swaying in place like a scarecrow in the wind.

Following her gaze, Gilbert saw them, too. "I'll go talk to Kaia."

Karen caught his arm as he started to get up. "Let them have fun. I'll go to the cabin and tell Cheryl to move the kids to Kaia and William's cabin. I'm sure they won't mind, given the reason for the sleepover. Wait until they sit back down and just let them know what's going on. I want them to enjoy themselves for as long as they wish, and Cheryl and the kids will probably be asleep by the time they get back."

Gilbert let out a breath. "Do you want to get something to eat? The line at the buffet is not long."

She put a hand over her belly. "I don't think I could take a single bite, but you go ahead. I'll be waiting in our cabin."

"Are you sure?"

"Yeah." She patted his arm. "I need to organize the kids, tidy up a bit, and then take a few moments to myself." She gave him a peck on the cheek, noting how hard he was clenching his jaw. "Relax. It's going to be okay. Negal finds me about as attractive as this chair, so you don't need to be jealous."

"That's absurd." Gilbert looked at her with incredulity in his eyes. "Any healthy heterosexual male would find you attractive."

"Thank you." She smiled. "That's sweet of you to say, but I'm no spring chicken, and I'm a mother of five children." She gave him a slight push. "Go, get something to eat. You'll need your energy tonight."

As he finally did as she asked, Karen let out a breath and refilled her glass with white wine.

It was a scary step, but she'd been preparing for it for weeks.

She had already spoken to Bridget, ensuring that the clinic was adequately equipped to monitor her in case it was needed.

Bridget and the nurses were busy tending to the victims who needed more medical attention than anyone had anticipated, and Karen didn't wish to add to their burden, but it was what it was.

Bridget understood and approved.

Glancing around at the joyous celebrations, Karen felt a pang of regret at the thought of missing some of the weddings. Each ceremony was a beautiful testament to love and commitment, something she had always cherished, but her successful transition took precedence.

Downing the glass of liquid courage, Karen pushed to her feet and looked at her mate, who stood in line at the buffet. She smiled and waved and then turned around and walked toward the exit doors.

Negal intercepted her just as she was about to exit the hall. "Is everything alright?"

"Yes." She gave him a reassuring smile. "I'm going up to our cabin to help my daughter move the little ones to Kaia and William's room. Gilbert is at the buffet," she added.

"I'll join him for a meal and come up with him when he's ready." Negal hesitated before adding. "Do you need me to thrall you now to make it easier for you?"

She shook her head. "Let's wait until everything is in place. The twins might be fussy and want their mommy, and then the whole thing would have to be postponed until tomorrow anyway. I don't want to have to be thralled more than necessary." She lifted her hand to her temple. "There is no point in living forever if this is not working right."

"You are a smart woman, Karen." He made a move as if to kiss her cheek but then grimaced and leaned away. "This is going to be more difficult than I thought."

She frowned. "Why?"

"Don't take it the wrong way, but your scent is," he rubbed a hand over the back of his neck, "how should I say it, unpleasant to me."

Karen's eyes widened, and her first instinct was to smell her armpits, but then she remembered what Casandra had told her about fated mates getting addicted to each other and their scent changing to deter other immortals from trying to seduce them.

That shouldn't be happening to her, though. She was still human, and she hadn't even been injected with anyone's venom. She'd never been bitten, and the reality of it happening tonight made her shiver, and not in a good way.

"What do you smell?" she asked.

"Gilbert." He grimaced. "His scent is all over you."

"Oh, I see. Will you be able to overcome it when the time comes?"

He nodded. "I won't breathe through my nose until I have my fangs in your neck."

Another shiver rocked Karen's body. "Can you please make it so I won't feel the bite?"

His eyes softened. "Are you scared?"

"A little."

"It only hurts for a second, and then there is bliss. But I'll make sure to muffle the pain with my thrall."

"Thank you."

Gilbert

W hen the loud music was replaced with a pleasant melody to complement dinner, Kaia and William joined the line at the buffet, and Gilbert took the opportunity to tap Kaia's shoulder.

"I need a word with you," he murmured.

"What's up?" She followed him to a quiet spot next to the kitchen entrance.

"There's been a change of plan. Instead of it happening tomorrow, it's happening tonight." He didn't have to spell it out. Kaia knew what he was talking about. "Karen went up to our cabin to help Cheryl move the little ones to yours. I hope it's okay."

"Of course." Kaia cast a glance at William. "But what's the rush? Even if Negal hooks up with Frankie's friend, that doesn't make them fated mates, and he can still offer his venom services. I don't know why Mom freaked out like that."

Gilbert took a deep breath. "Perhaps she had a gut feeling about it. In any case, I'm glad that it's finally happening, and Negal is perfect for the job. He's kind, polite, and your mother believes that he doesn't find her attractive, which I think is bullshit, but I'm glad she thinks that. It will make everything easier. Besides, after the cruise, Negal is leaving with Aru and Dagor, and it could be months before he's back."

It was beyond awkward to talk to the girl he had raised as his daughter about his sexual relationship with her mother, but it was unavoidable, given that he needed her help.

Kaia nodded. "That's why I didn't say anything. If she's ready, go for it. I wish you both the best of luck."

Gilbert placed a hand on her shoulder. "Thanks, Kaia. And thank William for us, too."

"I will." She kissed his cheek and returned to her spot next to William in the line for the buffet.

Scanning for Negal amidst the sea of guests, Gilbert spotted him at the bar, talking to Aru.

"Negal," Gilbert motioned for him to step aside. "I need a word with you."

The god said something to his team leader and walked toward Gilbert with a drink in hand. "How are you holding up?" he asked.

Surprisingly, Gilbert felt much calmer than he'd expected to feel under the circumstances, and he wondered whether Negal had already thralled him without telling him.

"I'm doing well. Thanks for asking." He looked around, making sure that no one was paying attention to them. "I'm heading upstairs. I'll give you a call once everything is set."

Negal clapped Gilbert on the back. "Don't start anything before I get there. I need to thrall you both before you two get busy."

"Of course. Is there anything I need to prepare for you in the other room? Something to get you going?"

The only thing he could offer was a lingerie catalog, so he hoped the god would say that he didn't need anything or that he would take care of it himself.

Negal laughed. "I might not look it, but the Fates blessed me with a vivid imagination. I don't need external stimuli."

"That's good." Gilbert gave him a tight smile. "How about a bottle of wine or perhaps Snake Venom? You know, the beer the immortals love so much."

"I'll be fine." Negal squeezed his shoulder. "Go to your mate and offer her some wine to soothe her nerves."

"Thanks, Negal. You're a good guy."

The god chuckled. "Karen said the same thing. I guess that's what happens when you are mated for as long as the two of you have been. You form the same opinions about people and use the same phrases."

Gilbert wasn't sure whether it was meant as a compliment, but he took it as such.

"That's what a good partnership is like. I wish for you to get as lucky as I did with finding a great partner. Life is blessed when you have someone wonderful by your side. Someone you are happy to wake up next to each morning and return to at the end of each day."

The god sighed. "I have given up hope of ever finding that someone special. I'm not as young as my teammates, and I've been all over the galaxy before getting assigned to patrol this sector. If I haven't found her by now, I never will." He affected a nonchalant smile. "Not that I made a big effort to look for her. It either happens or it doesn't. I'm quite satisfied with my bachelor status and having the freedom to sample a variety of lovelies wherever I'm stationed."

Karen

On the way to the cabin, Karen's mind raced with the thoughts of what she was about to do. She was no longer worried about the awkwardness of having Negal bite her while she was having sex with Gilbert.

If she wasn't aware of it while it happened, she could live with the fact that it had afterward. With that settled in her mind, the worry of survival returned.

If it was only about her, she wouldn't have thought twice about it, but she had five children, and only one of them was an adult with a mate of her own. The other four needed their mother, and losing her would devastate them in ways that she was all too familiar with.

After losing Kaia and Cheryl's father, Karen had functioned on autopilot because she had two little daughters to take care of, and her girls had been suffering in ways that they couldn't even fully express at such a young age. Things had gotten a little easier with time, but that wound had never really mended, not even after meeting Gilbert and falling in love with him.

Immortality wasn't going to cure it either. If she survived, she would carry the pain of loss for eternity.

With a sigh, Karen entered the code to the cabin and opened the door.

As she'd expected, Cheryl was in front of the television with the twins sleeping in the crib and Idina sprawled on the couch, clutching her blanket in one hand and her favorite doll in the other.

"You're back early," Cheryl said without shifting her gaze away from the television. "What happened? Someone spill wine on your dress?"

Instinctively, Karen looked down to examine her gown and then shook her head. "No, I came to tell you that you and the little ones are spending the night at Kaia's and to help you move them. Gilbert invited a couple of friends over after the party."

She hated lying to her daughter, but Cheryl was too young for Karen to share the truth about tonight with.

Kaia had promised not to tell her younger sister anything about the plan, and Karen hoped she'd kept her promise, but given the knowing look in Cheryl's eyes, she knew exactly what was about to transpire.

"Are Kaia and William back in their cabin?"

"No, but they know you'll be there when they are done partying for the night."

Cheryl yawned. "I watched the ceremony on television. It was hilarious before it became boring, so I switched to something else."

They had taken all the kids to the first wedding, but the twins had been fussy, and Idina turned into a terror, so Gilbert had offered Cheryl five hundred dollars for each night she stayed to babysit even though he could have hired one of the human staff to watch over the kids for much less than that.

Cheryl was more than happy to babysit for that outrageous amount and watch the weddings on the ship's closed-circuit broadcast.

"Are they still broadcasting?" Karen took off her high-heeled shoes.

"Yeah. But it's boring. People eating and dancing."

"That's what weddings are all about."

"Nah, they are about the ceremony and the vows. I think it's cool that the Clan Mother makes every ceremony unique." Cheryl yawned. "So, how are we going to carry the little ones over to Kaia's cabin? Do you want to put them in their strollers?"

"You can wheel the twins' crib, and I'll carry Idina."

Cheryl nodded. "First, help me pack a bag for them."

As they organized everything the kids would need tomorrow morning, Cheryl put the bag inside the crib and pushed it toward the door.

"Do you remember the code to Kaia's cabin?" Karen asked as she crouched next to Idina.

"Naturally." Cheryl opened the door. "The code is Kaia's birthday. I'll leave the door open for you."

"Thanks."

As Karen scooped Idina into her arms, she opened a pair of sleepy eyes. "Is everything okay, Mommy?"

Karen dipped her head and kissed Idina's warm cheek. "Everything's fine, sweetheart. You're going for a sleepover in Kaia's cabin, and tomorrow morning, you'll have fun with your big sister."

"Yay." Idina yawned. "Will you come to have fun with us, Mommy?"

"I will, sweetie." Karen carried her to the next cabin over and walked straight to the bedroom where Cheryl had already prepared the bed.

Cheryl covered her little sister with a blanket and kissed her forehead. "She's so adorable when she's asleep. I wish she was that cute when she's awake." She smiled at Karen. "Can you stay for a few minutes so I can get my things?"

"Of course."

As she waited for Cheryl to return, Karen looked at the sleeping faces of her children and wondered for the umpteenth time whether she was doing the right thing. Despite giving her transition the best possible tools for success, there was still a small chance that her gamble wouldn't pay off, and she might leave her children motherless.

On the other hand, nothing in life was guaranteed, especially for a mortal, and Karen would rather grab destiny by the horns and drive it to where she wanted it to go rather than be jostled through life by its whims.

"Qué será, será."

Gilbert

Gilbert tried not to dwell on what was about to transpire as he made his way to the cabin.

It was better that way.

He couldn't afford to be overwhelmed by irrational jealousy or fear for Karen's life.

As he opened the door, he was greeted by the familiar aftermath of his kids' chaos. There were toys strewn about, a few scattered pieces of clothing, and half-empty sippy cups on the coffee table.

"Given how much I'm paying Cheryl to babysit, she could've at least cleaned up," he murmured as he started picking up stuff off the floor.

"She would have if I didn't practically shove her out the door." Karen came out of the bedroom with a large bag and started picking up things on the other side of the room. "I think she knows what's going on."

He arched a brow. "Do you think Kaia told her?"

Karen shrugged. "Cheryl is just too smart for her own good. I bet she had it figured out, but thankfully, she had enough tact not to say anything and pretended to believe my story about inviting friends over after the wedding."

"It's the truth, just not the whole truth." He threw the items he'd collected into the bag and took it from her. "How are you holding up? Are you okay?"

"Yeah." She let out a breath. "*Qué será, será.*"

"That's the spirit." He pulled her into his arms and kissed her forehead. "Negal suggested that I pour you a glass of wine to soothe your nerves."

She chuckled. "That's not a bad idea. You know what I like."

Karen wasn't a big drinker. She had the occasional glass of wine, and when she was in a mood to celebrate, she liked a Moscow Mule, with just a tiny bit of vodka and a lot of ginger beer.

"I do, but this time, I'm going to pour double the vodka in your Mule. You need it to take the edge off."

She smiled up at him. "I'm not going to argue."

When he was done mixing the drink for her, he added ice cubes and handed it to her. "Here you go."

"Aren't you going to make one for yourself?"

He shook his head. "I'm doing mental gymnastics to not let myself get overwhelmed with unwanted feelings, and I need to stay sharp until Negal gets here and takes us both out of our misery. It would be nice to forget that he's about to intrude on our intimacy."

"He can't intrude if he's invited." Karen took a long sip of her drink and sighed. "This is so good. Thank you."

"You're welcome. I mixed it with love."

"I know you did." Karen reached for his cheek and cupped it. "So, how are we going to do this? I mean technically."

"Well, I think you should be on top." He swallowed. "Wearing a dress. I don't want him to see you naked even if you do think that he's not attracted to you."

"He's not." Karen frowned. "He said that my scent is unpleasant to him because I smell of you, but you haven't bitten me yet, so I don't know how that's possible. From what I was told, it's the repeated venom injections that affect the body odor."

"That's both reassuring and worrisome." He puffed out his chest. "The ape in me is very happy that I marked you with my scent, but now I'm worried that Negal won't be able to bite you because he'll be repulsed by the smell."

Karen's cheeks turned a deep shade of red. "He said he would hold his breath and do it quickly." She grimaced. "I'm so glad that I'm not the male in this relationship, or I wouldn't be able to get it up." She eyed him from under lowered lashes. "Will you?"

Gilbert threw his head back and laughed. "Do you have to ask? Since my transition, I have had the libido of an eighteen-year-old. My problem is getting it to go down, not up."

That was true, and she felt guilty for not being able to keep up with him. It was just one more reason to stop pussyfooting around and just do it. "Let's grab a shower and scrub really well. Hopefully, the aroma of the soap and generous spraying of perfume will overpower the scents Negal finds objectionable."

Gilbert winced. "In that case, we should shower separately. Otherwise, I won't be able to keep my hands off you, and we will have to get another shower. I don't think it's fair to Negal to keep him waiting."

"Right." She stretched on her toes and kissed him lightly on the lips. "See you in ten minutes."

He nodded. "I'll text Negal and tell him to be here in fifteen."

After taking a quick shower in Cheryl's bedroom, Gilbert put on a pair of nylon pants and a T-shirt. He straightened the room and covered the bed with the decorative cover that Cheryl had taken off. Negal would hopefully use the armchair in the corner, but just in case he wanted to use the bed, Gilbert planned on changing the bedding tomorrow.

When Karen emerged from their bedroom, her hair was wet, and she had a long nightgown on that would do well for what they had in mind but was too sexy, in Gilbert's opinion. It was made of satin, sleeveless, with only thin straps holding it up, and even though it wasn't form-fitting, it draped over Karen's body in a most enticing way.

"You look beautiful." He rubbed a hand over his jaw. "Too beautiful."

"Oh, stop it." She rolled her eyes and waved a dismissive hand, but he caught the small smile tugging on one corner of her lips.

As the doorbell rang, Gilbert cast another reassuring smile at Karen before opening the door.

"Hello, Negal. Thank you for doing this for us. Can I offer you a drink?"

"No, thank you. I've had enough for tonight." Negal walked in and smiled at Karen. "I'll start with you. Where would you like to do it?"

She looked confused for a moment, but when understanding dawned, she motioned to the couch. "You mean the thralling, right? I know what to expect."

As she sat down and Negal joined her, Gilbert sat across from them on an armchair.

"Here is what I'm going to do," Negal said. "I'm going to thrall you to relax and focus entirely on Gilbert. You will be dimly aware of my presence, but you will not be disturbed by it in any way. I'll be like a distant thought in your mind. Sound good?"

When Karen nodded, Negal looked into her eyes for a few moments, and when he was done, she pushed to her feet, cast Gilbert a seductive smile, and walked into their bedroom.

"I really need to learn how to do this," Gilbert murmured as he took her place on the couch.

"I'm going to do exactly the same to you," Negal said. "Ready?"

"One moment." Gilbert lifted his hand. "Before I forget that you are here, I wanted to ask if you would like to use the other bedroom or stay here in the living room."

"It doesn't make a difference to me. What's your preference?"

"The living room, if you don't mind. My children sleep in the other bedroom. I tidied it up, but I didn't have time to change the bedding."

"No need to go to all that trouble. This is going to be over very quickly."

"Thank you. You're making it all remarkably easy for us."

The god grinned. "I'm glad. Now, look into my eyes."

One moment, Gilbert was aware of looking into Negal's eyes, and the next, he was confused and didn't know where he was or what he was about to do. After shaking off the momentary fugue, he remembered Karen's seductive, come-hither smile. She had put on a sexy nightgown for him, and he couldn't wait to take it off her.

Something in the back of his mind reminded him that the nightgown had to stay on, but he couldn't remember why.

Oh, well. He could work with that.

Pushing to his feet, he turned toward the bedroom.

He found Karen sitting on the bed with her arms spread to the sides, her hands braced on the mattress, and her legs crossed under the long skirt of her nightgown.

"Hi, handsome," she greeted him with a throaty lilt in her tone. "I've been waiting for you."

As Gilbert's erection tented his nylon pants, Karen laughed and beckoned him forward. "I see that someone is eager to say hello."

Negal

Negal took the syringe he'd prepared ahead of time out of his pocket and put it on the coffee table. He didn't know how long his blood would remain viable after extraction, which meant that he had to do it at the last moment before biting Karen.

It wasn't going to be easy to do that when he was about to shoot his load, but he was determined to give the mother of five the best chance of survival he could.

Removing his tux jacket, he hung it on the back of a dining chair and sat on the couch in the living room. Next, he yanked the bowtie off and popped open several buttons of his shirt.

He leaned back and let his thoughts drift back to Anumati and the many goddesses he had bedded. Not all of them had stuck in his memory, but he remembered a select few who could get him excited just by thinking about them.

There had been overwhelming passion and vigor in those most memorable encounters, and yet he had never felt fully satisfied. He'd come close a few times with Evanitta, the one goddess whom he had hoped to mate, but even she had been distant. There had been no true intimacy between them, and their connection had been primarily physical.

If not for the great works of art in film and literature depicting fated love and the unbreakable bond between fated mates, Negal wouldn't have known that anything was missing. Perhaps he would have been satisfied with the physical pleasure and never missed the melding of the souls he'd witnessed so rarely among his acquaintances.

On Earth, though, his experiences had been different.

Earth had been a revelation to him, showing him facets of intimacy and relationships that were absent in his life back home.

Even though human women couldn't possibly match the physical perfection of goddesses or keep up with his stamina, they compensated by being livelier, for lack of a better term, or perhaps more playful and less stifling.

There was something to be said for shorter lifespans.

Negal had memorized the names of those who had left a strong impression on him, and he rifled through the archives in his mind for an exciting memory to get him aroused and ready to deliver the bite.

There was Emily, a petite brunette with a quick wit and infectious laughter. Sophia was a tall redhead who was a talented and passionate artist. Jasmine, with the most incredible ass and smiling eyes, was an ambitious business-woman. Lina, a voluptuous, naughty nurse with a great laugh.

Each of these women had left an impression on him and helped him understand what it meant to be human. Their uniqueness and individual strengths and vulnerabilities had given him a richer experience than he had ever known back on Anumati.

He finally settled on Rachel as an inspiration for his solo pleasure session. The biologist was perhaps the least beautiful of the women he had been with, but she'd captivated him with her exquisite mind and curiosity about the universe that he'd been happy to indulge, pretending to ruminate when he had actually been describing real phenomena.

Rachel was tall, thin, and modestly endowed, but she had a devious mind. Just thinking of her made him harder in an instant.

With a groan, Negal reached into his pants and gripped his swollen erection.

At first, he stroked it leisurely, his hand moving up and down without applying much pressure. It was like saying hello, a gentle communion before even the first kiss, just to let things warm up a little.

The image of Rachel sitting on the counter in her kitchen, her shirt bunched up over her small breasts, her nipples dark and stiff from the treatment he'd given them only moments ago, her legs spread wide, and her fingers threaded in his hair as he licked and sucked.

So wanton, so sexy.

The sound of her moans reverberating in his head, he cranked things up with his hand, his grip tightening as he moved up, squeezed the head, and then went down in a corkscrew motion.

After Rachel had orgasmed all over his tongue, he'd gripped her ass and impaled her on his shaft in one powerful thrust, and she'd come again with a scream that had reverberated through the small kitchen of her Lisbon apartment.

Given the sounds coming from the bedroom, things were getting heated in there, and as he swiped his tongue over his fangs, Negal tasted venom.

He was ready, in more ways than one, and when he heard Karen scream her orgasm, his own was triggered, barreling up his shaft with a nearly unstoppable force, but he couldn't let it happen—not until he fulfilled his task.

Squeezing the top off with a vice-like grip, he bit down on his lower lip, nearly slicing through it, and the pain was enough to halt the eruption.

Blood dripping down his white shirt, he hiked his pants up, stuffed his aching shaft behind the zipper, and reached for the syringe.

Gritting his teeth, he tore the package open and made a fist before sticking the needle into his vein.

The vial filled so quickly that he had to yank the needle out, and then he was spraying blood and had to lick the puncture wound closed.

Syringe in hand, he rushed toward the bedroom and the woman he was about to help induce into immortality.

Gilbert

As the aftershocks of Karen's climax subsided, she collapsed on top of Gilbert's chest. He wrapped his arms around her, holding her tightly while his heart still raced from his own orgasm.

"I love you," he whispered into her neck.

Panting, she didn't answer, and he felt a surge of anxious anticipation that felt familiar and justified, but when he tried to think of what he was waiting for, the thought slipped away.

There was a surreal, dream-like quality to the postcoital bliss, and as Negal quietly entered, Gilbert's mind couldn't process his presence. The god felt distant, like a shadow at the edge of Gilbert's consciousness.

As the specter's hand reached out, cradling Karen's head, Gilbert tensed, sensing that something monumental was about to happen. But it felt like part of a dream, and a veil separated the ghost of the god from reality.

Then, the ghost of Negal tilted Karen's head to the side, exposing the delicate skin of her neck and licking the spot.

Gilbert felt a surge of fear and possessiveness gripping him. Everything inside of him rebelled against what was coming, but he was paralyzed, held by invisible chains that were nonetheless unbreakable.

The god hissed, flashing a pair of monstrous fangs, and struck, piercing Karen's skin.

Gilbert expected her to scream in pain, but she only groaned softly. And then she was climaxing again while the fangs were still embedded in her neck.

He felt like his brain was about to explode through his scalp because he needed to stop what was happening but couldn't move.

It seemed like forever before the god retracted his fangs, licked the spot clean, and then was gone between one blink of Gilbert's eyes and the next.

Karen was still climaxing, her sheath gripping his rapidly hardening shaft, and soon, he was coming again.

When both their bodies stopped trembling, Gilbert held her tightly to his chest.

Suddenly, his thoughts cleared, and he knew precisely what had happened. Negal had thralled him and Karen, so they hadn't been fully aware of anything outside the bubble encompassing the two of them.

It was done. Negal had provided the venom necessary for Karen's transition.

Paralyzing panic flooded Gilbert, a choking sensation and nausea that he hadn't felt since he'd become immortal.

Karen was his world, the center of his universe, and the thought of anything happening to her was unbearable. If she didn't make it, he would find a way to end his own life. But he couldn't. They had three little ones to raise, and Cheryl was still a young girl. He would have to wait for their children to be fully grown and suffer through existing without Karen until they had families of their own and were well settled in their lives.

It was a morbid thought that he had to push to the back of his mind and put a blockade in front of it. For Karen's sake and the sake of their children, he had to remain optimistic.

A god's venom activating Karen's godly genes increased her chances of survival dramatically, and Gilbert was beyond grateful to Negal.

Still, the jealous monster living inside his head had him checking that Karen's nightgown was still on, draped over them both and hiding where they were still connected.

"Mine," he whispered against her neck, and tightened his hold on her. "Only mine."

Karen didn't answer, probably because she was floating on the euphoric cloud that the god's venom induced. Gilbert hoped she was enjoying the trip, but more than that, he hoped that everything would turn out well, Karen would successfully transition, and they would have many years ahead of them to explore a future filled with endless possibilities.

For now, though, he focused on the fragile woman in his arms.

Listening to her slow and steady breathing, feeling the warmth of her body against his, he beseeched the Fates to keep his mate safe.

Dagor

"This was fun." Frankie removed her shoes as soon as they entered the elevator. "I love dancing, but my feet are killing me."

Suddenly, she was so tiny next to Dagor, barely reaching the top of his chest, and his protective instincts were triggered even though it didn't make any sense. The high-heeled shoes didn't make Frankie stronger or more resilient, although he had to admit that dancing for over two hours without taking a break was impressive for a human. It had been tiring even for him.

Frankie was probably exhausted.

"You should have taken the shoes off and danced barefoot."

Casting him a sultry smile, she stretched on her toes and kissed his cheek. "I knew you would bite me later and make my little footsies all better," she whispered.

The guy standing behind them chuckled, and the woman next to Dagor grinned.

If they were alone in the elevator, he would have lifted her into his arms and started on the fun, but there were four other people riding up with them, and he wasn't about to give them a show.

Clearing his throat, he leaned down and offered quietly, "How about a foot massage?"

"Ooh, that would be wonderful."

As they exited on Frankie's deck, two of the females who had been riding with them exited too, and he had to wait until they entered their cabin to lift Frankie and kiss her like he'd wanted from the moment she'd made the comment about his bite.

He carried her to the bedroom and set her down on the bed. "Do you need help peeling this dress off?"

She turned and offered him her back. "You can get the zipper for me, but before you get any ideas, I need to shower first. I'm sweaty, and I need to wash all the makeup off before getting in bed."

"How about a relaxing bath?" he suggested as he pulled the zipper down. "I can scrub your back."

"That would be lovely."

He leaned down and kissed her forehead. "I'll start the bath for you."

"You are spoiling me, Dagor, and I love it." She let the dress fall to her waist, revealing the lacy bra underneath that was the same red color as the dress.

Swallowing, Dagor rushed into the bathroom before he could be tempted to do away with the pretty bra and deprive Frankie of the bath she wanted.

As the tub filled with warm water, his thoughts wandered to her transition. He knew it was still too early to start worrying about it working, but he couldn't help it.

They didn't have a lot of time, and it was crucial that she transition before the end of the cruise. If she didn't, she might give up.

What if he could expedite the process with another transfusion?

The other time hadn't done what Kian had been afraid it would do, but perhaps when combined with his venom and his seed, the addition of the blood transfusion would do the trick?

Then again, what if giving her more of his blood would be detrimental to her health?

He needed to consult Aru.

Standing by the bathroom door, Dagor watched the steam rise from the water as the idea of accelerating Frankie's transition solidified in his mind. There was no harm in doing that, and the only downside was that if it didn't work, they would both be devastated.

"Trust in the Fates," he murmured.

Turning back to Frankie, he saw her seated on the edge of the bed, wearing only her bra and panties and rubbing her feet. She looked tired but happy, and he dreaded spoiling her mood by voicing his concerns.

Perhaps it would be better not to tell her his plan yet and let her enjoy the aftermath of the party while soaking in the tub.

"Your bath awaits, my lady." He executed a deep bow. "Should I carry you?"

She smiled at him with love shining in her eyes. "Not tonight, my love. I want to take off my makeup before I get into the water, and it will take a while."

He didn't know why she needed to wash her face before getting in the tub, but he wasn't going to question her beauty routine. Apparently, there was much more to it than just applying color to her cheeks and painting her eyelashes black.

"Can I help?"

"A girl needs to keep a few secrets." She batted her eyelashes, which he'd just noticed were thicker than normal.

He lifted his hands in the sign for peace. "I'll leave you to it, then, and get out of the tux."

She pushed to her tiny feet, stretched on her toes and kissed his cheek. "Give me fifteen minutes to do my nightly routine, and then you can come in if you want."

He kissed the tip of her nose. "Take your time and soak those poor feet of yours."

When she closed the door behind her, he walked into the living room and wrote a text to Aru.

Is it safe to give Frankie another transfusion to expedite her transition?

Aru's response came a moment later. *Probably, but make sure it's a small quantity.*

'Probably' was not as good as a yes, but it was better than a no.

Dagor needed a syringe, and he knew where to get it.

After changing into a pair of jeans and a T-shirt, he made his way to the clinic.

The ship was quiet, with most of its occupants either still in the dining hall enjoying coffee and desserts or back in their cabins. Dagor didn't want to bump into anyone and have to explain where he was going and why, so he took the stairs instead of the elevator.

Reaching the clinic deck, he continued to the storage room and slipped inside. The cabinet where he had found the syringes before was locked, but he knew now where the nurses kept the key.

Securing the syringe, he closed the cabinet and turned to leave, but stopped to fill his pockets with a few toiletries just in case anyone wondered what he'd been doing sneaking into the storage room in the middle of the night.

Frankie

I n the bathwater's soothing warmth, Frankie let her
mind drift, and her body relax, the tension slowly
ebbing. She had half-expected Dagor to join her, but
as the minutes ticked by and the bathroom door remained
closed, she wondered what he was doing.

She'd needed a few minutes to take off her false lashes and
wipe off the layers of makeup, but once that had been
done, she wouldn't have minded his offer to massage her
feet and scrub her back.

A flicker of concern crossed her mind. After the lecture
she'd given him about always letting her know where he
was, he wouldn't just leave without saying anything.

As more time passed, her concern deepened into worry.
Maybe something had happened? She knew the ship was
safe, but Dagor's sudden disappearance was troubling. He

would have told her if something was going on and he had to go. He wouldn't just leave her in the bathtub.

Her mind began to race with possibilities. Was there an emergency? Had something gone wrong with the plan regarding the Doomers? Maybe the teams assigned to rescuing Luis had been called to depart immediately?

The thought sent a chill down her spine.

Nah, she was probably freaking out for nothing. He might be in the living room watching television or listening to music. If she had her phone with her, she would have called him, but she'd left it in her purse, which was on the bed, next to her discarded dress that she'd forgotten to hang back in the closet.

With a deep sigh Frankie leaned back in the tub, trying to calm her racing thoughts, but her eyes kept darting to the bathroom door, hoping to see it open and Dagor walk in.

When it finally happened, Frankie's head snapped up, and her heart skipped a beat. "What took you so long? I was worried about you."

He arched a brow. "You asked for fifteen minutes, and that's precisely how long I was gone."

She pouted. "It felt like longer. Now get undressed and join me in the tub. I'm taking you up on your offer to scrub my back."

Smiling, he sat on the edge of the tub. "You didn't ask me where I was."

She frowned. "I didn't even know that you left."

"So why were you worried?"

She let out an exasperated breath. "Never mind that. Where did you go?"

"I went down to the clinic to get another syringe."

Her gut twisted into a knot. "Why?"

"I think that another transfusion could help expedite your transition." He pulled out a couple of small, wrapped soaps from his pocket and then the syringe. "Only if you are comfortable with it, of course. It's up to you."

Frankie hadn't considered that before, but now that he was offering, it made sense to her, and she wasn't about to refuse the offer unless there were risks she wasn't aware of.

"Are you sure it's safe to give me another transfusion?"

"I asked Aru, and he said that it probably is, which means that he's not sure. But then he's not a doctor."

Chewing on her bottom lip, Frankie nodded. "There is probably nothing left in my system from your first transfusion, so it's probably safe to do another one. I don't think it can do any harm, and the worst that can happen is that it won't do anything." She smiled nervously. "But my feet will not ache tomorrow for sure."

Dagor regarded her for a moment before tearing the packaging open and pulling out the syringe. "One last chance. Yes or no?"

"Yes."

She couldn't suppress a small wince when the needle pierced his skin. It was one thing to know intellectually that Dagor was capable of healing quickly and quite another to watch the needle sink into his vein without the usual preparations like an elastic band to swell the vein. She hoped that this deviation from what she knew as standard procedure wouldn't cause any complications.

As he drew a small quantity of his blood, she wondered what it would look like under a microscope. Would there be millions of nanobots floating in it, tiny genetic machines that cured and repaired and facilitated transition in carriers of the godly genes?

She offered him her arm, trying to keep still, but her heart was pounding in her chest, and she felt queasy. When the needle pierced her skin at the spot where she previously had the IV, she felt a slight sting, but it was nothing compared to the emotional weight of the moment. She watched as Dagor gently pressed the plunger, his eyes locked on her face, searching her eyes for signs of discomfort or distress.

The sensation was odd, a slight warmth spreading from the injection site, but nothing more dramatic than that.

Dagor disposed of the syringe by putting it back into its torn wrapping and tossing it into the trash container under the sink.

"You'll need to dispose of it better than that," she said. "If anyone comes to clean the cabin, they'll see the bloodied syringe and might report it."

"You're right." He pulled his T-shirt over his head and tossed it on the counter. "I'll take care of it tomorrow."

Her concerns flew out the window as her eyes roamed over the perfection of his body. "Take your pants off and get in the tub with me." She scooted to the side. "I need to thank you for what you just did for me." She gave him a sultry smile.

Dagor pushed his pants down, revealing how excited he was about her offer of gratitude even before finding out what she had in mind.

"I did it for me as much as I did it for you." He stepped into the tub and got behind her back. "I want you with me forever."

Dagor

Morning light filtered through the parted curtains, casting a soft glow across the bed and the woman sleeping peacefully beside Dagor.

He'd been awake for a while, watching Frankie. Most of the time she seemed peaceful, with a faint smile on her lips, but from time to time a frown furrowed her forehead, and she stirred in her sleep.

Was she having bad dreams?

"Good morning," she murmured, her eyes fluttering open as she turned to face him. "What time is it?"

"It's still early." He leaned to plant a soft kiss on her lips. ""How are you feeling?"

"Good." Her smile widened. "In fact, I feel wonderful." She wound her arms around his neck and drew him closer. "You gave me a lot of yourself last night."

He chuckled. "Yeah, I did."

He'd given her his blood once, his venom twice, and his seed four times. If that wasn't enough to induce her transition, he didn't know what else he could do other than keep doing that every night until it happened.

"When do you need to leave? Do we have time to have breakfast together?"

He glanced at his watch. "I have a little over an hour."

"That's plenty of time." She stretched her arms over her head. "Let's eat in the cabin. I'm too stressed and worried to make small talk with people in the dining room. I want you all to myself."

He'd had other ideas about spending the morning, but Frankie seemed to need reassurances, and the best way to do it was to give her more information about the mission. The worst thing would be to leave her guessing.

"We both need to shower." He kissed the tip of her nose. "The rigorous activities of last night have left their mark."

"You go first." She yawned. "I want a few minutes longer in bed."

After a quick shower, he got dressed and started on the coffee. By the time it was brewed, Frankie emerged from the bedroom wearing a loose T-shirt and a pair of shorts that were almost indecent.

"I hope you don't intend on wearing that out of the cabin while I'm gone."

Smirking, she tilted her head. "Why? I'm much more covered in this than I am in my bikini. Are you telling me that you don't approve of me going swimming while you're away, either?"

Dagor had a feeling that he should tread carefully or find himself in trouble. "Of course, I don't mind you swimming in your skimpy bikini. It's just that those shorts are too sexy because they tickle the imagination, and I want you to wear them just for me."

"Good save." She sat down on the chair he pulled out for her. "But for future reference, the only types of comments I'm willing to accept in regard to my attire are how good I look in it."

"Noted." He poured them both coffee and handed her a cup. "You look very sexy in those shorts."

"Thank you. I appreciate the compliment."

"The bottoms of your ass cheeks peek from underneath the frayed hem, and all I can think about is nibbling on them. I bet the same thought will cross the mind of every unmated guy who sees you, and there aren't that many mated immortals on this ship."

She rolled her eyes. "Fine. I won't send you off to battle worrying about my ass being on display. I didn't plan on wearing them outside the cabin anyway." She lifted her chin. "This is my staying-inside lounging outfit. I like to dress more elegantly in company."

That was a relief for more reasons than one. The most important was that Frankie wouldn't be tempting all the other single males with her sweet bottom peeking from the too-short shorts, and the other one was that she felt comfortable enough with him to slouch.

Dagor pulled out a box of crackers from the cabinet and a tray of assorted cheeses from the fridge. "Is this good enough for breakfast?"

She shrugged. "If it's good enough for you, it's good enough for me. I'm not the one heading out to battle and needing good nutrition to fuel my body."

"That's not true." He put the items on the table and went back to get plates. "You are about to fight the most intense battle of your life. Your transition."

"Fates willing," She lifted both hands with fingers crossed. "Although after you gave me your blood, I'm not worried about me. I'm worried about you."

He put the plates on the table and sat down. "Maybe you will feel better once you know what the plan is."

Her eyes widened. "Are you allowed to tell me?"

"I don't see why not." He pulled out a bunch of crackers and put them on her plate. "The ship will get as close as it can to shore about two hundred nautical miles north of Acapulco. We will take one or two lifeboats to shore and then drive to the location. Turner has arranged for bullet-proof vehicles to await us, along with surveillance drones. We will stop several miles before reaching the place where we engaged the cartel and send out drones to scout the area. We are taking every precaution to protect ourselves from being ambushed, which is most likely what they are planning."

She shook her head. "I didn't even think of the possibility of an ambush. Just shows you how little I know about these things."

If anything, his explanation seemed to make her even more anxious.

Dagor reached out with his hand, brushing a strand of hair from her face. "You have nothing to worry about. I'm a god, and I can take hold of the minds of humans and immortals." He didn't add that he couldn't do that to a large group of people.

If they were all human, he and Negal together might have been able to do it, but the twelve immortals complicated things.

Her chin wobbled. "You're not impervious to bullets."

"I took two dozen bullets in my back, and it was nothing. It wasn't pleasant, but I was in no real danger. I possess strengths and abilities that far surpass those of the immortals and even Toven."

Frankie's eyes widened. "I knew you were more powerful than the immortals, but Toven? How?"

This wasn't a good time for a lesson in Anumati's history, but he'd promised to tell her more about himself, and he could condense the events that had taken place over thousands of years into a few minutes.

"Remember what I told you about the pods and the people inside of them?"

She nodded. "The Kra-ell, whoever they are."

"There are two species of intelligent beings on my home planet. Those who call themselves the gods and the Kra-ell. The Kra-ell are traditionalists who refused genetic alterations and followed a simpler way of life that was not based on technology. There is more to it than that, but I don't have time to dive into the entire history of our planet. At some point, the Kra-ell rebelled, demanding equal rights, and since the gods hadn't expected to have to defend themselves in their homes, they were not prepared. The Kra-ell were physically stronger and had had eons of tribal wars to develop their fighting skills. The gods had to resort to unconventional means to defend against the Kra-ell. They modified a class of robotic household servants, the Odus, transforming them into formidable killing machines. Long story short, the robotic servants were decommissioned after the rebellion and their manufacturing was outlawed. It was part of the peace agreement between the gods and the Kra-ell. To compensate, new genetic modifications were included for the new generations of gods. I was among those who received enhancements to increase our strength and speed to give us an edge against the Kra-ell. These enhancements make me more powerful than most gods, including Toven."

"So, you're like... supercharged?"

Dagor chuckled softly, appreciating her attempt to ease the tension. "Something like that, yes. I have abilities that are beyond the ordinary, even by the standards of my world."

"Oh, wow, that's so hot." She fanned herself jokingly, her eyes twinkling with mischief. "I'm one lucky girl. I can now boast that my boyfriend is stronger than Mia's."

"You might not want to do that. Toven is royalty, and I am not. He has a glow, and I don't."

"Yeah, the Clan Mother glows, too, but that's just a gimmick. It doesn't do anything. You have super strength."

"True, but Anumati's society is hierarchical despite purporting to be a democracy with equal rights and opportunities for all. At the top are the royal families, which have the strongest luminosity; below them are the nobles, who are distant relatives of the royal families who retained some glow; and at the bottom are the commoners, which is where I fall."

"What about the Kra-ell?"

"They have their own society and their own hierarchy. The Kra-ell queen is usually the strongest compeller, which is a hereditary trait, so the throne basically stays in the family even though any other Kra-ell female can challenge the queen."

Frankie listened intently, her gaze never leaving his face. "That's so fascinating. When you return from the mission, you must tell me more."

"I will." Dagor squeezed her hand. "Rest. Watch some movies to take your mind off the mission or spend time with Mia. I'll be back before you know it."

"Promise?" She gripped his hand, tears brimming in her eyes.

"I promise." He leaned over and kissed her lips, her nose, her cheeks, her forehead. "I love you, and I'll be back."

Kalugal

K alugal stood on the outdoor promenade, the cool ocean breeze whipping around him as he waited for his team to assemble.

He gazed at the lifeboats and contemplated how many were needed. Each was capable of carrying one hundred and fifty people, so one lifeboat was enough for their team of forty, but the idea of deploying two boats seemed like a good tactical move. If the Doomers somehow found out about them disembarking north of Acapulco and sent someone to investigate, they would assume that a much larger force was coming their way.

The ship was not full to capacity, so the remaining lifeboats would suffice for all the passengers if the unthinkable happened and the Doomers managed to sink the ship or a catastrophic storm appeared out of nowhere.

Kalugal very much doubted that was a possibility, but it was always better to err on the side of caution.

It had been a long time since he'd gone on a mission. The altercation with the cartel thugs hadn't been planned, but it had felt damn good to deliver justice and save the women, and it had given him a taste for more.

He'd been a businessman for so long that he had forgotten what it was like to be a warrior, and he had never been a warrior for justice before. The thrill of the fight had been dormant in him, overshadowed by financial strategies and corporate negotiations.

Kalugal had no illusions about being a savior, and he was well aware that one small operation like the one they had stumbled upon would not cure the world of its evils. He'd thought that InstaTock was a better way to influence minds and encourage them to think critically by providing pertinent information, but that had been naïve as well. People rarely bothered to dig deeper beyond the slogans fed to them by various instigators, and the more negative and harmful the slogan, the more viral it became. For those who wished to destroy humankind and Western civilization in particular, social media was the perfect breeding ground for malignant ideologies.

The spoiled brats who had never known any real hardship couldn't recognize evil even when it was staring them in the face with a loaded gun pointed at their foreheads. They parroted the malignancies they were fed, thinking that they were righteous when they were the absolute opposite of that.

Positive messages were ignored, trivialized, or twisted to mean the opposite of what was conveyed.

Kalugal let out a sigh. Perhaps nothing ever really changed because humans were so short-lived and had such short memories. Lessons of the past were forgotten, and the same mistakes were repeated time and again, bringing misery, death, and destruction.

Rinse and repeat.

"Hello, cousin." Kian walked over with Dalhu, with the brothers trailing a few feet behind them.

Dalhu was armed to the teeth and looking formidable.

"I've never fought by your side before," Dalhu said. "I'm eager for the opportunity."

"Don't get too excited. After I freeze them all, there won't be any fighting to do, but be ready to have lots of blood on your hands." Kalugal grimaced. "Tearing out hearts is messy."

Anandur chuckled, and Brundar arched one blond brow.

Dalhu grinned. "I'm a painter. Mess doesn't bother me."

The banter stopped when Bhathian arrived with Max and a contingent of Guardians.

They were all heavily armed, except for Kian who was staying behind, and Anandur and Brundar, who weren't joining the mission because they had to guard him.

Kalugal knew that Kian would have gladly allowed them to join the party, but his esteemed aunt insisted that her son always have two bodyguards by his side whenever he was away from the protective walls of the village.

"I wish I could join in." Anandur glanced longingly at the group of armed Guardians. "Wonder said that she was okay with me going on the mission."

"That's very considerate of her, but your brother is getting married tonight." Kian put a hand on the redhead's shoulder. "And his bride won't be happy if you come to the wedding with blood and gore stuck under your fingernails that no amount of scrubbing can clean."

"Callie won't mind," Brundar said.

Anandur cast a questioning look at Kian, but his boss didn't seem in the mood to relent. "It's a shame that Brundar is not getting a bachelor party. I had so many fun ideas."

Brundar shook his head. "I don't want a bachelor party. I've said it at least twenty times."

"You can still have one," Kalugal said. "Your brother and your boss are staying on board, and I'm sure you have many friends among the Guardians who are staying to protect the ship and can celebrate with you while being vigilant about safeguarding it."

Kalugal wasn't sure that Brundar had any friends, but pretending to think that he did was the polite thing to do.

"I don't want a bachelor party, period." Brundar cast him a glare that would have scared a lesser male.

Anandur sighed. "My brother has trouble enjoying anything other than being with his mate and killing bad guys. If you want to make him happy, take him with you."

Kalugal could have sworn that Brundar's lips curved in a shadow of a smile as he turned to Kian. "For once, Anandur is right. Can you assign someone else to your security detail?"

Kian hesitated for a split second before nodding. "It's your wedding tonight. Are you sure that Callie will be okay with that?"

That earned Kian an even deadlier glare than the one Kalugal had been treated to. "My mate knows who she's bonded to. As long as I show up to the ceremony, she'll be fine."

Kian nodded. "Then go. I'll get a replacement."

"Thank you." Brundar bowed his head, which Kalugal had only ever seen him do in the presence of the Clan Mother.

Anandur looked incredulous. "This is so unfair. I got turned down twice, and he gets to go after asking once?"

Kian shrugged. "If you want to go so badly, I can find a replacement for you as well."

The redhead crossed his arms over his chest. "Now, I don't want to go on principle. I'm staying."

Kian didn't seem affected by the theatrics, probably because he was used to them.

Bhathian, who had been listening to their exchange, walked over to Brundar. "You should get armed."

Brundar patted his chest. "I have all I need right here."

Dagor

As the winch detached from the lifeboat Dagor braced for impact, but as the vessel hit the water, it was minimal. Nevertheless, he and his companions got sprayed with ocean water.

When the other boat hit the water moments later, they were sprayed again.

"Damn," Negal cursed next to him. "Now I will have to smell the ocean on myself until we get back."

"It's not that bad." Dagor lifted his T-shirt and sniffed at it. "You've gotten spoiled."

"I have," Negal admitted. "It has been a long time since I've had to endure any hardship, and I don't miss it. I like wearing clean clothes, sleeping in a comfortable bed, and getting regular showers."

"I hear you," the Guardian sitting on Negal's other side said. "That's why I love our current mode of operations. We go in, free the victims, and take care of the scum who's holding them in one way or another, and the whole thing takes no more than six hours, including the drive to and from the mission. I never have to go to bed without showering."

"Do you go on missions every day?" Negal asked.

As the two continued talking about the rescue missions the clan engaged in on a regular basis, Dagor checked his gear once again, ensuring everything was in place. The weight of the weapons was unfamiliar, but it was somewhat comforting even though he didn't expect to make use of them. They were primitive compared to what he'd been trained on, crude even.

His strength, his speed, and his enhanced senses would most likely suffice, and he doubted he would need more than that to fight a few immortals and a horde of humans.

Even though the rebellion was a thing of the past and no one expected another Kra-ell insurgence, the powers that be had decided to ensure that the new generation of gods was built as efficient killing machines. He had never thought in those terms before getting drafted, but during training, it had been drilled into the minds of the new recruits. They were a protective shield for Anumati's society in case the gods' home was ever attacked again, either by the Kra-ell, who were their neighbors, or unknown outside forces. Their enhancements were insurance. The decision to enhance the physical strength of the next generation was made to ensure that they never got caught again with their pants down, as the human saying went.

There were only about twenty people in each boat, which was a fraction of what they could carry, but it was done to create the perception of a much larger force in case the Doomers and their cartel goons discovered their mode of transportation. Besides, as a rule, two were better than one in case one got damaged, or some other unforeseen event took place.

The truth was that Dagor was impressed with the level of planning that had gone into the mission.

It was always better to spend the time preparing and accounting for all contingencies than going in with a half-baked plan and fighting harder and longer than necessary. If everything went according to Turner's plan, the actual battle would be over in minutes.

The big question was whether the enemy had brought the hostages to the site or was hiding them somewhere else. The contingency for that was to capture the Doomers' leader and interrogate him to reveal their location.

It was also important to find out what these Doomers knew and whether they had reported the incident to their superiors on the island.

The sea was calm, but the waves breaking at the shore bounced the boat around. The boat slowed as it approached the designated landing spot, and the team readied themselves to disembark.

When they got within wading distance, Dagor and Negal followed the Guardians' example and strapped their rifles high across their chests before jumping into the water that reached below their waists.

After dragging the boats to shore, they put some effort into camouflaging the vessels so they wouldn't be visible from the highway, which was only a few hundred feet away, and then walked to where the vehicles were parked discreetly, hidden from casual view but easily accessible.

As the team divided among the vehicles, Dagor joined the lead car. He double-checked the earpiece he had been given, and then the convoy set off, leaving the shoreline behind.

His thoughts turned to Frankie.

He had left her safe and sound on the ship, and he already missed her. Even the thrill of the upcoming battle wasn't enough to overshadow the tight feeling in the pit of his stomach where an invisible tether connected him to her.

The farther he got from her, the stronger the pull got and the tighter the knot in his stomach felt.

Dagor had to remind himself that what he was doing was important. They were about to confront the Doomers, rescue the hostages, and bring justice to those who had caused so much harm.

Kalugal

K alugal signaled for the convoy to come to a stop five miles away from the rendezvous point with the Doomers. It was time to deploy the spy drones, which were an essential part of their reconnaissance strategy. He couldn't help but marvel at the technology that Turner's contractor had procured for them on such short notice.

These drones were unlike those he had seen the clan use before. They were smaller than the palm of his hand, designed to look like some kind of a bird, and their operation was impressively stealthy.

"Look at this." He put one on his palm. "Have you seen anything so advanced?"

The question was directed at Bhathian, but Dagor responded with a chuckle. "I guess Kian didn't tell you about our drones. You wouldn't detect one even if it was perched on your shoulder. They are the size of a mosquito."

Kian had mentioned something about the gods' technology, but since he'd also said that it was impossible to take it apart and reverse engineer it, Kalugal had lost interest.

"Good for you." He smiled at the god. "Did you bring anything with you on board?"

Dagor shook his head. "We didn't bring any of our equipment, and I've been lamenting that decision since the whole mess with the cartel started. Our disruptor would have disabled their weapons and communicators, which would have given us a clear advantage." He glanced at the Guardians standing around them. "We have enough power to easily win this battle and free the hostages, but it would have been less messy with better tools."

"Indeed." Kalugal cast him a smile. "Next time you join the clan on a cruise, bring everything you have. Trouble always follows wherever they go."

The god tilted his head. "They? Aren't you part of the clan?"

"Yes and no. I like to think of our community as a coalition. Annani's descendants are the clan, while my people and I are not connected to each other by familial ties. My men and I came together as a group that sought similar goals, which was freedom from the oppression of the Brotherhood and a peaceful life away from wars and conflicts."

Kalugal let out an exaggerated sigh. "And yet here we are, fighting alongside the clan to correct wrongs and do good."

Bhathian cleared his throat. "The history lesson can wait. We need to release the drones."

"Absolutely." Kalugal took the remote from the Guardian. "Let's see how these things work."

As the drones took to the sky, their engines emitted a low hum that was barely discernible. With the natural sounds of the surrounding forest, even the keen hearing of immortals would struggle to detect them.

Kalugal watched the drones ascend and then switched to the display on the remote, which provided a bird's-eye view of the area.

"Now we wait," he murmured, his eyes fixed on the monitor displaying the drone footage. "They will each do just one flyby. Less chance of them being noticed."

Peering at the screen from behind Kalugal's shoulder, Yamanu let out a breath. "I hope they didn't have time to set up traps on all the accessible paths. Our advantage is that they don't know which direction we are coming from.
"

Kalugal turned to look at the Guardian. "We are not in a rush, and we can progress slowly to make sure there are no makeshift traps on the way."

Yamanu let out a breath. "It's very easy to set up detonations along the way, and even with our keen eyesight, we might not see the wires strewn across the road in time."

When the drones reached the meeting point, Kalugal whistled. "Well, that's something I didn't expect."

It was impossible to tell the Doomers from the cartel thugs, but together, there were at least a hundred fighters there. But the most alarming part was not the number of adversaries but the weaponry they possessed. Among the standard firearms, Kalugal spotted two jeeps with armor-piercing machine guns mounted in the back.

"They have at least a hundred fighters," he muttered. "And armor-piercing weapons. They probably have RPGs as well."

Yamanu, who had been watching over Kalugal's shoulder, let out a breath. "This changes things."

Kalugal nodded, his gaze still fixed on the screen. "We need to adjust our tactics and approach in stealth, taking them by surprise."

"We need to ditch the vehicles and approach on foot," Bhathian said.

Dalhu nodded. "As we discussed, they will have sentries posted about two miles out in all directions. Four teams are the standard, but since they only have twelve immortals, there might be fewer. In any case, the sentry teams will probably have one immortal and one or two humans each."

Evidently, Dalhu remembered the standard procedures better than Kalugal, but then it wasn't surprising. The guy had left the Brotherhood five years ago, while it had been many decades since Kalugal had escaped his father's stronghold.

"We need to do the same," Bhathian said. "We need to dispatch four teams to take out the sentries first so we can make it the rest of the way without being spotted. We get within hearing distance, you use your megaphone, and it's all over."

Dagor

Dagor stood to the side, listening in on Kalugal's strategic huddle with his leadership team as they discussed the battle plan.

No one had thought to ask for his or Negal's advice, but the immortals didn't seem to mind that they were listening. Did that mean that they were interested in their input?

Clearing his throat, Dagor stepped forward. "If I may, I can offer a slight improvement to your plan." It was a big one, but he was downplaying it, not wishing to sound condescending or to offend.

Kalugal nodded. "Go ahead."

"You don't need four teams. Negal and I can go ahead and take out all the sentries. We are faster, stronger, have sharper senses, and we can shroud ourselves to become invisible. We can achieve the objective faster and with less chance of complications."

Kalugal's eyes rounded with appreciation. "Why didn't I think of utilizing your superpowers before? I can shroud myself from immortals, too, but I can't pull off a disappearing act. I can only make myself look like someone else."

Dagor eyed him with curiosity. "You have godly powers despite being a hybrid. How come?"

Kalugal's compulsion ability was so strong that few of the gods back home could compete with it, and only those that came from the same royal line as the Eternal King at that. And now he had revealed that he could also shroud himself from other immortals.

Kalugal smirked. "I'm special. I am the descendant of two powerful gods. That's why inbreeding was so popular among our people." He winked. "When genetic manipulation wasn't available to us, it was the method of choice to produce more powerful offspring."

"Which gods were your ancestors?" Dagor asked.

They knew that Kalugal was a descendant of the Eternal King through Mortdh, but who was the other one?

"That's a story for another time," Kalugal said. "Now, we need to focus on the task at hand. Since you two can pull a disappearing act, you're on."

That was easier than Dagor had expected. "Good."

Next to him, Negal grinned like he had just won a game of Barkada. "We can do more than that," he whispered so low that only Dagor could hear him.

He nodded. "If I may, I have another idea for improving our chances of success."

"I'm listening eagerly," Kalugal said.

Dagor cast a quick look at the other members of the leadership team to make sure that he wasn't stepping on anyone's toes, but they all seemed as eager as Kalugal to hear what he had to say.

"Both Negal and I can conceal one more person in addition to ourselves. Once we dispatch the sentries, we can come back to collect you and another person. We can get you right in front of the Doomers without them being any the wiser. Once you freeze them, the rest of the convoy can arrive to help with the cleanup."

A smile bloomed on Kalugal's face. "That's perfect, Dagor. Thank you. We don't even need to waste time on the sentries. You and Negal can sneak me and one more warrior past them right in front of the Doomers. The element of surprise will be complete."

Bhathian shook his head. "We need to take out the sentries. When you freeze those at the meeting point, the sentries will be too far away to hear you, so they will not be frozen, and they could cause plenty of damage to our convoy, which will still need to reach you. The sentries might activate booby-traps to blow up our vehicles. They might have armor-piercing bullets, RPGs, and Fates know what else. Eliminating them is a must."

Max nodded. "After the sentries are dealt with, we will follow slowly behind and check for traps. When you reach the Doomers and their patsies and freeze them, we will not be far behind."

Kalugal groaned. "What if taking out the sentries reveals our hand? I'm sure that they have to report to their cohorts every few minutes."

Dagor lifted his hand to get their attention. "That's a good point, which necessitates another change of plan. We need to take you with us, and instead of taking the sentries out, you will compel them to keep reporting that nothing is happening. We will take them out on our way back."

Kalugal grinned. "That's brilliant. Thank you, Dagor."

Negal pushed his hands into his pockets. "We can achieve our objectives much faster if Dagor and I carry you and the other guy on our backs. We can cover twice the distance in half the time."

Kalugal shook his head. "I draw the line on being carried."

Negal shrugged. "As you wish. But we can cut the time in half that way."

"Thanks, but no thanks." Kalugal squared his shoulders. "When the stories about today are told, I don't want them to include you carrying me on your back." He turned to Max. "Coordinate with the convoy to hold back until we give the signal that the scouts have been dealt with."

"Understood," the Guardian nodded.

Kalugal turned to Bhathian. "If anything changes back here, let us know right away. We need to adapt. The situation could evolve quickly."

"Of course." Bhathian looked offended. "This is not my first rodeo."

"I know." Kalugal clapped him on the back with a smile. "I like to reiterate things, even those that you might think everyone knows. That way, there is no room for confusion."

"Who do you want to take with you?" Bhathian asked.

Kalugal turned to Dalhu. "Do you want to come?"

"Of course." The guy grinned as if Kalugal had offered him a prize, which, in a way, he had.

Dalhu seemed to be spoiling for a fight, but if everything went according to plan, there wouldn't be much fighting to be done.

Dalhu

"So, here is how it's going to work," Negal said as the four of them collected their equipment. "We will scout the area and locate the sentries. Then we will come back for you."

When Kalugal nodded, Negal continued, "Dagor and I are not the best of shrouders, and shrouding others along with ourselves drains our ability. After we locate all the pairs, the four of us will get in position to take the first one, but Dagor and I will approach them first while shrouding only ourselves, which is much less draining for us, and incapacitate them. You will stay behind until they are ready for you. Then you come, and you do your thing with the compulsion."

Dalhu was disappointed. "Then what do you need me for? You can take just Kalugal."

Negal smiled. "Precautions. What if we encounter someone who is immune to compulsion? Or if we walk into an ambush? Dagor and I can probably handle that on our own, but you seem like a capable warrior, and having you with us might save the day."

Dalhu had a feeling that the god was just being courteous, but he wasn't going to argue. He was itching for action, even if it involved nothing more than running through the forest.

As he found out a short time later, though, keeping up with the gods was not easy. The dense forest around them was both a blessing and a curse. It provided cover, but the uneven terrain and the thick undergrowth made it challenging to move quickly and silently.

Dalhu was no stranger to physical exertion, but keeping pace with the gods was proving to be a herculean task. After more than an hour of running at breakneck speed, every breath he drew was a labored gasp, and his lungs were burning with the effort.

If they didn't slow down, the sentries would be alerted to their presence by his and Kalugal's huffing and puffing.

"Slow down," Kalugal finally whispered. "We don't need to run at top speed. We have plenty of time."

Kalugal's whisper was music to Dalhu's ears. The gods seemed to move with supernatural ease, and despite the speed at which they were running, their steps barely disturbed the forest floor.

He admired and envied their agility and strength, and those were not the only attributes of theirs that were superior to his and Kalugal's.

Even though the gods were at least a hundred feet ahead, they'd heard the whisper, which attested to their superior hearing. With all the ambient noise of nature around them, Dalhu doubted he could have heard a whisper from such a distance.

Dagor was the first one to switch from a run to an easy jog, and Negal reluctantly followed his example.

"Let's walk for a little bit," Kalugal whispered. "Dalhu and I need to catch our breath."

As they transitioned to a walk, Dalhu's chest heaved as he drew in deep, steadying breaths. When he and Kalugal were no longer huffing and puffing, the sounds filling the silence were the chirping of insects, the rustle of leaves, and the distant calls of animals.

Negal smirked. "We offered to carry you on our backs."

"There is no need for that," Kalugal said. "You were just going too fast."

Dagor, the more serious of the two gods, frowned. "Perhaps you should rest while Negal and I scout ahead. We can find where the sentries are and come back for you after we've dealt with them."

Kalugal cast Dalhu a sidelong glance. "What do you think?"

"I think it's a smart use of resources."

Dalhu might not have the godly abilities of Dagor or Negal, but he had his own strengths to bring to the table. He was a skilled warrior and a quick thinker, and he had a personal stake in the success of this mission. He might recognize some of those Doomers from his time in the Brotherhood, and if they belonged to the group of those he had vowed to one day eliminate, this mission would kill two birds with one stone, pun intended.

"Very well." Kalugal walked up to a tree and sat down, leaning against its trunk. "Go ahead."

Dalhu joined him, unstrapped his water canteen, and took a long swig.

"These gods are such show-offs," Kalugal murmured as he pulled out his own canteen. "They act so superior."

"They are superior." Dalhu grimaced. "Therefore, it doesn't count as showing off."

Kalugal took a sip of water, his gaze still fixed on the spot where Dagor and Negal had disappeared. "I know, I know. It's just hard to accept that they are better than us. We're supposed to be the elite, the best of the best. And then these gods come along, and suddenly, we're playing catch-up. When it was only Annani and Toven, it was okay. They are our royalty. But these are simple guys. Commoners."

Dalhu cast Kalugal a sidelong glance. "I'm a commoner compared to you, but I can still beat you on the sparring mat. You are a commoner compared to the Clan Mother and Toven, but you are a powerful compeller and a successful businessman. Each of us brings our own strengths to the table."

A hint of a smile tugged at the corner of Kalugal's mouth. "You're right, of course. I'm a prideful, competitive guy, but I admit that I'm grateful for their help."

Dagor

"Just as Dalhu anticipated, there were four sentry pairs," Dagor reported. "Each one seems to have one immortal and one human. The Doomers stationed them about a mile away from the meeting place, though, not two. They are covering all the accessible pathways."

Kalugal nodded. "What about surveillance equipment? Did you detect any?"

Negal shook his head. "Unless it was very well hidden, we didn't see or hear anything, but that doesn't mean there isn't any. We are good, but without our equipment, we can't be sure." He sighed. "We shouldn't have left it behind."

"It was supposed to be a vacation," Dagor reminded him.

Now that they knew where the sentries were located, there was no reason to keep whispering.

"Are they within shouting distance of each other?" Kalugal asked.

"They are about an hour's walk away." Negal smirked. "At your speed, not ours. When we are within earshot of them, we will stop. Dagor and I will go first, subdue and gag the first pair, and only then will you and Dalhu emerge. After you compel them, we will remove the gags. We will do the same with the other three pairs."

Kalugal nodded. "Good plan."

"Let's do it." Dalhu strapped his rifle over his chest.

As the group set out, moving quietly through the dense underbrush, Dagor's senses were on full alert.

When they were close to the first sentry pair, Dagor held up his hand, signaling everyone to stop.

The forest around them was a symphony of sounds, but Dagor and Negal were as silent as shadows, their footsteps muffled by the thick undergrowth.

It was possible to shroud sounds as well, but Dagor had found that he couldn't make himself perfectly invisible and soundless at the same time. Perhaps as he grew older he would develop the ability to do both, but for now, he had to rely on his training for the silent approach.

Evidently, he and Negal were doing a good enough job because both the human and the immortal seemed oblivious to them. The two spoke in low tones, and then the immortal laughed at a crude remark made by the human.

Dagor's stomach turned over at the blatant disregard for human life and dignity evident in their conversation. He focused on the immortal and motioned for Negal to aim at the human.

Negal wasn't happy about getting the easier target, but they could switch targets with the next sentry pair.

With another hand signal, Dagor initiated the attack, and they struck in perfect coordination. Dagor lunged at the immortal, clamping a hand over his mouth to stifle his scream and twisting his arm behind his back to immobilize him.

Negal tackled the human sentry just as swiftly, with a hand covering the man's mouth while his other arm secured a firm grip.

The human's eyes widened in shock and fear.

It was satisfying to watch the two freak out because they couldn't see their assailants, only hear and feel them. The immortal was most likely aware of shrouding, but since most of the immortals couldn't manipulate the minds of other immortals, he had no idea what was happening to him.

Working quickly, they gagged their captives using strips of cloth they had brought along, tying them securely around the mouths of the sentries. Next, they hogtied their limbs, using fortified rope they'd brought from the ship to use on the immortals. With that done, he and Negal released their shrouds.

As fun as it was terrorizing the two, it was a waste of energy to keep up the shroud for any longer than necessary.

"Nice job." He high-fived Negal.

A low-pitched bird call was the signal for Kalugal and Dalhu to come forward.

As Kalugal approached the subdued sentries, Dagor watched intently, ready to intervene if necessary. He had seen compulsion at work before, or rather its effect on Frankie when Toven had compelled her to keep immortals and gods a secret from anyone outside the ship, but witnessing Kalugal's power was fascinating.

Kalugal knelt before the human sentry first.

The man's eyes widened with fear and confusion, but as Kalugal's deep, commanding voice washed over him, they glazed over. The sound of compulsion was potent, almost tangible in the air, and Dagor could see the human's body slackening as Kalugal's influence took hold.

"Please release him," he told Dalhu. "He won't move from this spot or say a word other than everything is fine, all is quiet, or there is no one here."

After Dalhu did as Kalugal had instructed, the human sat up, leaning against a tree with a line of drool forming in the corner of his mouth.

"He looks like a zombie," Dalhu murmured.

Turning his attention to the immortal, Kalugal repeated the process. The immortal initially tried to fight the compulsion, but he was overcome in seconds. His eyes became blurry, and the tension left his muscles.

"You can untie him as well," Kalugal told Dalhu.

When Dalhu positioned the immortal next to the human, Kalugal smiled evilly.

"What's your name?" he asked the immortal.

"Badsor."

Negal chuckled. "It sounds like a bedsore."

"Badsor." Kalugal used his commanding tone. "Put your thumb in your mouth and suck on it."

The guy's eyes bulged out, but he did exactly as he'd been ordered.

"Good." Kalugal crossed his arms over his chest. "Take off your boots and socks and suck on your big toe."

The veins on the guy's neck swelled as he tried to fight the compulsion, but his hands obeyed immediately, untying the laces, removing the boots and the socks, and then contorting to put his big toe in his mouth.

Negal laughed. "Can I take a picture?"

"Go ahead." Kalugal waved a hand as he turned to the human and gave him similar instructions.

When the human had his toe inside his mouth and was drooling all over the dirty digit, Kalugal uncrossed his arms. "You will keep sucking on your toes until it's time to report to your superiors that there is nothing going on and that everything is quiet."

Dagor watched the display of Kalugal's formidable abilities with a mix of fascination and discomfort. He was not affected by the compulsion, but he knew that there were gods capable of taking control of the minds of other gods.

The Eternal King was the most powerful compeller in the history of Anumati, and it was very likely that his granddaughter was a formidable compeller as well, but so far, he hadn't seen the princess using her power on anyone.

Hopefully, she wouldn't use it on him or his friends.

"We are done here," Kalugal said. "On to the next pair."

Kalugal

Once all the sentries had been taken care of, Kalugal activated his earpiece. "The coast is clear. You can start moving."

"That's not a report," Bhathian grumbled in his ear. "I need details."

Rolling his eyes, Kalugal activated the earpiece again. "Negal and Dagor located four sentry pairs within a one-mile radius of the meeting place. They caught and subdued them, and I compelled them to keep reporting that everything was fine and nothing was happening. The four of us are about to continue, with Dagor and Negal shrouding me and Dalhu. Once I'm in front of the demon horde, I will pull out my trusty megaphone, order them to freeze, and let Dalhu loose. He's been itching for some action. So, if the rest of you want to join in the fun, you'd better hurry up."

"We are on our way," Bhathian said. "But don't let Dalhu loose before we get there. We need the leader of the Doomers alive for questioning."

"Even if Luis and his family are found?"

The contingency was to capture the leader in case they were not there, and leverage was needed to get them released.

"Yes. Kian wants us to bring the leader to the ship for questioning."

"I don't know how wise that is," Kalugal said. "Leadership positions in the Brotherhood go to the older members of the order. The leader might recognize me even though I left a long time ago, and even if he doesn't remember me, he will recognize Lokan for sure. Getting rid of him as soon as possible is the safest strategy."

"Don't worry. He's not leaving the ship alive. You and Lokan are safe."

Kalugal didn't trust reassurances that weren't backed by an iron-clad plan. "I'd rather err on the side of caution. I want to know exactly what Kian plans to do with the Doomer."

"I give you my word that the bastard won't live after we are done questioning him. I'll personally see that he's dead."

Kalugal was sure Bhathian had every intention of fulfilling his promise, but the law of unintended consequences was a bitch, and shit happened.

"Just make sure that he's subdued the entire way. I don't want the bastard to have a chance to escape."

"I will. We will knock him out with venom if necessary."

"Thank you. I appreciate it." He ended the conversation and turned to Dagor. "When do you want to start shrouding?"

"We should start now. It will take us fifteen minutes to get to the meeting spot, and both Negal and I can easily shroud for that long."

Kalugal waved a hand. "Then let's do it."

As Dagor and Negal's shrouding enveloped them, rendering their small group invisible to the outside world, it was an eerie sensation.

Seeing Dalhu and the two gods disappear was a very disconcerting experience.

Kalugal knew they were there, but he couldn't see them, and he could barely hear them. Would he feel it if one of them touched him?

"You will need to drop the shroud when we are in position, or they won't hear me. Please touch my shoulder if you got it."

"I'm not shrouding for sound," Dagor said. "Negal and I are trained to move nearly soundlessly, but from now on, we shouldn't communicate verbally."

Kalugal felt the god's hand on his shoulder. "I was afraid that I wouldn't feel that. Can you keep your hand there? I don't want to accidentally veer off the path and walk away from you."

The hand on his shoulder tightened a fraction in confirmation.

As they progressed, Kalugal found himself adjusting to the sensory deprivation this new mode of operation created. It was a strange dance, moving in sync with an invisible partner, especially since Kalugal wasn't the trusting type.

The only person in the world he trusted implicitly was Jacki. He would follow her blindly wherever she led him. But Dagor wasn't even a friend, and relying on him was a struggle.

Dagor

As their group made its way through the last mile separating them from their enemy, the dense foliage around them rustled gently in the breeze. The canopy of trees swayed, casting shifting patterns of light and shadow on the ground, and the sunlight filtering through the leaves played tricks on the eye, creating an almost surreal atmosphere.

Occasionally the distant call of a bird pierced the air, adding a layer of authenticity to the scene, with the subtle hum of cicadas and the occasional buzz of a mosquito providing a backdrop to the anxious anticipation.

As they entered the clearing and Dagor's eyes fell on the immortal and human scum, his jaw clenched. They looked so nonchalant, lounging in their roofless jeeps, chatting and laughing as if they and their comrades hadn't committed the most heinous crimes just days before.

Scanning the treetops surrounding the clearing, he expected to find goons hiding in their canopies, but there were none. Evidently, the leader of the thugs was confident in their numbers and their firepower and did not think that posting hidden snipers was needed.

Dagor would have loved to finish the job the other immortals had done and tear them apart with his fangs, but their firepower was too formidable. The armor-piercing bullets could do massive damage, and while he was incapacitated for even a few brief moments, they could end him by beheading him or tearing out his heart.

It had to be done the way they had planned.

Squeezing Kalugal's shoulder, Dagor let him know that he was about to drop the shroud.

Kalugal activated the megaphone, put it next to his mouth, and nodded.

Dagor dropped the shroud.

"Don't move a muscle," Kalugal said, the compulsion in his voice reverberating through Dagor so strongly that he was frozen in place for a moment as well. "And don't say a word."

The shock on the faces of the Doomers was a sight to behold. Their sudden shift from arrogance to fear was a vindication that Dagor savored. It was a reversal of fortunes. The hunter becoming the hunted.

He relished the stunned and terrified expression on the males' faces, the knowledge that they were going to die.

A smile tugged on the corner of his lips.

The poetic justice of the situation was not lost on him. These were the monsters who had thought themselves invincible, untouchable, but now they faced the inevitable consequences of their actions.

"Payback is a bitch, vermin," he murmured under his breath. "How does it feel to be helpless in front of a superior force? How does it feel to know that you are about to die?"

His whisper had been too low for the Doomers to hear, but Dalhu stood right next to him. The guy turned to him and put a hand on his shoulder. "Patience, my friend. Retribution is moments away."

Dagor nodded.

"Members of the Brotherhood of the Devout Order of Mortdh," Kalugal's voice boomed through the megaphone. "Come forward," he commanded.

Eight males broke the ranks and walked toward them.

"Stop ten feet in front of me," Kalugal ordered.

Dagor observed the rage on their faces with pure satisfaction. It was like balm for his soul.

He would enjoy killing them slowly.

They halted precisely ten feet away. The distance was negligible for someone like Dagor, who could close it in the blink of an eye. But it wasn't the physical space that mattered, it was Kalugal's complete control over them.

Their eyes burned with hatred and frustration, a reflection of their impotence in the face of overwhelming power. Dagor could almost taste their fury, and it thrilled him.

The thought of prolonging their suffering, of savoring their fear and desperation, was tantalizing. Dagor imagined the various ways he could inflict pain, each more satisfying than the last. It was a dark, exhilarating thought that danced in his mind, an unpleasant reminder of his predatory nature, but at this moment, he embraced the side of himself that he normally sought to stifle.

There was not an ounce of pity in his heart for these people. Earth would be a better place without them to taint its soil.

Kalugal

Kalugal scanned the faces of the Doomers, but he didn't recognize any of them. They must have been born after he had run away because there was no recognition in their eyes either, only intense hatred and fear.

Good.

The rumble of vehicle engines announced the arrival of the rest of their team, the graveled ground crunching under their tires until they stopped some distance behind him.

Kalugal didn't turn to look. "Who is the leader of this operation? Raise your hand," he commanded.

When the hand of one of the eight shot into the air, Kalugal ordered, "Take two steps forward."

The guy looked like a robot whose legs were operating independently from the rest of his body.

It was so comical that Kalugal had a hard time keeping his menacing expression. "Tell me where Luis and his family are being held!"

There had been enough compulsion in his voice to topple an army, and he got several answers at once.

"The van," one Doomer said.

"In the back," another said.

"In the van in the back," the leader spat.

Kalugal thought that he recognized the voice of the one who had called him, the one who'd said his name was Bud, but he wasn't sure. Still, it was easier to refer to him as Bud than the leader.

When Bud opened his mouth again, Kalugal lifted a hand. "Shut up. You are not to speak unless I tell you to."

He motioned for Negal to step forward. "Go get Luis and his family."

Negal hesitated. "If they heard your command, they will be just as affected as the others and unable to move. I can carry two or three at most, and there are more of them."

Kalugal didn't want to chance releasing anyone else from his immobilizing compulsion. Even using the megaphone to tell Luis to move wouldn't work because there might be another Luis among the humans. It was a popular name.

He could send Dagor and Dalhu along with Negal, or he could wait for the Guardians to get out of the vehicles and send them instead.

"You don't have to carry them," Dagor said. "You can just drive the van over here, and the Guardians will take them to safety."

"Good idea," he said. "Do what he said."

Kalugal offered a prayer to the Fates for the family to be found safe and sound. Until they were in the hands of the Guardians behind him, he didn't intend to do anything and was content with keeping the enemy frozen and waiting.

The longer he made them suffer, the better.

Negal broke into a jog, weaving between the vehicles on his way to the back where the lone van was parked.

Bhathian and Max took up position next to Kalugal.

"Can we get to work?" Max asked.

"Not yet." Kalugal watched Negal throw the van door open and hop inside. "I want Luis and his family to be out of here before we start."

He waited anxiously until he heard Negal in his earpiece. "They are all here, and they are alive."

Kalugal released a relieved breath. "Thank the merciful Fates."

Negal hadn't said unharmed, just alive, but Kalugal hadn't expected them to be unharmed. He just prayed that the harm had been limited to being terrified or getting roughed up. Hopefully, Luis's wife and teenage daughter hadn't been violated.

The sound of the van's engine revving up broke the tense silence, and Kalugal watched as Negal skillfully maneuvered the vehicle towards them, somehow managing not to drive over anyone even though the plan was to kill them all anyway.

Perhaps Negal was looking forward to killing them up close and personal?

Kalugal could understand that. It was how he'd felt when he'd killed those who held the kidnapped women. But then another thought crossed his mind. Perhaps there was a soul or two worth saving from this Sodom and Gomorrah?

Some of the humans looked as young as sixteen, and perhaps they didn't have the blood of innocents on their hands. If so, he would spare them. He would ask the Guardians to enter each of the humans' minds to decide who lived and who died.

As the van pulled up close, he motioned for the Guardians to approach the van and assist with the extraction.

As the van's driver door opened, Negal jumped out and jogged around to slide the passenger door open. He and several Guardians carried the family out of the van and into the vehicles behind them.

Given that their eyes were closed and their bodies were limp, Kalugal assumed that Negal had thralled them to sleep. It should have occurred to him to tell the god to do that, but it hadn't, and he was glad that Negal had taken the initiative.

Luis and his family had been traumatized enough.

Once the family was out of harm's way, Kalugal turned to Max and Bhathian. "Now, we can proceed with our plan, but I don't want us to kill indiscriminately because it will make us no better than them. Look into their minds and kill only those with the blood of innocents on their hands."

Bhathian arched a brow. "What if some of the Doomers didn't kill with their own hands but commanded the humans to do it?"

"Then the blood of innocents is on their hands as well. Though I doubt you will find even one Doomer worth saving."

Kalugal wondered if that was true for him and Dalhu as well and preferred not to dwell on it. He'd never killed innocents intentionally, but some might have been unintended casualties in the wars his father had sent him to fight.

"You heard Kalugal," Bhathian addressed the Guardians. "If you find anyone who deserves another chance, spare him. The leader is to be taken in for questioning."

Kian

Kian had been receiving typical military-style succinct progress briefings from Bhathian, so when his phone rang with Kalugal's ringtone, he was glad to finally get the complete account of events from his cousin.

"Hello, Kalugal. How are things going out there?"

"I thought you knew. Bhathian said that he reported to you."

"He did, but all I got were bullet points. I know that Luis and his family are alive and safe, but Bhathian didn't say anything about their physical and mental state. Did you check on them?"

"I did. Negal had the foresight to thrall them to sleep when he got them, but we had to wake them up so I could release them from the compulsion not to move. Luis's wife couldn't stop crying, and his daughter was curled into a ball and trembling. The younger children were a little better, but they were also terrified and traumatized. The bastards kept threatening them with all the terrible things they planned to do to them. If not for the compulsion I put on Bud to keep them safe, I don't want to think what would have been done to them. Anyway, I thralled them to calm down and rest when they get home."

That was good, but Kian wondered what would happen when Kalugal's thrall faded. Hopefully, Luis could get counseling for his family. Acapulco was a modern city, which should imply that it had well-equipped hospitals operated by well-trained physicians, but Kian had no idea if mental health specialists were easily accessible and covered by health insurance.

"Bhathian said that you got the leader and disposed of most everyone else."

"I didn't want to order everyone killed indiscriminately in case there was an innocent among them, so I played the biblical God and tasked Dagor, Negal, Dalhu, and several of the Guardians to find some that were worth saving among these modern Sodomites and Gomorrahites. They found two teenagers who had been recently recruited and hadn't taken part in the atrocities."

Kian grimaced. "Those two are monsters in training. Their teachers are gone, but new ones will come, and if you leave them alive, they will become as bad as the others."

"They won't because I did a number on their minds. They now believe that a powerful Colombian cartel is moving in, and that it's taking out all the competition. The Colombians killed all the members of the cartel they belonged to, including the leaders, and left them alive as a cautionary tale. If they stay out of trouble, the Colombians won't kill them, but they are coming for anyone who dares operate in the area. My main objective was to ensure Luis and his family's safety so they could go home without fear of retribution, but it will work to keep these teenagers out of trouble as well."

Kian shook his head. "What does one have to do with the other?"

"It has nothing to do with the imaginary Colombians, but I made up another story for Luis. I'll tell you about it when I get back. I'm bringing Bud as you have requested, but I don't understand why you want him on the ship. We can question him out here and be done with it. We are making a big pyre with all the bodies, and I would love to throw his on top after I've played with him a little. Or a lot. He's the one who gave the order to massacre the villagers in the most brutal way imaginable to scare everyone in the area into compliance."

"I want to interrogate him at my leisure and then execute him." Kian smiled. "Even my mother approves."

"That's a big change in her attitude. I wonder why now. I'm sure the Doomers have done worse in the past."

"Perhaps, but these are different times, and it was shocking that such cruelty and barbarism still exist. Things were supposed to become more civilized, and we believed that the Brotherhood was becoming more sophisticated. We knew they were dealing in drugs and trafficking, and both are bad, especially the trafficking, but to order the horrific slaughter of an entire village is just so demonic that even my mother doesn't believe these Doomers are capable of redemption." Kian sighed. "I wish she had realized this years ago, and that it didn't have to take this catastrophe to drive the point home that some people are beyond redemption and need to be eliminated. Being soft-hearted toward perpetrators of evil ultimately leads to more innocents suffering and dying."

There was a long moment of silence, and then Kalugal released a breath. "If left unchecked, evil will spread like cancer and kill everything in its wake. The problem is that good people who champion and revere life can't comprehend what evil is and what it wants. They can't understand the thirst for death and destruction, so they try to rationalize evil deeds."

"What can we do, cousin? You are the mastermind with global domination ambitions. Can you think of a way to eradicate evil for good?"

Kalugal chuckled. "Contrary to what you think, I don't have delusions of grandeur. There are things that even I can't achieve. But if you want, I will be more than happy to discuss this with you over whiskey and cigars. Brundar has already celebrated his bachelor party by cutting out hearts and other organs that I won't mention, so you and I can enjoy a quiet hour on your balcony before his wedding tonight."

"That sounds delightful, but I need to interrogate the prisoner first, and I'll need your help to compel him to talk. If we have time after that, I'll gladly share with you a glass of whiskey or two and a cigar."

Frankie

⤟⤞

"I have good news." Mia put the phone down. "Toven said that everything went more or less according to plan, none of ours got hurt, and Luis and his family are safe."

Frankie released a long, relieved breath. "What do you mean by more or less?"

"He didn't say." Mia frowned. "Why are you still sweating? Dagor is obviously fine."

"I'm not sweating." Frankie wiped the back of her hand over her forehead and slumped against the couch cushions. "Well, not anymore now that I know no one got hurt. What about Luis and his family? Are they going to be alright? It must have been horrifying for them."

"I don't know." Mia turned her chair around and drove to the kitchenette. "Do you want something to drink? I can make you another vodka with cranberry juice."

Frankie shook her head. "No, thanks. All this stress has made me a little dizzy. I don't know how the Guardians' mates handle it when they go on their rescue missions. I know that it's really hard to kill immortals, but it's not impossible. I would have gone crazy with worry."

"Yeah, me too." Mia poured cranberry juice into two glasses. "It's easier when you are part of the action. When I went on a mission with Toven, it was stressful, but in a good way. I felt like a badass."

Frankie's jaw slacked. "How the hell did you go on a mission? Did he carry you on his back?"

"Actually, that's exactly what he did on one of the missions." Mia put one of the glasses in the cup holder attached to her chair and held the other one as she drove back to the living room. "I've been on more than one."

Frankie shook her head. "Who are you, and what did you do with my timid best friend?"

Mia smiled. "I've never told you this, but I have a very special paranormal talent. I'm an enhancer. I make other talents stronger, and on several occasions, Toven needed me to fortify his compulsion ability. Two of the missions were nothing special because there was easy access for my chair, but one of them was in a remote region in Karelia, and he had to carry me. That was the stressful one because we were in enemy territory, but it was probably the most excitement I've had in my life, and that's including my Perfect Match adventure."

"Un-freaking-believable." Frankie felt her head spinning. "I want you to tell me all about it." She took a sip from the sweet juice, but it only made her feel nauseous, so she put it back on the coffee table. "I don't know what's wrong with me. I'm nauseous and dizzy, and everything I try to eat or drink makes it worse. I really don't handle stress well."

Mia frowned. "Are you sure it's stress? Maybe you are transitioning?"

"I don't have a fever."

"You are sweating, and the air conditioning is on." Mia maneuvered her chair to get closer. "Let me feel your forehead."

"I don't have a fever," Frankie insisted but leaned her forehead into Mia's extended palm to humor her.

"You're a little warm." Mia pulled her phone out of its holder. "I'm calling Bridget."

Frankie swallowed. "I can't be transitioning yet. It hasn't been long enough."

Except, she'd received a booster, so maybe she was.

Dagor had given her a blood transfusion last night, and that was in addition to the venom. It was very possible that she was transitioning.

"There is no harm in calling the doctor and asking her opinion, right?"

Panic constricting her throat, Frankie nodded.

What if she lost consciousness before Dagor returned?

What if she was out cold for the rest of the cruise?

She'd been looking forward to telling Margo about all the wonders of the immortal world and introducing her to Dagor, and now she would miss all that. Margo would be so disappointed.

Mia put her phone back in the holder. "Bridget says that you should come down to the clinic."

Frankie had been so up in her head that she hadn't even heard Mia speaking with the doctor.

"What did you tell her?"

"That you were nauseous, dizzy, and felt a little warm to the touch. She said she needs to run some blood tests on you to rule out a reaction to the blood transfusion."

As panic rose in Frankie's chest, her head swam, and bile rose in her throat.

How did Bridget know about Dagor's blood transfusion? Had she guessed?

"Don't look so scared." Mia patted her knee. "I don't think it's an allergic reaction to the transfusion. It didn't happen in the first twenty-four hours, and the chances that you are reacting to it now are very slim. I'm sure it's the transition."

"Oh, right." Frankie let out a breath. "That transfusion. I forgot about it."

Bridget had referred to the one she had administered to replenish Frankie's lost blood. She didn't know about Dagor's.

Mia looked at her with worry in her eyes. "Your fever seems to be getting higher. We should get you to the clinic before you pass out."

Dagor

Dagor wiped his hands on his pants and grimaced. As soon as they got back to the beach where they had left the boats, he was going to dunk into the water and wash all the grime away.

It had been a lot of work to get rid of all the bodies, old and new.

This time, they had made sure that no trace remained. The vehicles, the rifles, and the ammunition were going back with them to be donated to Turner's contractor, who had supplied them with the transport and the drones.

Next to Dagor, Negal sat with his arms crossed over his chest, his eyes closed and a smile on his face.

"What are you so happy about?" Dagor asked.

Negal opened his eyes and looked at him. "I enjoy a job well done. We cleaned up the area for these people, at least for a little while. New goons will fill the vacuum, but not immediately."

Dagor grimaced. "I'm glad that killing makes you happy."

Negal's smile got even broader. "Why? Are you sad for those monsters?"

"Not at all. I'm sad that monsters exist and that good people have to dirty their hands with their tainted blood to make life bearable for those who can't defend themselves."

"I'm with you on that." Dalhu turned around to look at them. "But I also enjoyed the killing." He turned back to look at the road ahead.

Dagor had no doubt. After the particularly gruesome way he'd killed four of the eight Doomers, the guy looked calmer and more relaxed than he had ever seen him before.

What Dagor wanted to do was call Frankie, and now that he had calmed down a little from the rush of the battle, he felt centered enough to do that, but he was in a jeep with three other people, and it would be awkward.

Maybe texting her would be better.

Pulling out his phone, he turned sideways so Negal couldn't see the mushy love words he was about to type.

Hello, my love. I'm on my way back. It will take us about three hours, maybe a little longer, and I'll be counting the minutes until I can hold you in my arms. After I shower first, that is. You don't want to know what I'm covered with.

He hit send before it occurred to him that it wasn't romantic to mention that he was dirty and covered in gore.

When she didn't return his text right away, his gut clenched with worry, but then the three dots started dancing, indicating that she was typing a message.

When several minutes passed with the dots blinking but no text, he wondered what was taking so long. Was she writing and then erasing what she'd written?

Finally, when the message appeared, he let out a relieved breath.

I'm so glad that you are coming back to me. I was worried, but then Toven told Mia that none of ours got hurt, so I knew you were okay. I have a surprise for you. It's a good one. Something both of us have been waiting for. I love you.

"No way!"

"What?" Negal asked. "What's going on?"

"I don't know for sure, but I think Frankie is transitioning."

"Congratulations." Negal clapped him on the back. "What did she say?"

"That she has a surprise for me."

Negal's smile faltered. "It might be something else, you know."

"She said that it's something we have been waiting for. What else can it be?"

"Maybe her friend flew in by helicopter," Dalhu said. "Just ask her."

"She won't tell me. She wants it to be a surprise."

"Just ask her." Negal pushed on his back. "How are you going to survive the next three hours, not knowing for sure?"

His friend was right.

Dagor typed. *I know that you probably don't want to tell me news like that in a text, but I have to know, or I'll go crazy. Are you transitioning?*

The answer came a moment later. *Yes. Maybe. Bridget thinks I am, but it's not a sure thing.*

Dagor had no doubt that Frankie was on her way to becoming immortal, and he finally let the floodgates of his love open and fill his heart to bursting. He felt so buoyant that he expected to start floating above the seat.

His hands trembled as he typed back. *Thank the merciful Fates, my prayers have been answered. I love you so much.*

Frankie

~~~

Frankie lifted the back of the hospital bed to a sitting position. "Are you sure you need me here?" she asked Bridget. "I'm perfectly fine."

Well, she was fine except for the nausea, the dizziness, the elevated blood pressure, the faster-than-usual heartbeat, and the mild fever. But she didn't feel faint, and she didn't expect to lose consciousness.

"You're doing well now," Bridget said. "But that can change rapidly, and you have no one to watch over you in your cabin. If you slip into a coma, no one will know."

"I can watch over Frankie," Mia offered without much conviction in her tone.

"That's okay." Frankie gave her a thankful smile. "I'll just wait for Dagor to return. He can watch over me."

Bridget shook her head. "I prefer that you stay in the clinic where I can monitor your vitals even if I'm not here. I can see the readouts from the blood pressure and heart monitors on my tablet while I'm doing other things."

"Look on the bright side," Mia said. "At least you're not hooked up to a catheter and an IV. You can use the bathroom and drink coffee." She cast a sidelong glance at Bridget. "She can drink coffee, right?"

"Water is always better, but a few sips of coffee won't kill you." The doctor winked at Frankie.

"Ugh, Bridget. Is that what doctors consider a joke?"

Bridget shrugged. "A bit too morbid for you?"

"Yeah." Frankie rolled her eyes. "I'm transitioning, and I might die."

Mia gasped. "Fates forbid, Frankie. Don't talk like that."

Bridget smiled. "You'll be fine. Thanks to Dagor's venom, you are doing better than most transitioning Dormants. I was worried because of your fainting spells, but it must have been something that the venom cured as well."

It was a combination of venom and blood.

"I'm so lucky," Frankie murmured. "I didn't think it would happen to me."

Mia reached for her hand and clasped it. "I was sure of it. It wasn't a coincidence that the Fates brought you and Dagor here so you could meet."

Frankie chuckled. "Does Toven have a third nickname that starts with an F and ends with an E? Because he's the one who made it happen."

"Kian had something to do with it as well," Bridget said. "The Fates don't work in a void. They move chess pieces to arrange the board for the game they have in mind."

A knock on the door had Frankie's heartbeat spike, and the monitor beeped a warning before the door opened, and Dagor rushed in, looking like he'd just showered with his clothes on and didn't bother to dry off.

"You're awake," he whispered. "I was afraid that by the time I got here, you would be unconscious."

A smile spread over her face. "You've been texting me every fifteen minutes to ask if I was still awake. I answered the last text about ten minutes ago."

He smiled sheepishly. "I didn't want to push my luck."

Bridget patted Dagor's wet shoulder. "We will leave you two alone." She motioned with her head for Mia to follow.

"I'll see you later." Mia gave her hand a little squeeze before letting go.

When the door closed behind them, Dagor walked over to the bed and took her hand. "I want to kiss you, but I don't want to drip water all over you."

As it was, he was making a puddle on the floor.

"What did you do? Swim to the ship?"

She wouldn't put it past him. He was so strong that he could probably swim faster than the lifeboat's engine could propel it.

He chuckled. "I dunked in the ocean before getting on the lifeboat, and when I got on board, I used a hose to wash off the seawater. I just needed to see you right away, and I didn't want to waste time on a shower."

That was so sweet.

Leaning over, she reached for his shirt and pulled him to her for a scorching kiss. When she got dizzy, this time from oxygen starvation, she let go and sucked in a breath. "I love you, Dagor, and now we can be together forever. I'm never letting you go."

His eyes blazed blue light as he regarded her with such fierce love that it took away what breath she had left in her lungs.

"I'm not letting you go either. I know it's selfish of me, but I'm taking you up on your offer to accompany me on my mission. The good news is that we have all the time in the world, and after my mission is over, I will implore Toven to let us both become testers for the Perfect Match adventures so you won't have to give up on your dream."

Happiness filling her heart, Frankie laughed. "A better use of our talents will be for me to do the testing and you to work on the code."

He leaned over and kissed her softly. "Only if we work in the same building and can see each other whenever we want. I don't want to ever be separated from you."

Frankie's heart swelled with love. "I can't wait to start this new chapter with you. We will have so many adventures together."

"Fates willing."

He leaned down and took her lips in a kiss so passionate and filled with so much love that it left all other kisses behind.

COMING UP NEXT
Margo's Story
The Children of the Gods Book 80
DARK HORIZON NEW DAWN

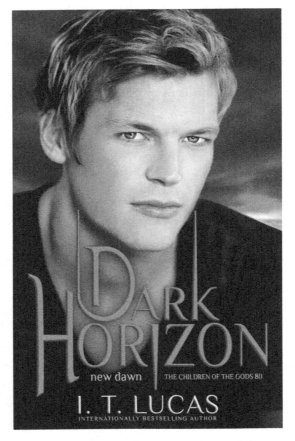

To read the first three chapters, JOIN the VIP club at ITLUCAS.COM.

After breaking up with my boyfriend, I vow never to date a physician again and avoid workplace romances like the plague. Seeking an escape from bad memories and hospital politics, I apply for a job at the Perfect Match Virtual

Fantasy Studios, where I hope to explore fantastical scenarios and beta-test new experiences.

I have no intention of entering a new relationship anytime soon, but it is difficult to ignore Kayden, a fellow trainee who's good-looking and charming but regrettably has aspirations of becoming a physician.

Hoping never to get paired with him to beta test an experience, I choose the Valkyrie adventure. It seems like a safe bet to avoid a guy like him, who would never select an experience where the female is the kick-ass heroine and the man only gets a supporting role. However, the algorithm has other plans in store for us. It seems to think that we are a perfect match.

Join the VIP Club
To find out what's included in your free membership, flip to the last page.

Note

Dear reader,

I hope my stories have added a little joy to your day. If you have a moment to add some to mine, you can help spread the word about the Children Of The Gods series by telling your friends and penning a review. Your recommendations are the most powerful way to inspire new readers to explore the series.

Thank you,

Isabell

Also by I. T. Lucas

PERFECT MATCH
Vampire's Consort
King's Chosen

CAPTAIN'S CONQUEST
THE THIEF WHO LOVED ME
MY MERMAN PRINCE
THE DRAGON KING
MY WEREWOLF ROMEO
THE CHANNELER'S COMPANION
THE VALKYRIE & THE WITCH

THE CHILDREN OF THE GODS SERIES SETS

BOOKS 1-3: DARK STRANGER TRILOGY—INCLUDES A BONUS SHORT STORY: **THE FATES TAKE A VACATION**

BOOKS 4-6: DARK ENEMY TRILOGY —INCLUDES A BONUS SHORT STORY—**THE FATES' POST-WEDDING CELEBRATION**

BOOKS 7-10: DARK WARRIOR TETRALOGY

BOOKS 11-13: DARK GUARDIAN TRILOGY

BOOKS 14-16: DARK ANGEL TRILOGY

BOOKS 17-19: DARK OPERATIVE TRILOGY

BOOKS 20-22: DARK SURVIVOR TRILOGY

Books 68-70: Dark Alliance Trilogy

Books 71-73: Dark Healing Trilogy

Books 74-76: Dark Encounters Trilogy

MEGA SETS
INCLUDE CHARACTER LISTS
The Children of the Gods: Books 1-6

The Children of the Gods: Books 6.5-10

PERFECT MATCH BUNDLE 1

CHECK OUT THE SPECIALS ON
ITLUCAS.COM
(https://itlucas.com/specials)

FOR EXCLUSIVE PEEKS AT UPCOMING RELEASES &
A FREE I. T. LUCAS COMPANION BOOK

Join my *VIP Club* and gain access to the VIP portal at itlucas.com

To Join, go to:

http://eepurl.com/blMTpD

Find out more details about what's included with your free membership on the book's last page.

**TRY THE CHILDREN OF THE GODS
SERIES ON
<u>AUDIBLE</u>**

2 FREE audiobooks with your new Audible subscription!

FOR EXCLUSIVE PEEKS AT UPCOMING RELEASES &
A FREE I. T. LUCAS COMPANION BOOK

JOIN MY *VIP CLUB* AND GAIN ACCESS TO THE
VIP PORTAL AT ITLUCAS.COM
TO JOIN, GO TO:
http://eepurl.com/blMTpD

INCLUDED IN YOUR FREE MEMBERSHIP:

YOUR VIP PORTAL

- READ PREVIEW CHAPTERS OF UPCOMING RELEASES.
- LISTEN TO GODDESS'S CHOICE NARRATION BY CHARLES LAWRENCE
- EXCLUSIVE CONTENT OFFERED ONLY TO MY VIPs.

FREE I.T. LUCAS COMPANION INCLUDES:

- GODDESS'S CHOICE PART 1
- PERFECT MATCH: VAMPIRE'S CONSORT (A STANDALONE NOVELLA)
- INTERVIEW Q & A
- CHARACTER CHARTS

IF YOU'RE ALREADY A SUBSCRIBER, AND YOU ARE NOT GETTING MY EMAILS, YOUR PROVIDER IS SENDING THEM TO YOUR JUNK FOLDER, AND YOU ARE MISSING OUT ON **IMPORTANT UPDATES, SIDE CHARACTERS' PORTRAITS, ADDITIONAL CONTENT, AND OTHER GOODIES.** TO FIX THAT, ADD isabell@itlucas.com TO YOUR EMAIL CONTACTS OR YOUR EMAIL VIP LIST.

Check out the specials at
https://www.itlucas.com/specials

Published by Evening Star Press

EveningStarPress.com

ISBN: 978-1-962067-21-8

Made in the USA
Las Vegas, NV
13 July 2024

92269751R00243